DELIVER US FROM EVIL

A DARK NEW ADULT REVERSE HAREM ROMANCE
(THE SINNERS OF SAINT AMOS BOOK 3)

LOGAN FOX

WARNING

This dark romance is a work of fiction. The aim of this book is to entertain, not educate. While it includes elements of BDSM, it in no way depicts a healthy relationship (kinky or otherwise). That being said, you can expect some pretty dark content such as non-con, dub-con, public humiliation and degradation, violence, knife play, breath play, choking, murder, mention of suicide and abuse. Please tread carefully if you have triggers.

JOIN THE FOX DEN

Can I send you my secret dark romance novella that's never been published…?
Join my VIP newsletter and you'll receive your own exclusive copy of My Darling, and I'll keep you up to date with my new releases and promos!
https://authorloganfox.com/my-darling-signup

PLAYLIST

Theme Song
everything i wanted — BILLIE EILISH

Playlist
Dangerous — SON LUX
Ma And Pa — LONDON TEWERS
See the Light — SOFA SURFERS
Temple Priest — MISSIO
Repeat After Me — KONGOS
Serpent of Old — SEVEN LIONS
Lake Of Fire — NIRVANA
Poacher's Pride — NICOLE DOLLANGANGER
Joan of Arc — IN THIS MOMENT

To view this playlist, please visit my website at https://
authorloganfox.com/playlists.

1
TRINITY

It's amazing, the things you don't notice the first—or the hundredth—time around.

She kept you, Trinity. She kept you because you were special.

When I first came to the bell tower with Apollo I never noticed the stale, chalky smell inside this small room.

Do you know why you were special, Trinity?

Gabriel is a handsome man, especially with his warm brown eyes. But I never noticed the spots of bronze in his eyes before.

Because you're mine.

I never noticed his shaggy eyebrows. The shape of his nose. How similar his eyes are to mine. Suddenly, it's impossible *not* to notice.

I wouldn't let her.

Gabriel—my *father*—scans my face like he has so many times before. But this time, there's hidden meaning in his gaze. He's not checking to see if I've finally found God. He's staring at his daughter's face. Picking out his likeness, or perhaps my mother's.

He brushes his thumb over my lower lip. The intimate gesture sends a surge of panic through me that freezes me solid.

But only for a moment.

Then self-preservation kicks in.

I shove Gabriel away and whirl around, bolting out of the tiny room. But I barely take two steps before he grabs my hair and yanks me back.

I fly into him, and we both crash backward into the wall. He slips an arm around my waist and drags me back. When I realize he's taking me further into that tiny room, I put everything I have into my struggles.

I grab the door frame as I pass. Gabriel makes an angry sound in his throat, then he rips me free with a hard tug that leaves behind some of my fingernails.

I scream again, as loud as I can.

He throws me away from him, and I catch a glimpse of the enraged snarl twisting his face before I hit the wall.

Bright pain lances through my head.

Gabriel crouches at my side, face disturbingly blank even after our scuffle. I groan and try to sit up, try to move away, but that makes my head hurt even more.

He touches the side of my face. "I didn't want it to be this way. I wanted to tell you. I wanted you to know the truth. But they fought me on it. Both of them. Said it would confuse you."

Gabriel shakes his head, breaking eye contact for a second. "I should have fought harder, child. I should have insisted. But…"

When he looks at me again, there's something terrifying in his eyes.

Despair.

"I loved them, Trinity. Both of them. I know it's impossible to understand, but it's the truth." His voice goes hoarse, and he runs those same fingertips down my cheek. "I did it for them. And I'd do it again."

He smiles, but it's faint and more sad than happy. "They're gone now. It's just us. But we can start again. Me and you. We can be a family again."

He wants me to be his daughter? If I could have, I would have laughed in his face. How the hell can he think I'd want a sick, perverted man like him for a father?

But I can't even stand, let alone argue. "Please, just let me go," I whisper. "I won't tell anyone."

He grabs my shoulder, squeezes it. "Shh." He shakes his head. "It'll be perfect, you'll see. Now you wait here. I'll be back with something to help you sleep. And when you wake up, it'll be a new day. A new life."

It's amazing, the things you don't notice.

I'd always thought that tiny spark, that delightful little gleam that Gabriel got in his eyes was a kind of righteous joy.

Now I see it for what it truly is.

Madness.

Gabriel leaves, locking the door with a finality that makes my skin crawl. I have to get out of here before he comes back. But there's no way I can open that door and this room has no windows.

My heart starts knocking in my chest.

I'm trapped.

2
RUBE

I open my eyes to darkness and cigarette smoke, a combination that never fails to give me heart palpitations.

Triggers come like a thief in the night. Ambushing my mind, my body. I've stopped fighting them because I'll never win. Same reason I stopped fighting my Ghost.

As if my sudden panic wakes him, Cass fumbles a hand down my arm. "Jus' Zach," he murmurs, still half asleep as he laces his fingers through mine. He squeezes my hand, and then he relaxes, already asleep again.

In the basement, sleep was our oblivion. I was always exhausted and Cass was fucked on heroin more often than not, so it was easy for him to slip away with me.

But I'm wide awake now.

Trinity is gone.

I shake loose Cass's hand, tugging on my shirt as I step out from behind the curtain.

Zach is sitting in the armchair, smoking a cigarette.

Darkness and smoke.

"Where is she?" My voice is still raspy from sleep.

"Probably halfway to Sisters of Mercy by now," he says, and then takes a long drag at his cigarette without looking up at me.

"She left without saying goodbye?" I inch closer as I wait for his response. Because I'm pretty sure it's going to piss me off. And if that's the case, I might go for his throat.

I consider myself calm. Reasonable. I think things through a hundred times before I act on them. But when I'm triggered it's like a switch inside me flips. All that calm, all that reason...it's decimated by rage. Like a town flattened by the shock wave of a nuclear bomb.

Zachary can trigger me at will. He's had that power ever since I found out who he really was. I couldn't reconcile the fact that he'd been living a normal life above us while we hunkered in the dark waiting for our next visit.

I spend a lot of time dredging up memories of the Utopia that had existed above us. Replaying them. Wondering if the sounds I'd so often heard were made by him. A patter of fast, light footsteps—was that Zach on his way to school? A faint thump—Zachary sitting down in front of the TV, eating a PB&J sandwich while he watched Sesame Street? Sometimes we'd hear voices, but only if the Keepers shouted. And then the words were usually unintelligible because they'd made sure to soundproof the basement as much as possible.

All except one. A name.

Mason.

"Didn't want to wake you," Zachary says.

I have no way of telling if he's lying. He's had years to perfect the art of twisting the truth.

Fuck. Why did I let myself sleep that deeply?

Because I was happy for the first time in a long time. And it felt good. And it felt safe. And I let my guard down.

This is what happens.

"And she said she's going to Mercy?"

We can fetch her when we're done with Gabriel. I know a few of the sisters who work there. Shouldn't be too difficult to find her if she wants to be found.

Zach takes another drag before replying. "She's an orphan. Where the fuck else would she go?"

So callous. But I knew him when he was still vulnerable. When he was still human. The first week he was down in the basement with us, he'd been crying for his mother. Begging his father to open the door and let him out. That he didn't belong down there with the 'other kids.'

He eventually realized he wasn't special. Not to them, not to us. He was exactly like the 'other kids.'

We'd been planning escape long before he arrived, but we were suspicious of each other because we were each treated differently. Cass had a regular dose of drugs to keep him warm and fuzzy while abominable things were done to him. Sometimes he even seemed to be enjoying it. Apollo only had two ghosts, and they only ever spent time with him on the weekends. Zach and I? Our Ghost treated us like scum. We were kicked and bitten and had foreign stuff shoved in us all the fucking time. We were tools—objects of pleasure for a sick man. Sometimes he would visit us together, make us watch what he did to the other one. Or he'd take us away to one of the upstairs rooms. Play us against each other. We'd get treats when we were alone with him, while our brothers in the basement starved.

That shit really messes with your head.

Other boys came and went. So many we didn't bother finding out their names. Weak, shattered, hollow. Nameless shapes in the gloom, some of who never made a sound, despite how brutally they were used.

Some who, after a few days or a week, would stop moving altogether.

We don't know why they brought the boys there to die. Not until we'd escaped, anyway. Then it became so clear.

A lot of things became clear after we were free.

But that would never have happened without Zachary. We wouldn't have been able to get out of there without his help. He knew the layout of the house. He knew his parents' schedule. And he had a solid plan. But it would take four, possibly even five kids to pull it off. He sat and watched. Chose us, because he saw strength and resilience.

If Zachary hadn't come to the basement, we'd have died there like the other boys.

If we hadn't been there, Zach would never have escaped.

Everything happens for a reason. Trinity's arrival only strengthened that belief. She came to Saint Amos—to us—for a reason. It wasn't a coincidence.

I thought it was a sign from God. A reminder that there was more to life than revenge. That love *could* exist in a void. Until we discovered who she really was.

She wasn't a Godsend.

She'd been sent by the Devil.

There's movement at the partition—we woke Cass. He moves aside, letting Apollo into the room.

"She's gone?" Apollo asks. The disappointment in his voice hits me harder than it should. Apollo has changed so much since Trinity arrived. I don't know if the others see it, but he's started interacting more, not just sitting quietly in the corner absorbed in whatever toy Zachary lavished on him. When Zachary isn't around, he starts talking about what we'll do after we've found our Ghosts and ended them, as if he's obsessed with starting a new life.

Before, he'd been drowning in the past. Trinity had brought him to the surface. Had breathed life back into his cold, dead mind.

"Yeah," Zach says, "and we should get going too."

How often he's sat like that. Slightly hunched, cigarette dribbling smoke from one end as it dangles from his fingertips. He's lost weight again. It happens when things come to a head. He stops eating, and his body takes sustenance in any form it can —even if it's from his own flesh.

He locks eyes with me. Green to my green.

Green...but outsiders only see black. My Ghost liked my eyes. Forced me to keep them open. Forced me to watch. And then told me how pretty they were when I cried. So, like Cass shaves his head, I hide behind colored contacts. I've worn them for so long, so religiously, that I hardly notice them anymore.

"Now how about we get a move on?" Zach stands and crushes out his cigarette in the designated mug.

"First, coffee," Cass mutters. He doesn't seem that pained that Trinity's gone. I guess she was just a piece of tail to him. It's easy for him to pick up girls. He simply has to look in their direction and smile.

"I'll bring you some," Apollo says. "I need to grab my stuff."

"Yeah, me too." Cass stretches. "I'll walk with you."

Zach turns on them with narrowed eyes. "The fuck you will. We're sticking with protocol until Gabriel's tied up in that fucking cabin. Got it?"

Apollo nods, even dropping his gaze. Cass scoffs and gives him a dismissive wave. "Fine, whatever." But there's a shift in his eyes I've seen too many times not to know what it means.

The moment they're out from under Zach's watchful eye, they'll meet up. They might even walk together anyway, despite what he says. Because although he's taken command, Zach doesn't control us.

I guess, after going through what we did, we'll never let someone have that much say in our lives.

Apollo and Cass leave, and I make to go after them, to warn

them. Because they might not like it, but Zach's right. We have to be careful. If Gabriel slips through our fingers again…

But a hand catches my arm, squeezing my bicep hard, almost cruelly.

And I have to let the other two go.

I glance over my shoulder. Zach's face is stone.

"Gotta run some things by you," he says.

Code for "I need you." Always has been.

So I stay.

We smoke a cigarette together. We have a shot of whiskey. And we listen to each other recite exactly what we'll do to our Ghost the day we find him.

3

CASS

Where the fuck is Apollo? I'd have stuck with him after we left the library, but he said he needed to take care of some shit. I thought he was being literal—I wasn't hanging around for that. But that was ages ago, and he's not answering my calls.

I need to make sure he's okay, and that's pissing me off.

I *hate* needing things.

Sleep.

Sex.

Coffee.

Sleep replaced the heroin. Coffee replaced the adrenaline. And sex replaced…Huh. I guess it didn't replace anything. I suppose my brothers need things too, but they're not addicts like me.

The least I can do is fucking own that shit.

Denial's for pussies.

I could slip into the kitchen and make myself a cuppa. That wouldn't raise too many eyebrows for Cassius Santos, the Hall

Monitor. After, I'll track down Apollo and find out why he ditched me.

The kitchen's pretty bare. Can't even find a kettle. Looks like everything's been locked up for the big exodus. Guess then there's less stuff to dust off when everyone gets back after summer break.

One of the kitchen guys comes out of what I assume is the pantry with a bag of what could only be potatoes and calls out, "Hey, man," when he sees me.

I walk over. "Hey. You seen that blond guy who works here?"

The kitchen guy frowns. "Apollo?"

"Yeah, him."

Kitchen guy shrugs. "Nah, man. He was supposed to be here to help me with this shit." Kitchen guy cocks his head to the bag of potatoes.

"'Kay. Thanks."

"You tried his room?"

"Yeah," I call back without looking around. Idiot. Why wouldn't I have—

"Bell tower?"

I stop walking. Turn back. "Bell tower?" Why am I suddenly in a modern-day remake of the Hunchback of Notre Dame?

The kitchen guy puts down the sack of spuds. "Yeah. He goes up there to smoke a spliff."

Well fuck me sideways. And here I thought I knew all there was to know about twinkle toes.

"I'll take a look. Thanks, man."

Kitchen guy nods. "If you find him, tell him Dave says fuck him." He shakes his head, picks up his sack, and heads off to wherever bags of potatoes are destined during summer break.

It takes me a few minutes to find the stairs leading up to the tower. Another few minutes to climb them. And Christ, I'm fucking done when I reach the top.

Really gotta quit smoking.

But the little shit's not in the tower either.

"Fuck."

I pull out my phone, try and call him. It's probably a lost cause, seeing as he didn't answer before, but—

I hear it ringing.

Not through my phone. I actually hear Apollo's Nirvana rip off ring tone rocking it out somewhere nearby. I look to where the sound is coming from, and it feels like every hair on my body is stretching for sunlight.

There, barely visible behind the mass of the bronze bell, is a metal door.

It's standing ajar. Beside it, smeared on the stonework, is a bloody handprint.

Ice coats me from head to foot, and then I'm running.

Running so fucking fast.

But I know I'm already too late.

4
APOLLO

I'm going to miss this view. I hope there'll be enough time to sit up here and smoke a last joint before we leave Saint Amos forever. I could bring the crew here when we're done. We could all sit up here and stare out at the forest.

Because we *will* find Gabriel.

He *will* tell us where to find our Ghosts.

And then we just have to go and kill them.

I fill my lungs with sweet forest air. I'll miss this old stack of stones too. Probably the only one who will. The others hate it here. Always have.

I like gloomy places. Even the basement—but only when there weren't any Ghosts around.

And the forest.

Shit, I'm going to miss that forest.

But I have to get going. When I move, keys jingle inside my pocket.

Did Trin find the envelope? I didn't want to put it in her room in case Jasper found it before she did. Now I'm worried she didn't come up here again after I cleaned out the place. Or, if she did, that she didn't check the drawer. Shit. Maybe I should have left it out in the open.

Trin didn't mention anything about finding the photo, and I have a feeling she would have. Maybe give me a knowing look or something. A kind of a thank you.

The photo means a lot to her. I wish I knew why.

I've stared at it so many times over the years, I have it memorized. Especially Gabriel's face. He was young back then. He looks so innocent in that photo, if a bit of a prick. Guess that's no surprise. Maybe that's how she'd prefer to remember her father. Innocent.

I saunter over, glancing at the view as I try to drink in every leaf on every tree.

I unlock the door and push. It swings open, then gets stuck like there's something in the way.

The hell?

I push against it, shove a little harder. There's a groan.

My eyes go wide, lungs tight and hot and bursting.

I squeeze in through the gap and stare down at Trinity. It takes me way too long to process what I'm seeing because there's blood down there and blood makes me feel like gravity has stopped working.

I grab onto the thin edge of the metal desk behind me, holding on, trying to stay rooted to the floor so I won't float away.

Her eyes are open, but she looks out of it. Concussed maybe. I've seen it plenty of times. Ghosts playing too hard with their toys. Sometimes they break them and those toys don't always heal.

"Trin." My voice comes from far away.

Shit, man. Keep it together. She needs you!

But there's blood pooling on the floor by her head. More on

her legs. She's still wearing the white dress, and her skin is so pale. The red looks neon against all that white.

Focus on her eyes, man. Look at *her*. *Help* her.

I push away from the desk. Start rambling. "Hey. It's okay. I'm here. Trin. Trin! Can you hear me? I'm here, pretty thing."

She groans again, her eyes fluttering closed. I get closer. See all that blood is actually her dark hair. Only a little blood. A small splash. Almost less than the streaks on her thighs.

We did that.

No. Can't be. I saw blood yesterday, but not that much. Not enough to make me float away.

I touch her shoulder, scoop a hand under her head. Help her sit up.

Got to be careful with a possible head trauma. So, *so* careful.

"Hey, you there?" I ask. "Can you hear me, Trin?"

Her mouth moves, but no sound comes out. Is that good or bad?

"I'm here, pretty thing. You're safe now. Everything's fine."

Best thing ever—someone telling you shit's fine. Even when it's not, it doesn't matter. Because you give them hope, right? Would have been like those other kids if we didn't have hope. The ones that came to the basement to die.

"'Ming," I think she says.

"Shh. Don't speak, okay?" I can carry her, but not down all those stairs. Not without jarring her. And that can't be good.

Gotta get help.

I take out my phone.

Shit! Cass has been trying to reach me. I must have forgotten to take my phone off silent this morning. I turn on the ringer now. Then I go to call Cass.

"Coming," Trinity says, and this time I hear her fine. But it's too late, because her eyes are already wide, her lips peeling open in dismay.

Maybe if I'd understood sooner, Gabriel wouldn't have had the upper hand. But he works out. Stays fit.

I don't. Hate getting sweaty. Hate feeling tired and stiff.

When Father Gabriel comes at me from behind, slings an arm around my throat, and puts me in a chokehold, there's nothing I can do about it.

Sweet fanny fuck all.

I swat at him, try and scratch out his eyes, but he dodges like a snake.

Trinity watches, eyes brimming, lips distorted. Angry, scared. But just sitting there like a broken doll propped up against the wall in some filthy playhouse.

I finally make contact. Scratch his cheek.

But the light's fading. I can't fend him off much longer. And once he's rid of me...

"They're coming for you, you piece of shit," I manage through a collapsing windpipe. "I'd run. Run fucking far."

God, it takes everything I have to say those words. Not just physical effort, because taking a nap right now is all my body wants to do.

I'm giving up everything we've tried so hard to conceal. No vote. No consensus. But I can't let him take her. And I know that's what he's going to do after leaving her here like this. Probably had to go fetch some ropes, or a carpet to roll her up in like those old spy movies.

Life is more important than revenge. Trinity's life especially.

I don't care if she's Gabriel's daughter.

I don't care if she was sent to spy on us.

I care too much about her for that shit to matter.

My brothers might never forgive me, and that's fine. I can handle that. But I'll never forgive myself if I didn't do everything in my limited power to protect her.

"They? They who?" Gabriel says. It sounds like he's trying not to laugh. Like he thinks I'll say anything to drop his guard.

"My brothers. They're coming up the stairs. You're trapped."

"Brothers? You don't have any brothers." He laughs outright now, so hard his chest shakes. That vibration goes through me. Fills me.

The Guardian wasn't one of the sick fucks who took turns offloading their unrighteous perversions on us. He never touched us.

But he orchestrated everything.

The feel of him so close against me, it's worse than cleaning out the fucking grease trap.

It turns my stomach, gives me the shakes, and just when I think I'm about to puke…

It flicks a switch.

I'm useless, a victim. Then suddenly I'm not. Because all that rage, all that horror, all that shame and humiliation and pain rises up in me like a motherfucking tsunami.

And wherever it goes, it leaves devastation in its wake.

I let go of the arm around my throat. It clamps tighter. Lights sparkle in the darkness that's eating away ten times as fast at the edges of my sight.

I clasp my hands. Throw back my arm. Drive my elbow into Gabriel's stomach.

He makes a soft sound that sends a puff of ashtray breath against my face. His grip relents, but not enough. So I do it again. Then I stamp on his toes.

Fighting like a fucking girl, but still fighting. That's what counts.

He folds forward, and I push back, shoving him against the edge of the metal desk. It must catch him somewhere painful— his hip, his ass, his kidneys, I don't fucking know—because he yells out and loses hold of me.

I swing around and throw a punch. It lands solidly on his nose.

Blood gushes.

I start floating away.

Gabriel comes at me, teeth shining red through the blood. And all I can do is stand there as he rams into me. Drives me over Trinity's legs and into the wall.

She's lying on her side now, and I can only hope I didn't hurt her. Trample her pretty legs, or bruise her beautiful skin.

Gabriel takes hold of my hair, twists it, rams my head into the wall. And then steps back as if to check out his work. The darkness comes, and with it some flashing lights. Pain is there, but distant, because I'm already fading. I slide down, my legs refusing to keep me up.

He puts a hand to his nose, coating it with blood. Looks stunned that there's so much of it. Then he's crouching, poking a needle into Trinity's arm.

I want to tell her it's going to be okay. That we'll find her, somehow. That we'll make Gabriel pay for whatever he's planning to do with her.

Somehow.

But he's already scooping her up. Her head lolls back, and I know it's not because he might have broken her earlier, but because he set her mind free and it's flapping away like a bird.

That's something at least.

Whatever he does, she won't mind it one bit anymore. That's how that shit works.

Maybe I'll tell her now, when I leave my body.

Because there's nothing else left for me to do now but float away.

Float away and never come back.

5

CASS

That bloody handprint feels like an accusation the closer I get. A blatant stamp of the Universe's disapproval. I slam into the metal door, and barely manage to catch hold of the handle to stop it flying inward.

Inside, Apollo's phone rings a last time before going silent. I hope that means that I'm not too late. But that glaring smear of red says otherwise.

Need to calm down. Need to get control.

But as soon as I'm inside and I see Apollo crumpled up against the wall, fury obliterates what little control I had left.

My hand shakes as I lift my phone. It's already locked again, and now it doesn't recognize my fingerprint, beeping impotently at me once, twice, fucking five times before it unlocks and lets me dial.

I go to my knees, trying to be gentle when I thumb back Apollo's eyelid. Left, then right. No fucking clue if anyone's still left behind those pupils though. I pat his cheek. He comes around with a groan. His head tips forward, but I push it back with fingers on his jaw, but gentle. Could be gay for him that's how tender I'm being.

"Gabriel?" I ask. Meanwhile, my phone rings in my ear then goes to voice mail. I redial. Why the fuck isn't Zach answering? "He did this?"

I mean, who else, right?

But how? *Why*? That's what I need to know.

Apollo's eyes roll around in their sockets as he tries to focus on me. He eventually gets out a pained, "Trinity."

I frown, huff out a laugh. "Yeah, no. Try again. Gabriel, right?"

"He's got Trinity."

My blood turns into a raspberry slushie.

All that shit I was spouting about denial? Well, I guess I'm a pussy after all. I couldn't have given less fucks when I found out Trinity had left. There was even a whole good-riddance vibe in my head. Because obviously she couldn't handle the four of us. We were too much for that pretty little slut. Who wasn't a slut after all, and I guess that goes a far way in explaining why she bolted in the first place.

But now?

Christ fucking Jesus.

I was bullshitting myself at a master level. Because if I didn't give a fuck, there'd be no way I'd be outright getting heart palpitations at the thought that something bad might happen to our little girl. And that makes no sense, because we were just having a good time. I don't do feelings. I don't—dear God—do relationships. There's no way you can date someone like me.

So why do I feel like someone's gone and dug up my future grave, poured lighter fuel over my corpse, and set it alight?

The phone goes to voice mail. I call Reuben without missing a beat.

Apollo's eyes flicker, about to close.

"Nuh-uh," I tell him, gripping his jaw harder. Next I'll be putting my nails in him. "Tell me what happened."

He winces, but whether that's from whatever blunt trauma he experienced or my grip is difficult to say. I won't call him an outright pussy, but he's never been able to handle pain, or blood, or any of that shit. Despite what he claims when we get pissed and rage about the deliciously dark shit we'll do to our Ghosts, I know he'll be the one standing outside, keeping watch. Or digging the grave. Or something that doesn't include binding, torturing, and killing.

It's not that he can't hurt a fly. He swats them all right. But he only does it hard enough to daze them, and then tosses them out the window.

"Apollo!" When he doesn't respond, I try, "Trevor!"

His eyes go wide. He winces again. Mumbles, "He took her."

"Yeah, you said that already, Christ. *Where* did he take her? Did he say anything? Does he know?" Too many questions, but I can barely stop myself from yelling at this point.

"He...I dunno. Didn't say where." Then he closes his eyes, and I'm convinced he's about to start crying.

"Cass?" Reuben's voice legit makes me flinch.

I turn away from Apollo, letting go of his head and glancing around the tiny room as I talk to Rube. "Yeah, buddy? We got a serious fucking problem on our hands."

6

ZACH

I'm headed to Gabriel's room when I get the call. I shouldn't even have checked who it was—my mission is set in stone. I must find Gabriel before he leaves Saint Amos.

We know he's staying behind to oversee the repairs to Saint Amos. Him and him alone. Which is perfect, because by the time they figure out Gabriel's missing, we'll be lost in the woods. Even if they send out search parties, the chances of them finding that decrepit hunting lodge is slim to none.

Reuben is on his way to the admin offices. We want to make sure Gabriel doesn't have a chance to escape if he happens to catch wind of his own death. Fuck, for all we know, he has a direct line to Satan and Old Scratch sends him prophetic messages every now and then.

Cass and Apollo are probably disobeying me and having a joint together somewhere. They take things like summer break too fucking seriously. It pisses me off, but I can't really blame them for acting like the kids they are.

My phone rings as I step into Gabriel's hallway. I hurriedly take it out of my pocket to silence it, cursing myself for being idiotic enough not to have done that already. When I see it's an unknown number, my curiosity is piqued. Only a handful of people have this number and none of them would phone from an unknown number.

I hurry back down half a flight of stairs before answering, fully expecting to hear Gabriel's voice on the other end of the line. Not that he's one of the handful. But the feeling's impossible to shake for the precious second before an old lady says, "Hello. May I please speak with Mason Price?"

It takes another second before I can answer. "Speaking."

"Mr. Price, it's Beverley from California Key Realty. Is this a good time?"

I stop breathing. My back's against the wall, and I use it as support to slide down until I'm hunkered in a crouch.

I force myself to take a breath.

"No time like the present," I say, and even manage a faint chuckle. "What can I help you with, Beverly?"

I stare at my phone for a few minutes after the call ends. My fingertips are still tingling. My chest still feels too tight. But for the first time in a long, *long* time, those feelings bring relief—even joy—and not anxiety.

It's done.

It's fucking *done.*

We got the house.

Soon as it's out of escrow, it'll be ours.

There's a grin on my face, and I can't seem to shake it. Fuck, I don't even want to. I draw in a huge breath as I stand, and for a moment it feels like I'm still rising, like a fucking balloon some sweaty kid lost at the fair.

Christ. Why am I so surprised? In this economy, with my generous offer? But I *am* surprised. Fuck it, I'm shocked. Because honest to God I thought the Universe would send a last fuck-you to the four boys it's been such a motherfucking cunt to all these years.

Nothing's ever been easy.

Getting out of the basement.

Trying to keep us together. Focused.

It's been hard fucking work all the way.

I can't remember how many times I've wanted to give up. How often I've wanted to let the Universe win.

But then I'd think of them.

Of my brothers.

And I'd find my second wind. I'd get the strength I need to tell them we need to push on. And they'd rally. They *always* rally.

I shove my phone in my pocket and head for Gabriel's apartment again. But my euphoria starts fading the closer I get. My steps become reluctant.

About a yard from his door, I slow down. Then stop.

This means everything to them, to me...but I can't stop thinking about the house. I'm even getting fucking feels about it. All I want to do is spill my guts to them. I'd call them, but it has to be in person. I want to see their faces light up as I tell them about the infinity pool and the dance room and all those big fucking windows. Light everywhere. The coast so close you can taste salt in the air.

Fuck.

I rake fingers through my hair.

Fuck!

He's one man, Gabriel, but suddenly I feel like I'm facing off against an army. And it's just me this time. I don't have any of them. Yeah, I'm only supposed to find out where he is. Track him until we've got everything in place to grab him. But it's suddenly too real. And, at the same time, surreal.

I'm walking into a nightmare, when I should be heading for the life of my dreams.

That house is everything we've always wanted—

I close my eyes, shake my head.

What the hell am I thinking? Of course they won't be happy. This—I open my eyes and glare at Gabriel's door—*this* is what they want.

What *I* want.

What we've *always* wanted since that first repulsive hand touched us. Since that first voice whispered to us that everything was going to be fine, as long as we play along.

It's just a game. You like games, don't you, Mason? Can I call you Mason?

My skin crawls at the thread of unwanted memory, but I'm too agitated to push it away. So it slithers in deeper, grabs hold of my conscious mind.

I fold my fingers around Gabriel's door handle. Open the door. It should be locked, but it isn't.

This game, I call it hide and seek. But we'll be playing it a little differently, okay?

My Ghost's voice raises goosebumps on my skin. I grit my teeth and step inside Gabriel's apartment. The next door is standing open. I swear I can hear sounds coming from inside.

I'm going to take this chocolate—you see it?—and I'm going to hide it. You like chocolate don't you, Mason? You must be hungry. If you find the chocolate, then you can eat it.

My heart hammers inside my rib cage like a fist trying to break down a door. I slink to the side, pressing my back to the wall.

There's a clatter from inside Gabriel's room.

Fuck. He's here. I have to leave. Go wait by the stairs. Watch him. Send a message, let my brothers know—

Now close your eyes, Mason. Close your eyes so I can hide the chocolate. Good boy. Keep them closed. I'm hiding it now. Good boy. Keep them closed. Give me your hand. Yes, good boy. Now I want you to find it. Go on. Don't be scared. Put your hand in, Mason. There. You feel that? Feels good, doesn't it?

Nausea wells up so fast, so bitter, I taste bile in my mouth before I can swallow it down.

The world swims, and for a second I'm convinced I'm back there in that room. My first night with my Ghost. Playing hide and fucking seek with a sicko.

I cataloged them all. My Ghost, their Ghosts. They're all saved neat and tidy inside my head. Their voices, what their aftershave smelled like, the size and shape of their dicks. Any rings, or freckles or scars on their hands. Those that showed their faces? They'll be the easiest to find. But we'll find them all.

Each and every last one of them.

Keep them for as long as it takes. Until *we're* satisfied.

And then burn them at the motherfucking stake. A sacrificial offering to the God who abandoned us, left us to rot in that basement with those demons.

My phone trembles as I bring it out of my pocket. The memory retreats. Finally have my body under control again. Sticking to the plan.

But before I can back out, something slams closed inside Gabriel's room. Thankfully, instinct takes over. I throw myself against the wall, crowding into a corner by the small key table. Holding my breath, closing my eyes.

He swarms right past me.

I catch a whiff of his aftershave as he disturbs the air, and like I always have, compare it to the database inside my head.

Unless he's changed what he wears, he's not one of them. Not one of the men who abused us.

Gabriel leaves his apartment in a rush, not bothering to close the door behind him. I wait for my arms and legs to stop quivering, and then slip out of the room and follow him down the hall.

I start to type out a message, but then I hesitate.

I almost lost control back there. Teetering on a knife's edge. Me. Them. I'm good at bringing myself back from the void, but they aren't. It's their one weakness.

I'll follow Gabriel, see where he's going. If he looks to be leaving, then I'll let them know. Then we can take him down.

I lick my lips as I wait for him to hurry down the first flight of stairs, then I follow him.

Silent.

Wary.

I'm always thinking of traps. Still not entirely convinced he doesn't know exactly who we are. That's my paranoia of course. Not as easily turned off as old memories.

You feel that, Mason? It feels nice, doesn't it? Oh, you're such *a good boy.*

G abriel goes to the bell tower. And that makes no sense, but I follow him anyway. I follow him all the way up the stairs and then hang around out of sight behind the first twist in the stairwell.

What's up there? A big fucking bell. Is this part of his provostial duties or something? Does he have to ring the bell to signal the end of term or some shit?

I still feel sick. My skin feels oily. I could use a shower to wash that debilitating memory off me. But I'll watch Gabriel first.

My phone's still on silent, so it vibrates furiously when someone calls.

Cass.

But I can't take it now. I need to listen. I need to be a few steps ahead when Gabriel comes down again.

And then he does. But something's different. His footsteps sound heavier than before. Little details like that don't get past me. I was on full alert back in that basement...I don't think I've ever gone back to normal.

I sneak down the steps as fast as I can, and it's too easy to stay ahead of him, silent like this. Because he's moving slower. Carrying something, maybe. Something heavy enough to slow him down. It's driving me mad trying to figure it out, so I just fucking stop with the mental gymnastics. I concentrate on staying ahead, keeping the sound of his heavy footsteps within earshot.

I slip into a nearby alcove when the stairs exit on the top floor landing. I'm sure the shadows are hiding me, but I'm quivering with adrenaline when Gabriel finally shows.

What?

No.

I blink, hard. Then again.

Is that...?

I watch Gabriel walk past with Trinity in his arms. If I ever had any doubt they were father and daughter, seeing them together eradicates it.

Same dark hair. Same nose, even. His is slightly larger, of course, and there's a fan of blood leaking from it that makes me think Trinity must have put up quite a fucking fight.

I follow as soon as he has a big enough lead on me. I expect him to go to his room seeing as it's only one hallway to the left, but instead he takes the stairs.

My phone vibrates again, but I don't bother checking. I know I should be calling my brothers and updating them on the situation, but there's a question that plays on repeat in my mind, crowding out all other thought.

Why is she still here?

Why is she still here?

Why *the fuck* is Trinity Malone *still* here?

When I squeeze into our lair the first thing I see is Apollo on his armchair with a washcloth pressed to the back of his head, wincing as he stares at nothing. Cass comes out of the bedroom like he heard me struggling to get in but for once he isn't wearing a look like he's about to tell you the punch line of a joke. He looks grim and serious and it scares the living shit out of me.

"Tell me everything."

But it doesn't help when they do, because they don't know all that much. Apollo got knocked out before Trinity said anything useful.

"And Zach?" I ask, still standing near the exit, barely moving.

Cass drops his gaze. "No answer."

"What if he got him?" Apollo says, and from the frown that flashes over Cass's face, he's only stating what we're all thinking. "He was supposed to keep tabs on Gabriel's room. He could be—"

"Cass, go check."

"Should we really be splitting up right now?" he asks.

I'm about to tell him to go check anyway, but he's right. Even though we have a huge school to search, splitting up will leave us vulnerable and exposed.

The trick is working out where Gabriel will go. We have to get into his head and figure out his plan.

The fact that Trin had been lying there, waiting for Gabriel to come back…that makes me think she surprised him. Perhaps they fought over something. That room is so far out of the way —maybe that's where they'd been meeting all this time.

The thought makes my heart calcify.

We'd trusted her.

But Apollo said she was injured. So things must have soured between her and her father. Now he's taking her away, but where to? Where in Saint Amos could he—

"He's leaving," I say, already turning on my heel. "We have to get to the road, try and stop him."

"How? We'll never make it!" Cass calls after me, but I'm already sprinting down the library's main aisle.

They'll either follow me or go look for Zach. We shouldn't split up, but I know deep down Gabriel's leaving. We'd only be at risk if we tried to stop him. I can take him on my own, unless he has a gun. But if he had one, he'd have used it on Apollo.

Not every criminal runs around wearing a pistol on his belt. Not like in the movies. I've known plenty of bad people in my life, and not a single one of them would even know how to fire a weapon.

I do. We all do. But we don't keep guns on us because we know there's a chance one of them might go off. And who the fuck knows who'd be at the receiving end of that bullet?

Guns are too easy to use, and too difficult to keep hidden. Especially around a bunch of boys still struggling with the fact that they're men.

The exertion of the sprint hits me when I'm halfway across

the lawn. I circle around the side of the dormitory, heading straight for the road.

We don't know how long Apollo was unconscious for, but the sun's barely warming up the land yet. It feels like everything's *just* happened.

I can't bear to let her slip away. Not a second time.

When my legs and lungs start burning, I push harder.

And I'm rewarded for my effort. Despite my heart clanging like a race horse's in my chest, despite the fact that I'm breathing fire, I make it in time.

I turn the corner.

I see the car.

Gabriel's car.

I'm in exactly the right place to watch him drive off, a shadow slumped beside him in the passenger seat.

He doesn't notice me because I'm yards away. If he did, I doubt he'd care.

Because I'm too late.

I ran too slow.

I didn't give it my all.

My legs collapse. My teeth clack together as I go down.

I'm still there, staring at the last place I saw them, when Cass runs up to me. He's out of breath, muttering something about stairs and smoking, and then his hand is on my shoulder.

I slap it away. I'd stand and face him, but I can't.

Muscle failure is a bitch.

"Gone?" he asks, but it's more a statement than a question.

Fucking gone.

And I was so close. If I'd pushed a little harder, if I'd thought just a little faster…

Cass helps me up. The ground feels spongy as we head back to the library. Something catches my eye.

I turn.

Zachary's standing on the front steps of Saint Amos. The big doors are open wide—Gabriel must have left that way. Zachary turns and disappears into the blackness without a word.

And then it all comes together.

I'd be mad, but I've got nothing left. I burned up everything in the useless sprint over here. It'll take time for my tank to refill.

I don't say anything to Cass, and I probably should. But sometimes it takes me a while to process things.

Like the fact that we were just betrayed by our brother.

8

TRINITY

It was all a dream. Saint Amos, the Brotherhood, Ghosts and Keepers and Guardians. Nothing but a nightmare. Sure, it makes no sense, but how else do I explain waking up in my old room back in Redford with groggy memories of photos and men with knives and losing my virginity in a library with four psychopaths?

My core aches when I try to remember details of the dream though. How they used my body for their own pleasure until they were spent.

Until *I* was spent.

I've had sexy dreams before, but nothing like that. Nothing that intense, that...vivid.

I force myself to picture the Brotherhood's faces.

Zachary with his intense green-eyed stare and that serpent tattoo on his chest. Apollo with his long, sandy-colored hair and light-brown eyes. Cass—mouthwateringly handsome, but those blue eyes so heartless. And Reuben. Black eyes and such a kind heart.

I sit up in bed, staring around blearily at my room as I

scratch my tummy. Daisy wallpaper. French-pane windows. Pastel pink curtains.

My body is stiff, my muscles sore. The itch is what woke me, I think, but it's hard to remember more than that.

I tug down the sheets and stare at myself. I'm still wearing the lacy white dress. There are a few spots of blood on it. More blood on the inside of my thighs—dried, smeared. My neck feels stiff. When I touch the back of my head, I find a bump on my skull. It should hurt, probably, but it doesn't. Not really.

The aroma of onions trickles into the room, wiping out my own stink of sweat and dried blood. There's a distant thump. Someone's in the kitchen.

Mom? Dad?

Awesome. I should go say hi.

Somehow, I make it to the top of the stairs, even though it's like I'm walking on clouds. From here I can only see a slice of the kitchen floor—I still don't know who's making the noise. The smell of cooking is intense now. I should be hungry, but instead I feel empty inside. Hollow, like a chocolate Easter egg. But in a good way.

I don't know why, but everything's good. And if it wasn't, I'm pretty sure I wouldn't give a damn anyway.

I cling onto the railing as I make my way downstairs because my legs feel kind of unreliable. Cigarette smoke comes to me in between the breakfast smell.

Wait. That's not right.

Dad's not allowed to smoke inside the house. He didn't even do it when Mom went to the shops.

Where *is* Mom?

She died in a car accident.

I falter halfway down the stairs.

Oh my God. They didn't both die. All this time, Dad's been living in our house in Redford while I was sent from pillar to post. While I had to bear the shame of being stranded in a school full of boys, an orphan girl who no one liked. No one except the Brotherhood.

Why would he do that to me? How *could* he?

The thought is visceral, but with no emotions attached. In fact, I don't feel anything. Except for a sudden itch behind my neck.

"That you, child?"

Dad called me that. Child. Like I was one of the kids in church. Maybe he got it from Gabriel.

I clear the stairs. I can see in the kitchen now.

There's a man by the stove. He has his back to me. There's a whole fog of smells now—bacon, onions, cigarettes, coffee, burned toast.

The man turns, smiling fondly when he spots me.

I'm convinced it's Dad, even though I know he's dead. So convinced that I see him there, right there. So convinced that, when my brain tries to interject, to correct me, I write it off as the fact that he's got a big Band-aid over his nose, and his face is a little puffy, and that's why he doesn't look quite like Dad but just enough that it *must* be him.

Dad beckons me closer with a spatula as he turns and starts dishing up food onto the plates standing ready on the kitchen island.

"Is this a dream?" I ask him through numb lips. Might as well make sure, after all.

"Would you like that?" he asks. And it's not Dad's voice at all. It's Gabriel's.

"Dunno," I say, but actually, I don't care.

Unsteady legs take me deeper into the kitchen. I stand next to a stool, but I can't even imagine how much effort it would take to get up.

Gabriel puts the pan back on the stove, dusts his hands, and comes around the island. His damaged face should scare me, but instead it intrigues me. I feel like I should know how he was hurt, but I can't seem to find the memory. He slips his fingers under my armpits and lifts me onto the stool like I'm a toddler.

"Morning, daughter," he murmurs, close to my ear, before he walks around the island and takes his seat on the opposite side. "Sleep well?"

When he slides my plate over, I try and pick up the fork propped on top of a piece of blackened toast. My fingers can't seem to get it right though.

Something is wrong.

With this setup.

With me.

"Hasn't worn off yet," Gabriel says, as if talking to himself. He takes a bite of his food and then points his fork at my plate. "You're probably not hungry. Should I put it in the microwave?"

The fork drops from my fingers, and he chuckles at me as he comes around to my side again. He pushes away the plate and grasps my chin with his fingers, turning my head to face him.

"How are you feeling?" he asks, staring deep into my eyes.

"Not feeling anything."

He smiles. "That's good." He drops his gaze, and it takes me a second to realize he might be staring at my body. I think I should care about that, but I don't. Not even when he rubs his hands up and down my arms like he's trying to warm me up. "You're so dirty. We'll have to get you cleaned up after breakfast."

He cups my face in his hands, wiping a strand of hair from my cheeks with his thumb. "You look just like her. It's uncanny."

Is he talking about Mom? Where is she, anyway?

"Where's Mom and Dad?" I should know the answer, but I don't. Another memory that refuses to come when called.

His smile fades a little. "Don't worry about them. We'll get along just fine on our own." He goes back to his side of the island.

I watch as he eats while my stomach grumbles quietly to itself. It probably means I'm hungry, but the thought of putting food in my mouth isn't in the least appealing. There's a soft pattering nearby, and I turn to look at the kitchen window. A gust of wind blows rain against the panes, smudging the world outside.

It's difficult to tell the time of day with the sun hidden behind the clouds, but I'm sure it's not breakfast time. Closer to midday, perhaps even past. And we're all the way back in Redford, a trip that takes hours, but I don't remember a single moment of it.

And then I do.

The bell tower. Gabriel has a needle. Apollo tries to stop him but he can't. It hurts going in but then my fear, my resistance, it all melts away into warm, cotton candy nothingness.

After that, there's only bits and pieces floating around in my head.

A long car drive tainted with the stink of cigarette smoke.

Stopping in front of my old house.

The overwhelming conviction that everything was right with the world, and I was exactly where I belonged.

"What did you give me?" I ask him. Not angry, not even scared.

Gabriel studies me over the brim of his coffee cup for a moment, and then takes a small sip before setting it down.

"Heroin," he says. Then he gives me a small, secretive little smile. "You'll love it. Your mother did."

"You must be getting cold," Gabriel says as he starts washing his breakfast plate in the sink. I'm still where he put me, and I have a feeling I'll stay here until he decides to move me again.

"No," I tell him, and quite truthfully. It feels like I'm wrapped in a thick, invisible cocoon. I don't even feel air moving against my skin.

"Let me just finish up here, then we'll go get you cleaned up and into something warm."

He's so nice. Always thinking of others.

"I loved them both, you know," Gabriel says, turning to me as he flicks soapy water off his hands. "It probably sounds strange." He smiles, laughs softly. "How can you possibly love two people?" Wiping his hands against his jeans, he deepens his smile as he comes closer. "But truly, I did."

He holds out his hand.

I take it.

It's still a little damp, but so warm. His grip is tight as he pulls at me, urging me to slip off the stool and follow him upstairs.

"We met at Saint Amos. Of course, back then, it was called Friends of Faith." He clicks his tongue. "Horrible place. Horrible." Sighs. "Better now, after the church took over. The new administration was a breath of fresh air."

He opens the bathroom door, pulls me through, and lowers me onto the closed toilet seat. I sit there and watch as he turns on the tub's faucet.

"Bubbles?" he asks, holding out a bottle of purple liquid.

I shrug a little. "Sure."

He tips some in and bubbles boil up and start spreading like a plague.

"You probably think I'm a hopeless romantic." Gabriel toes

off his shoes and goes onto his knees on the carpet in front of the bath. He sticks a hand in the water, agitating it so more bubbles form. "But truly, I was in love. I believe we all were." He pauses. "That's why we named you Trinity. Because you were *our* child. All three of us."

I nod. Love is a wonderful thing.

He catches sight of the movement from the corner of his eye. "Have you ever been in love?"

"I am."

He frowns a little at this. "Really? With who?"

"The Brotherhood."

His frown deepens. He sits back on his heels, putting his head to one side. "I don't follow."

I shrug. "Weird. I know. But I am." Talking is easy. Once I get going, I can't seem to stop. "I'm not sure about Zach. He scares me. But I love Reuben. And Cass. And Apollo. Different, but the same, you know?"

Gabriel reaches over and turns off the faucet, his eyes not leaving mine. When he speaks, it's slowly and carefully, like he wants to make sure I understand every word.

"You mean you *like* them. You were friends with them?"

"No. I slept with them. All of them."

The slap comes out of nowhere. I don't even realize it's happened until after. Suddenly, I'm facing the wall by the bath, and there's a fierce tingling ache on the side of my face. I turn back to face Gabriel, working a jaw that feels rusty.

White spots pop up on his cheeks. He turns back to the tub, twisting open the faucet so hard it squeaks.

"A whore," he says quietly as if to himself. "Your father said this would happen. Said you'd take after your mother."

I lift a hand to my cheek. I should be insulted, but it feels like I'm watching this all play out from the back of my mind. When my body moves, it's like someone else is doing it. When I speak, I'm hearing those words for the first time. "But I love them."

Gabriel swipes a hand through his hair, leaving a clump of bubbles on the side of his head. They start popping, and I swear it sounds like a hissing snake.

"She could have had her pick," he says, shaking his head. "Any boy at that school would have been happy just to have her look in his direction." He nods fiercely, whipping up more and more bubbles. "But she chose my Keith. Always wanted what she couldn't have, your mother."

His head snaps around. He looks me up and down, a disgusted sneer pulling at his mouth. "You're filthy," he says, in much the same tone of voice he's been using the whole time. "I hate filth."

"Is it because of the basement?" I'm dimly aware that I shouldn't be saying this stuff. That I should be keeping quiet. But my mouth's on automatic. Words spill out before I can filter them. "Because maybe if you'd cleaned the boys more, you wouldn't hate filth. It's psychological. Must be. You hate yourself for what you did. So you hate whatever reminds you of that place."

Gabriel stops with the bubbles. He doesn't look at me as he sits back on his heels, hands dangling over the side of the tub and dripping water and bubbles. Then he leans over and closes the faucet.

After the last drop falls, the bathroom is quiet but for the faint hiss of the bubbles.

He clears his throat, but it doesn't make his voice any smoother. "What basement?"

"The one you kept the boys in."

He whips his head to face me, eyes wide. "I don't know what you're talking about," he says, but his words sound so hollow, I wonder why he bothers trying to lie.

"You kept them there for years. Four little boys. More, I think. But those four were special. You kept them the longest."

Gabriel tries to stand, but there's something wrong with his legs. They tangle, and he ends up sitting on the edge of the bath. The whites of his eyes gleam, his eyebrows almost at his hairline.

"I don't know what you're talking about," he says again. Voice hoarse now, but still so rehearsed.

My fingertips start tingling. At first, I think it's because I'm scared. Terrified even. At least, I should be, somewhere deep inside. It only makes sense.

But then I realize it's the heroin wearing off.

Can't let him know, though. I have to take whatever advantage I can get, even a tiny one. So I make sure not to move. I try and keep my breathing at the same steady pace. And I continue talking.

"Apollo."

Gabriel's lips part suddenly, as if he's about to object. But he says nothing. Just sits there on the edge of the bath, gripping the porcelain with white-knuckled hands.

"He's the one that broke your nose."

His eyes flinch. He shakes his head. "I don't know what—"

"Cassius."

Gabriel's chest moves as he takes a deep breath. He suddenly seems to break out of whatever spell he'd been under. Standing, he steps closer, towering over me.

His expression is neutral as he slides his hand under my armpits and lifts me onto my feet.

And I let him.

Because if I try to fight him now, there's no way I'll win. And then he'll know I tried to trick him. I can't take a chance like that —I don't know how many I'll get. Right now, he's preoccupied. I've pushed him off course.

"I guess they probably changed their names or something," I say.

I expect him to deny it again. But this time he's silent. I guess he's trying to ignore me, but I can tell from the aggression in his movements that what I'm saying is hitting home.

The way he tugs at my dress to get it off. How his face contorts when I do nothing to help or hinder him. The way he draws back, as if startled by the fact that I'm not wearing underwear.

I have to use everything I can.

"They cut my panties off with a knife," I tell him. Lying is so easy. Maybe it's something to do with the residue of the drug floating around in my brain. I have no idea how they work, but it's as if it's annihilated every single filter I've ever had.

"Trinity." His voice is unsteady. He steps back, watches me. "Stop."

"Why?" I tilt my head to the side. "I thought you like this kind of thing."

His eyes go wide again. "You don't know anything," he whispers furiously. "You're a child playing with—"

"I thought you liked children," I say. It's becoming more difficult to keep my voice neutral. Emotions are coming back. Shame. I don't want to be standing naked in front of a priest. In front of a man I once thought of as my only friend.

But I also don't want to stay here, with him. I don't want to find out what he planned to do with me here, alone in my old house. The fact that he keeps comparing me with my mother, a woman he claims to have loved, when I can see only hate in his eyes.

"What are you insinuating?" He takes another step back. He's almost at the closed door now. Can I drive him out completely?

I put my head straight again, fight every cell in my body not to cover my chest or twist my legs. "I'm saying I know about the children you kept in the basement. The ones you hired out to those men."

I step forward.

His back hits the closed door. His eyes go even wider, and they start searching my face, frantic. What are you looking for, Gabriel? A sign that this is a nightmare, and not real life?

Trust me, that wish never comes true.

"I don't know what you're—" he says hoarsely.

"And they know about you." I stop walking because I can't bear to be closer right now. My skin feels like it's crawling with insects. Hundreds of them. The kind with little hooks all over their legs. And those legs, those hooks, they keep snagging on the fine hairs all over my naked body.

"No," he whispers, giving his head one shake. "No, you're wrong. You've got it all wrong."

And that's when the cold hits me.

I don't know how those boys kept the cold out, because I can't. I've never been able to. It's like I was wearing a blanket, and some invisible hand snatched it away.

A shudder ripples through me so hard that my teeth clench.

Gabriel looks at me. At my trembling body. And I guess he realizes what's happening. Something switches on in his head. Or off.

Because where I was convinced—*convinced*—he was about to tell me everything, perhaps even break down in a fit of conscience—

Gabriel throws back his head and laughs. Just once.

He grabs me.

On instinct, I struggle.

But I guess he's had a lot of practice dealing with unruly kids, because he kicks my legs out from under me and tips me to the side in one smooth motion.

My shin slams into the side of the bath, but that barely slows me.

One minute I'm standing, the next I'm under a sea of hot water and bubbles. My gasp of shock has me choking, my throat burning as water goes where it shouldn't.

I fucked up.

I pushed too hard.

I thought I was ready, but I clearly wasn't. My struggles are weak and pathetically ineffectual against Gabriel's strong arms.

He easily holds me under the water. When I reach up and try to gauge out his eyes, all I'm really doing is brushing his face with my fingers.

I manage to close my mouth. Hold my breath. It hurts like nothing I've ever felt, because my lungs still want to expel the water that went down my windpipe. And I'm trying to suppress those convulsions best I can.

Pain flickers red hot inside me. Building. Building.

My eyes are open, and they burn too because the water's too hot.

I don't know how long I can hold my breath, but it already feels like it's been too long.

My limbs are so heavy. My body weighs a fucking ton.

I can't even reach Gabriel's face anymore. So I try and grab onto his shirt.

Can't hold on.

Hands slap into the water.

My body convulses on its own, this time I can't stop it, and my lungs empty themselves. It takes forever, but then it's over in a heartbeat.

Only pain and emptiness left now.

And the faint sensation of his hands on my shoulders, holding me down.

9

RUBE

"Anything?" Apollo asks quietly as soon as he spots me. I'm sitting on the couch, Trinity's big white bible on my lap. I was reading it, but not with enthusiasm like I usually do. More just paging through, hoping for a sign that she'd read it too. A dog-eared corner. Some notes in pencil.

But there's no trace of her on here.

Maybe she never even opened it.

Which means I have nothing to remember her by.

"I'd have told you," I say, closing the bible and letting out a sigh.

It's been hours since I watched that car drive away. I've been waiting for a contact of mine who has an in at the Bureau to run Gabriel's plates and see if he comes up anywhere. But it's as if they disappeared off the face of the planet. For all I know, they switched cars as soon as they hit Redwater.

I rub my eyelids.

Zachary's been MIA. I saw him last at the front entrance of Saint Amos, a fact I reluctantly laid out to my brothers as we began piecing together what had happened this morning.

None of them reacted like I'd expected when I told them what Zach had done. Cass just stared, and Apollo let out a rueful snort like I'd told him he lost a bet he hadn't been expecting to win anyway.

I don't even know if he's still here at Saint Amos. We'd know when we go to the garage. And that'll be soon, because we have to leave.

That much we've decided on at least.

But where do we go? Anywhere past Redwater could be taking us further away from Trinity, from Gabriel. And we'd have no way of knowing.

We tried everything. Searched every record of Gabriel and Trinity's in the admin office. All we found were dead ends. Gabriel had cleaned house.

I don't blame Zach for hiding. I would too if I got a message like the one I sent him earlier.

WE WILL NEVER FORGIVE YOU

I didn't have to ask the others. I know they feel the same. Apollo's chewed his nails to the quick. I'm surprised Cass hasn't passed out from oxygen deprivation from chain-smoking.

They're fucked.

We're fucked.

And Zach did nothing. He just stood there and watched. For all we know, he helped Gabriel carry Trinity to his damn car. Maybe even wished him well as Gabriel sped off.

"Might as well head to Redwater," I say, standing. "Nothing more we can do here."

"I'll get Cass," Apollo says, turning.

I go to put Trinity's bible on the coffee table, but then hesitate.

I should take it with.

If we find her, I want to give it back to her.

Not if. When.

When.

When.

"What were you reading?" Apollo asks.

I frown at him. "Nothing specific."

"I mean…" Apollo rolls his eyes. "Read it to me." He lifts his shoulders.

"You want me to read to you from the bible?" I know my frown is deep, but Apollo looks hurt at my expression.

"Well, yeah." He flicks his hand. "Wanna know what it says."

I turn my head a little to the side. "It's the bible," I repeat. "It says a lot."

He crosses his arms over his chest. "Never mind then," he mutters and heads for the door. Apollo's never once shown an interest in religion. Spirituality, maybe, when he's high. But that's always been a more Universal Mind thing.

I didn't even stop for a moment to think what he and Cass are going through right now. How losing Trinity, then Gabriel, then Zach, affected them.

I clear my throat, and Apollo pauses by the door. Quickly scanning the page, I pick the first verse that stands on its own.

"Moreover, brethren, I would not that ye should be ignorant, how that all our fathers were under the cloud, and all passed through the sea. And were all baptized unto Moses in the cloud and—"

Apollo cuts me off with a wave of his hand. "Stop, stop. What use is that?"

"What were you expecting?" I ask, sitting back, closing the book, and putting it down on the cushion beside me. "A map?"

"Something inspiring," he says. "Not random—" He waves his hand again. "Forget it. I'll go find Cass and meet you at the garage."

I shake my head, letting out a long sigh as he closes the door behind him. Something inspiring?

I should have flipped to Revelations instead, read him chapter twenty verse ten.

And the devil that deceived them was cast into the lake of fire and brimstone, where the beast and the false prophet are, and shall be tormented day and night for ever and ever.

Maybe knowing that God had special plans for our Ghosts once they passed over would have *inspired* him.

My apartment door bursts open.

Apollo stands there in the doorway, hair disheveled, eyes wide.

I'm already on my feet, ready to attack whoever's behind him. But he just grins at me, claps his hands.

"I love that fucking book!" he yells, pointing at Trinity's gold-trimmed bible.

"What—"

He waves away the question, beckoning me to follow him. "We have to get to town, now!"

"Apollo, what—"

"I know how to find her, Rube!" His grin is infectious, especially paired with the exact words I've been waiting to hear all day.

I know how to find her.

"Wifi password," I bark out at the first waitress I see.

Her head moves back as she gives me a filthy stare, then she clicks her tongue. "All right," she says. "Settle down." Still frowning, she points with her chin. "Where you sitting?"

I'm about to frisk her for the damn password when someone's shoulder brushes mine. The waitress turns from me, and her frown dissolves instantly.

Should've listened to Rube. He told me to let Cass go in first. Nothing loosens lips like Cass's face.

"Hey, darlin'," Cass says, slipping in front of me. "We're outside, table twelve. Can't pass up a chance to watch that glorious sunset, now can we?"

I don't even know what accent he's putting on. But it doesn't matter, because it works. He's barely done speaking before the waitress is fumbling in her apron. "We got these paper thingies now," she's saying, her eyes glued on Cass as she rummages around. "They're changing it like every day."

"I hear you," Cass says. He sticks his arm around his back and pushes me away with his fingertips.

I guess he can't work his magic when I'm glaring at his conquest from behind his shoulder and willing them to get on with it. I grit my teeth, but I back off and go back outside.

Rube looks up as I thump down on the wrought iron chair. We chose a spot a little away from the rest, although this time of day, the town is pretty quiet. Everyone looks a little tired, like the drove of students they must have had in this place earlier today exhausted them.

Redwater's only diner is a nice enough place, but I'm itching to be on the road and headed toward wherever Trinity is. And that waitress back there has my hands tied.

Rube had to hot-wire Sister Miriam's old Ford to get us here. No idea why she left it behind—maybe she went on the bus—but it saved us because Zach's SUV wasn't in the garage. We'll have to switch cars before we leave here, of course. Rube's been eyeing an old truck parked next to the liquor store that has dust on the windscreen. If we can get it to start, then hopefully it won't be missed before we're far enough along to where we need to go.

Soon as I figure out where the hell that is.

"Coffee?" Rube asks.

"Yeah. Can we get something to eat?"

He frowns, and then nods. "But no lobster."

With Zachary gone, we only have a handful of cash between the three of us. We never figured a day would come when Zach wouldn't be there, swiping a card for whatever we needed.

How naive.

I still can't get over what he did, even though I kinda expected something like that to happen eventually. He's never been on board with Trinity. He's been treating her like the enemy from day one. And we went right along, because he laid it out so logically that it only seemed right.

I guess we've trusted him for too long.

Cass saunters back a minute later with a piece of paper dangling from his fingertips. I snatch it from him before he even has a chance to sit down.

I snort when I see what's written on the back. "She gave you her number?"

Cass shrugs, lounging in his chair like he was born without a spine. "Told her I wouldn't call."

Reuben rolls his eyes and then watches me type in the password.

It's one of those generated ones that are supposedly so secure. But the more random a password is, the easier a hacking program can crack it. It's passwords made out of words or phrases that are the hardest to crack. That's why Bitcoin wallets are usually protected with a seed phrase—a string of twelve random words that are easy enough to remember, but near impossible to crack without the use of a supercomputer.

That's why I know for a fact that the password to Gabriel's secret archive is some kind of phrase. My program's still trying to crack it, but I doubt it'll happen any time this century.

Soon as my laptop connects to the diner's wi-fi, I start looking for Trinity.

The world dissolves as I hunt through every database I can access.

Baptism.

Reuben laughed when I told him. We all laughed. Because it was so damn basic, we should have thought of it hours ago.

Trinity was baptized. Had to have been. Catholic parents and a priest as a family friend? No way around it.

And parishes keep baptism records. They have all kinds of useful shit on them like parent information, addresses, stuff like that.

I have Trinity's date of birth from the admin file. Her parent's first and last names too. But the rest of the file was empty. There were a few notes sent to Social Services requesting more info, but I guess their turnaround time is longer than she's been at Saint Amos.

All I need to know is which parish keeps her records.

I hop around the Internet, finding bits of information to add to my search.

Someone shoves a cup of coffee my way. I drink it down without tasting it, but fully appreciating the jolt of caffeine. A plate of food arrives, and it smells damn tempting, but I'm already down the rabbit hole so it grows cold beside me.

The light changes. Hues shift. Streetlights come on. The temperature drops.

And then I have it.

An address.

I look up. Cass and Rube are staring at me. "Well?" Cass says. "Tell us."

"It's not much." I grab a fry off my plate, swallow it down despite how cold it is. "But it's a start."

11

ZACH

I'm driving down the I-44—going too fast and giving way too few fucks. The joint I'm smoking helps. The bottle of whiskey in the glove compartment I sip at every now then, that helps most of all.

I never thought it would be this hard walking away from them. Or, in my case, driving away. Never thought I'd feel compelled to go back to them. To her.

But I am. And it is.

I hit the joint again. Tasteless. But I guess that happens if you keep smoking the same shit over and over.

No it doesn't.

I could have stopped Gabriel. If I didn't want to get my hands dirty, I could have called my brothers, warned them. *They* could have stopped him.

But I didn't.

They said they'll never forgive me for that.

Fuck—*I'll* never forgive myself for that.

A part of me was grateful he was leaving. And that part of me managed to take control long enough to sit back and let him walk away. But the rest of me? Numb, because it felt like I was losing something more important than my charred and blackened soul.

"That's because I *am* more important."

I glance in the rear-view mirror. A jolt goes through me when I see Trinity sitting in the back seat.

"What the fuck are you doing here?" I peer at her over my shoulder.

She's wearing the same lacy white thing she did when we took her virginity. Except now it's freshly laundered and her curls bounce around her shoulders like she's just come out of the salon.

And her lips are red.

Like the Whore of Babylon.

"You should watch the road," she says, an easy smile tugging at those cherry-red lips.

I smile back, glance at the road.

And almost lose control of the car as I swerve out for a truck. It blares its horn at me, the near miss rocking my now stationery rental like Trin and me are fucking in the back seat.

I turn around. She's not there anymore.

When I straighten and look ahead, she's standing by the hood of the car with her back to me. A gust of wind toys with her curls as she looks over her shoulder and beckons me with a crook of her finger.

I fumble for the car door, my composure shattered by the fact that I almost died. That I almost got Trinity killed.

Impossible. She's with Gabriel.

But that doesn't change the fact that when I walk up to her, when I grab her arm, when I turn her to face me, she's as real as I am.

I press her against my body, testing the theory. But there's no mistaking the way her hips press into the tops of my thighs. Her breasts into my ribs. And she makes a sound, a protest to my manhandling, as if I'm hurting her.

So delicate, like a dandelion. One breath and she'll scatter.

But I won't let her. Not again. The parts of my brain that held me frozen on Saint Amos's front steps aren't here right now. Maybe they clocked out after the deed, I don't know.

I grab the back of her neck and I kiss her right then and there on the side of the road.

Hard.

Relentless.

Forgetting how easy it was to break her. How much I enjoyed it.

"Here?" she murmurs against my mouth. "Right here?"

I don't know what she's talking about until she pulls back and climbs onto the hood. Spreads her legs.

Black underwear, which is wrong, because that's not what she was wearing. But maybe she changed, right? Girls like her don't go around commando.

My dick's out a second later. Too eager, but I can't help myself. I have to be inside her again. Feel her suffocating me. Milking me.

I thrust into her pussy with enough force to make her cry out.

Her fingers bite into my shoulders. "Harder," she says.

Her curls bounce. Her mouth forms a perfect 'o'. A car comes past, hoots at us. I give it the finger without looking. And then I yank down the top of Trinity's dress so I can draw one of her nipples into my mouth.

This isn't right.

Fuck it. I'm sure plenty of people have fucked on the highway.

No, this isn't right.

It's the way she rocks into me. So steady, so perfect. Like she gets paid by the fuck, blow jobs extra.

And that's not her.

That's not Trinity.

But I fuck her anyway, because it feels almost as good as the first time.

Maybe even better—this time there's no strange uneasiness floating around in my head. Because back then, with her, it wasn't just sex, and I still don't know why.

People fucking. Sometimes consensually. Sometimes not. That's all sex is to me. All it will ever be.

But it wasn't that way with her.

It's ridiculous, and pathetic, and stupid, but that doesn't change how it *felt*.

Like it meant something.

Like it would mean something every single time.

Except now.

This feels different.

Empty.

Fake.

I slap her thigh, but I can't feel that sting on my palm. She cries out though, and that helps. I fuck her harder, until her moans of pleasure become yelps of pain.

A normal man would stop. Maybe even apologize.

I'm not normal. Not even close.

Her pain is my pleasure. Nothing about that will ever change. She tenses around me, resisting me now. And that arouses me more than it should. More than what's moral or acceptable.

When she starts begging me to stop, that's when I finally feel a climax approaching. But it's taking too long. Like it's just out of grasp.

I pull back, wanting to kiss her again. Trying to capture

something of the first time.

But the face of the thing I'm fucking is no longer recognizable. It's still wearing the dress, but that fabric is dirty and tattered. Stained with blood and cum. The dead thing's face is bloated, disfigured, brutally beaten.

I push away from it, a yell trapped in my throat, but my dick is stuck inside it.

It's drawing me closer, arms wrapped impossibly tight around the back of my neck.

Its puffy, scarlet lips pucker as if for a kiss.

And then I'm coming inside it. The feeling goes on and on. Hollowing me out. As if it's not my semen I'm ejaculating, but my organs, and my bones, and my flesh.

My eyes fly open, a horrified gasp rattling deep in my throat. I push into a sit, clamping a hand over my heart. I can feel every violent clang as it pumps adrenaline through my body.

Jesus.

My body's stuck in some corporeal purgatory between Heaven and Hell. A dopey kind of pleasure from coming on the sheets. A skin-crawling horror from the memory of what I was pumping my load into.

I stumble out of bed, and almost crash into a wall I didn't expect so nearby.

Where the fuck am I?

Then my memories settle, and I'm back in the real world.

A motel room on I-44. I'd driven until I'd almost fallen asleep at the wheel, and then driven some more until I'd found a place to crash that wasn't my rental car.

Christ, that dream. No, that fucking *nightmare.*

I hit the shower before I'm even fully awake, washing the dream and the feel of decaying pussy off my dick.

I almost puke, but manage to choke it back.

Then I slide down the wall and curl into a ball, letting the water pound onto the top of my head until my scalp feels numb.

Until *I* feel numb.

It doesn't help. Body and mind, they're two separate entities.

I wish I could say the basement taught me that, but it didn't. *Mom and Dad* taught me that. They believed in discipline of the corporal kind. Mom with a wooden spoon. Dad with his belt.

I wasn't a naughty kid, I was high maintenance. Energetic. And they weren't. When I wanted to play outdoors—they'd lock me in my room. I'd end up breaking things, and then they'd punish me, even though I knew they had enough money to replace anything I ruined.

Only years later did I figure out what the problem was. I had ADHD, and an acute sensitivity to sugar. They never gave a shit about what I ate in between meals. And they'd keep replacing the sweets I ate. Maybe they didn't realize how bad it was. How it fueled my disobedience.

I guess I'm partly to blame. I never told them how it made my muscles ache and ache and ache until I had to move. Until I ran in circles, or threw things, or bounced on the bed.

My young body was a hormonal shit show. I either couldn't concentrate, or couldn't stop concentrating. Especially when I was punished. It was like my brain was working overtime to figure out why I invited pain.

It took years for me to realize that I was inviting it because I *did* enjoy it to some extent.

Because when they punished me, I wouldn't let any of the hurt show. And that confused them. And their confusion brought me great, great pleasure.

I was in my teens before I figured out that I enjoyed causing people harm. Emotional or physical, it didn't matter. They were the same thing, but experienced at different frequencies.

Cass was the one responsible for that epiphany. He claims

the basement turned him into a masochist but I think he was probably one all along.

When Cass ran out of dope or wanted something different to tune out to, he sought out pain. The others refused to give it to him. Me too, at first. Back then, my brothers didn't know about my darker side. The side that wanted to inflict suffering.

And I resisted him, until he goaded me past the point of no return.

Somehow, he'd figured out my secret.

So I hit him, just like he wanted. But a lot harder than he'd anticipated. I'll never forget his gasp of pain, and the shock in his eyes. Watching the confusion on his face as he tried to figure out what had happened? It felt fucking amazing.

That's when things changed. When I began to understand who the mind inside the body was. Me. My soul.

My brothers led me to that discovery, each in their own way...and I'm grateful.

But I still betrayed them and they deserve better.

That's why I left. Because my brothers deserve a life without me.

But not like this.

Not while the thing they—we—so dearly want has been taken from them.

I know they'll never forgive me. I knew before I read Reuben's message. But I don't need their forgiveness.

I need them to accept my help this one last time.

When the water turns cold and I start to shiver, I know it's time to get out.

I leave that place feeling like a dick for not cleaning up, but I couldn't stay a second longer.

I can't believe it's taken me so long to realize it, but I've been heading in the wrong fucking direction this whole time.

"**B**lack coffee," I say as soon as the waitress behind the counter looks up at me. I immediately break eye contact, but I see her watching me for a second longer before she goes to get my order.

Because I look like shit.

I didn't dare stop again, so I've been relying on caffeine and sheer willpower to keep me awake. It's been a rough road, like trekking up a crumbling mountain track, and I'm sure the downhill's even worse. But hopefully, by that time, I've found them again.

I didn't bother calling. Knew they wouldn't pick up. But technology has its perks.

The coffee arrives, and I blow on it to cool it faster. I order a sandwich—not because I'm hungry but because my body needs fuel.

I could have carried on driving to California. Set myself up in a hotel until the transfer papers for the house were signed. Until they gave me the key.

But then I'd have resigned myself to a life of misery. Probably a short one, at that.

They don't need me…but I need them. It's painful to admit, but I've had more than enough time to come to terms with the fact.

I detoured soon as I located their phones. I'm surprised they didn't ditch them…but I guess they weren't expecting me to come back.

Fuck, *I* wasn't expecting me to come back.

I stick a hand down the front of my shirt and fish out Trinity's crucifix. The wood feels smooth, almost oily, between my fingers. I lift it a little and squint through what looks like a clear gem stuck near the top as the smell of roses fills my nose. The Virgin Mary peers back at me, resplendent in front of her golden halo. Face serene. Like she knows everything's going to be just peachy, as long as I have faith.

I found it on the floor a few steps from Saint Amos's front doors, right after I'd locked eyes with Reuben. The clasp was bent —must have fallen off her neck as Gabriel carried her out of the building. I meant to give it back to Rube, perhaps put it somewhere he would find it, but then all I could think about was leaving.

Found it in my bag when I was pulling out clothes to change into. Hung it around my neck in case I lost it, because one thing is for sure…I will find my brothers. And when I do, this is going back to Rube.

My coffee is almost finished before my food arrives. But I don't complain, because I need the break, and I wouldn't have given myself that luxury.

My brothers are nowhere close to Saint Amos like I'd thought. They're in some small town in Virginia. I'm guessing they have a lead on Gabriel. Makes me want to find them even more, and I hate it. But revenge really knows how to get its claws into you. And fuck, does it latch on.

Was that way with my parents, too.

First week I was in that basement, my sadistic little mind was having a fucking field day. Oh, the beautiful, brutal things I did to them in my head. Holding them at gunpoint. Forcing them to do despicable things to each other. Thoughts of their fear, their humiliation—it kept me going for a while.

I'd keep banging on the door, begging them to let me out. Pleading with them. Trying to convince them that I wasn't one of the others.

Yes, I wanted my limited freedom back. But more than that, I craved the pain I knew I would inflict on them soon as I was free. Vengeance for hurting me. For hurting all the boys they'd kept in that dark hell.

To this day, I can't believe those tortured souls had been under my feet all that time. That I'd been living mere yards away from so much pain and suffering.

Some part of me still believes that's how my mind came to be so fucked up. That, unknowingly, I'd absorbed all that abuse through the pores in my skin. Like radiation, it began poisoning me.

I pay my bill. Leave.

The rental reeks of cigarettes, but I couldn't care if they kept my entire deposit because of it.

All I care about is one thing—getting to my brothers.

What happens after I arrive, that's up to them.

12

TRINITY

"Trinity."

"Trinity!"

I'm cold. So cold compared to the warm hands on my body. Behind my neck, between my shoulders. Pushing me onto my side.

I retch. Throw up. I choke on the water and bile burning my nose and throat. It hurts a lot, but at least now I can breathe.

Hands on me again—so warm—helping me up. A towel to cover my nakedness.

Those hands guide me down a passage and into a room.

Halfway across the soft carpet I recognize where I am. A bedroom, but not mine.

Mom and Dad's.

I'm still in Redford.

Oh God, I miss them so much. The smell in here, although stale, pushes pins through my heart. But why is everything still the same? It's been more than a month. Surely someone would have bought the house? Moved in? Made it their own? Why is it still exactly the same as the day I left?

I shiver, and then try to resist when the hands lead me to the bed.

I was never allowed in here.

It was *their* room. They made that very clear.

I never once ran in and clambered over them to wake them up when I was a little girl. No snuggling between them if I had a nightmare.

Because I was a good girl. I obeyed them. Even now, even though they're gone, I feel like I'm disobeying them.

But when someone pulls away the sheets, revealing a warm nest I can burrow into, I go. No hesitation. Because I'm tired. I'm hurting. And I'm so cold.

As I slip between sheets that still smell like my parents, I hear a voice. Mom's. Not singing—she never sang—but reciting a prayer.

...hallowed be...

Oh, right. I know this one.

I burrow into the bed, cringing as my wet hair makes my cheek itch. I'm not clean enough to be on these sheets. I can still smell myself. But there's lavender too, and that makes me think about bubbles and that makes me want to climb out of bed and run away.

But I'm too tired.

...give us this day...

So I stay where I am, curled into a ball, trying to warm up. I cough, and clear my throat, and try to get rid of the awful feeling inside me. The rawness where water went but shouldn't have.

...forgive us our...

I lie there even when someone gets in behind me and holds me. Even though I know who it is. Even though I know what he's capable of.

I'm even fucking grateful, because he's so warm, and I'm so cold.

...lead us not into...

I lie there in his arms until I fall asleep. And I'm still there when I wake up.

But I only wake up a long, long time later after he wakes up. After he brushes hair from my face and kisses my cheek. Only after he squeezes me tight and whispers, "Morning, daughter."

...deliver us from evil...

Now I'm not tired anymore. I'm not hurting as much. I *am* scared. But I'm also angry. And I want out.

...thine is the kingdom...

My mind races as he snuggles his face into the back of my neck, as if he's smelling me.

...the power and the glory...

This is not my new life. I'm getting out of here, whatever it takes.

...forever and ever.

Amen.

13

TRINITY

I think Gabriel has fallen asleep again. I guess it's tiring, holding someone captive. But he should be used to it though.

The thought leaves a bitter taste in my mouth. I shift a little, then pause, waiting for his reaction.

Nothing but a soft breath against the back of my neck. His arm is still slung around me, his fingers dangling over my hip.

It would be so easy to stay here. Although I don't feel as shit as I did when I woke up on the bathroom floor after he tried to drown me, my body is still weak. I haven't eaten in…days?

So easy just to let it happen.

To go somewhere else inside my head.

But that's not what *they* did. Those four boys in the basement fought back. They stayed strong, and they found a way out.

But they were four.

I'm just me.

So easy to feel sorry for myself right now. To think it's useless. That I'd make Gabriel angry and he'd try to hurt me again.

Even though right now he's peaceful. Almost like the Gabriel I used to know and love. But he won't stay this way. I'll say something and it will trigger him to the violence, and he'll try to hurt me again.

I gently grasp his wrist and lift it. Slow. Easy. I keep it suspended as I carefully wriggle to the side.

The tendons in Gabriel's wrist go tight. He murmurs something inaudible as he tries to hold onto me in his sleep.

I freeze, eyes squeezing shut, and send a prayer to any higher power who might be listening.

Our father, which art in heaven.

Hallowed by thy name.

The prayer becomes a mantra that cycles over and over in my mind as I slowly make my way to the edge of the bed. As soon as I'm clear, I put his hand down on the sheets.

The instant I let go, he turns over, dragging the bedding with him. Leaving me exposed and naked on the far side of the bed.

I slip out and stand hunched over, my heart thudding relentlessly in my chest. With his back to me, I don't know if his eyes are open. They can't be—why would they?—but that doesn't change a thing.

Deliver us from evil.

All I need is for him to stay exactly as he is. Lost in whatever perverted dream he's having right now.

I back up out of the room, hesitate at the threshold, and then pull the door closed as I creep into the hallway outside. I'd have locked it, but the key's gone.

I know I shouldn't be wasting a millisecond, but I can't run into the street naked. And it will only take a few seconds to put on clothes. Just pants and a shirt. I won't even bother with underwear or shoes.

That's the plan, anyway. But when I step into my room, it's as if the world does a somersault around me.

I freeze.

It looks like a tornado went through this place.

My closet doors are wide open. Everything inside them has been dumped on the floor or on the bed. Little ornaments—the kind of knick-knacks you accumulate when you're young—are everywhere. Some shattered. Tears and scuffs on the wallpaper where he threw things against the wall.

Was he looking for something? Or did my accusations really piss him off that much?

Move, Trinity! He could be waking up any second now, and you're just standing there? You've established he's a nut job—now how about you get on with escaping?

I force myself deeper into my room, but it's like I'm in a trance. There's so much chaos in here I can't find anything.

I pick up a jacket that doesn't have a zipper or buttons —pointless.

A scarf.

That goes around my neck, because, well, that's where scarfs go.

I find leggings. Pull them on. They're not fully opaque, but they're better than nothing.

Finally, the last piece of the puzzle. A sleeping shirt. Picture of a grumpy cat on it. Something about needing coffee. I tug it over my head as I turn to head out the room.

Gabriel's standing by the door. Chin down as he watches me. Hands opening and closing at his sides.

Panic slices into me like frozen razor blades. I wrap my arms over my chest and take a step back. "I was getting cold," I say.

He's wearing only a pair of sweatpants. I hadn't even realized that when he was in bed with me. I don't think I've ever seen him bare chested. I had no idea he was so muscular. So strong. No wonder I couldn't fight him.

He lifts his chin. "You have to accept the things you cannot change." He turns his palms to face me, arms still at his sides. "I'm your father. That's never going to change."

His body fills the doorway. I can only get out if he comes closer. It's that or jump out of a second-story window. There's a tree outside—I could maybe catch hold of a branch.

That's a big maybe.

How badly would it hurt if I missed the tree?

Maybe I can try and find out what Gabriel wants. I mean, I could be over-thinking this. What if he just wants to take me to the mall, watch a movie together, eat some take out?

As long as I don't mention the Brotherhood, or the basement, I should be fine. Even now, he looks calm.

"I…"

Lord, why is this so difficult?

He puts his head to the side, waiting. Always so patient.

"What are…we doing?" Another swallow. "Here, I mean?"

He frowns, glances around. Then he reaches out and straightens a framed picture I drew when I still believed in unicorns and how *awsum* they were.

"I've always liked this house," he says. "Spent much more time here than I should have."

His eyes fix on me again. I don't know how I could ever have thought those brown irises were warm, or comforting. Now they look cruel. Calculating, even. "They left it to me, the house."

"Don't you have a house? Why don't we go there instead?"

I don't know if it's better being here or in a different place, but we'd have to be in a car, on a road, out in public to get there. If I can convince him—

"My house?" Gabriel purses his lips. Shakes his head. "No. My house is no place for a little girl."

Ghostly fingers crawl up my back and start toying with my hair. That's what he thinks of me? A little girl? Does he even know how old I am?

It sickens me to think about it, but maybe that's the only card I have to play right now. He keeps calling me daughter— maybe I can count on his paternal instincts to get me out of this jam.

"I'm kinda hungry," I say, putting a hand to my stomach. "Can you make me something to eat?"

The kitchen has knives. Pans. Several objects I can use to hurt him with. It's also closer to the front door, which has a lock I can turn from the inside without needing a key.

If I can get to the front door, I can get out of the house. I can run down the driveway and scream at the top of my lungs. The neighbors would hear. They'd have to look out their windows. And they'd see me running like a lunatic—

"No."

My shoulders sag a little. "But I'm—"

Gabriel's eyes narrow. "Do you really think I don't know what you're trying to do?"

Fuck.

Fuck!

I try and look innocent. "Really, I just want some—"

"You've been bad," he says, stepping closer.

Yeah, come closer, you fucking creep. Close enough that I can run around you and out of the room. Down the stairs. To the front door.

I wish I'd thought of that yesterday. I'd been a few yards from the front door. But I'd been so doped up on heroin, I hadn't even thought about it.

No. I'd been convinced my father was in the kitchen cooking breakfast.

Ha, ha, ha. I guess he was.

"Slut like you, you don't deserve to eat."

Oh Lord. It's all coming back to me now. The things I told him when we were in the bathroom. Boy do I regret that plan.

I need to turn this around.

I wish it didn't have to come to this, but I can't think of any other way of doing that.

"Father, please."

There's a flicker of something in his eyes.

"Please, I'm sorry." Denial isn't the way to go. But confession might just work. "I sinned. I know that now, I see it. I just…"

I drop my head. The tears that come aren't all that forced. I've had a lot of practice with feeling sorry for myself.

I've been doing it my whole life.

I pitied the fact that I had such strict parents. That I could never do all the fun stuff other kids did.

Then I pitied myself because I'd been orphaned by a random twist of fate. That God had let two of his sheep die. Then came Saint Amos, and oh boy did my pity party turn into a rager.

Now this.

I used to challenge the Universe. I'd shout "What else you got?" in my head when I was feeling particularly downtrodden.

But I've met a group of men who could have pitied themselves day in and day out. I can't believe how weak I am, compared to them. How little it took to defeat me.

The attention of one man, when they've had to withstand many.

Two days, when they lasted years.

So yeah. I think I can suck it up and play pretend for a while.

"Will you help me, father?"

Gabriel's chin lifts a little higher. "Help you?" His voice is faint. He frowns, opens his mouth. But I cut him off with a sob that's not at all feigned.

Every cell in my body is screaming at me to stop, but this is the only way.

That's how you overcome fear, right? You face it.

I walk up to him, stumbling over the things scattered over the floor, and I put my arms around him, and I hug him hard.

When I close my eyes, I can almost believe it's my first day at Saint Amos, and he's just arrived outside my room.

The familiar smell of his fabric softener, his aftershave, him...wafts up to me. When he wraps his arms around me so tight.

"Please, father." Another sob. "Help me find the light."

His chest expands as he inhales, and I shiver when he kisses the top of my head.

"Of course, child," he murmurs.

Hands find my face. He draws back my head and stares down into my eyes. His smile is wide, and warm, and genuine. It shouldn't, but it lights a candle inside me.

He strokes away a tear with his thumb. "Come. Let's eat."

My body is ten pounds lighter as he grabs my hand and laces my fingers with his. I float behind him, barely touching the ground as he leads me down the stairs. I force myself not to look at the front door as we pass it, and my body complies.

A gust of wind slams raindrops hard against a nearby windowpane. And then he turns away from the kitchen.

My hope shatters like a glass trinket hitting a stone floor.

The hand around mine is suddenly too tight. He's pulling me a little too hard.

"Father—"

I cut off with a pained sound as he yanks me after him. "You want to find the light?" he yells, glancing back at me with wild eyes. "I know just the place." He turns again, and my heart sinks deep into the churning depths of my stomach when I realize where he's taking me.

I kick back, scream.

He pulls at me until I'm close, and then grabs me. Slaps a

hand over my mouth. All the while still walking toward the door at the end of a long passage.

Hidden away like a nasty secret. Even the keypad beside the door is flat and discrete. You probably wouldn't see it unless you were close.

Gabriel keys in a combination—so fast, I only catch the first two numbers, 4 and 2. When he opens the thick door, the smell of damp earth and crawling things slams into me.

He slaps a hand against the wall, and the basement light flickers on. It's not much—a bare bulb that only seems to solidify the shadows into something more sinister than before.

Gabriel brings me in front, an arm around my waist to keep me tight, a hand over my mouth to keep me silent. He forces me down the stairs one at a time. I struggle as much as I can, despite the fact that we could both take a tumble and land up with broken necks.

Especially when the sagging metal frame of my old single bed comes into view. Because then I know a broken neck is the only winning hand in this game.

I'd wondered about the lock on the basement before—the pilot light is down here, so we'd be stuck if he wasn't around to light it again if it ever went out. But who was I to question Dad's wisdom? His quirks and his rules? How could I, when Mom didn't?

I've never been down here before. Hell, I wasn't even allowed in the passage back there. The space is surprisingly small, until I realize the walls are soundproofed. Someone closed up this space on purpose. Turned a massive basement into a much smaller, more intimate space.

Someone? You know exactly who did this.

But my mind rejects the thought.

My old mattress is still on that rusting bed frame. There's even a sheet over it, but its moth-eaten and stained.

And then I see my old potty trainer.

And then I see the ropes still attached to the bed frame.

I start kicking up my legs, twisting and wriggling, but it doesn't help. Gabriel holds me with ease. His voice doesn't even sound strained when he speaks.

"No better place to look for the light," he murmurs into my ear, "than down here in the dark."

And then...then I see the video camera.

14

TRINITY

I wish I knew a bible verse by heart right now. Or lots of them. Then I could choose the perfect one. Something Old Testament about going to hell for your sins.

Probably wouldn't have helped. I mean, Gabriel's a priest. He knows the bible back to front, and not one verse ever swayed him toward the light.

He shoves me away from him. My hands fly out and barely catch me against the plastic sheet lining the floor.

I scramble onto my back, ready to kick out if he comes close.

The room is small, claustrophobic even. The bed takes up most of the space. If I can distract him, I can try and get past him and up to the stairs.

Like I haven't tried that before.

"What do you want?" I try to keep my voice calm in case he lunges at me to keep me quiet. Or maybe it doesn't matter down here with all this soundproofing.

I've certainly never heard sounds coming from the basement. Or had I dismissed them as my imagination?

Gabriel lifts his hands, showing me his palms. As if he wants me to trust him.

What a joke.

"You said you want to find the light." His voice is tight and unsteady, like he's barely keeping it under control. "Many boys have found the light down here."

I shake my head before I can stop.

"You don't believe me?"

"Dad would never—"

Gabriel's bitter laugh cuts me off. He walks up to me, dodging effortlessly when I kick. Then he grabs me by the hair and hoists me to my feet, shaking me mercilessly.

His other hand grabs my chin, turning my face and forcing me to look around the small room.

"Who do you think built this place?" he hisses in my ear. "It wasn't me, child."

If I could shake my head, I would. The things he'd said after I hobbled up to his room at Saint Amos and told him I had to show him something in the bell tower…

But my mind rejects what he's telling me.

"No," I murmur. "Dad was a good man. A holy man. He would never—"

"Your *dad*?" Gabriel croons, mocking me. He's becoming unhinged again, like he did back in the bathroom.

"I'm sorry," I blurt out. "I'm sorry, Father, I didn't mean—"

He shakes me into silence. "Always blameless," he whispers as he drags me close against him. "No one ever suspected. Not even you."

Of course not. Why would they? My dad kept to himself and both my parents were quiet people. But they loved the church. They loved people. I never heard them say a bad thing about anyone. Oh, they'd fight behind their closed bedroom door, but I wasn't idiotic enough to believe they had a perfect marriage. Dad was gone a lot and Mom didn't like staying home to look after me. She never said it, but I could see she missed him when he wasn't around.

When I was younger they'd sometimes go away for a week or two, but that stopped as soon as I hit puberty. It was Dad who told Mom to stay at home. He probably thought I would lure a boy back home or something. He seemed to think I was a whore as much as Gabriel did.

I always thought he was strict because of his faith, but maybe he was actually trying to protect me from people like him? Deviants and pedophiles who would see me in a short skirt and obsess about what they could do to me if they had me to themselves?

Somewhere hidden. Somewhere secret.

A dark, soundproofed room like this.

"Please," I whisper. "Please stop."

I can't let him destroy my past. It's all I have.

"Forgiveness requires confession, child," Gabriel says, his lips brushing my ear. He shakes me again, kisses my temple. "Only through confession can we be cleansed of sin."

"P-please."

"I told your mother that so many times. But she wouldn't listen, just like you."

My heart stutters in my chest.

Mom knew?

Oh Lord, who am I kidding? Of course she knew. But logic doesn't ease the pain of realizing my mother kept Dad's secret.

I stab my elbow into Gabriel's stomach.

I get lucky. He's distracted, and I manage to hit him hard enough, and in just the right spot, that I knock the air from his lungs.

He doubles over with pain, his grip releasing just enough for me to wriggle free.

I make a dash for the stairs, for the door, for freedom.

My foot lands on the first stair, and then Gabriel kicks it out from under me. I fall face first, my chin slamming into the wooden step. Blood leaks into my mouth from the cut my teeth sliced into the inside of my cheek.

But I'm already scrambling up, ignoring the pain, ignoring the sound of Gabriel's furious breathing behind me.

I don't reach the door.

Halfway up the stairs, Gabriel latches onto the back of my sleeping shirt and *tugs*. I go flying down the stairs, missing all of them. I land on my back on the plastic sheeting with a loud *crump*.

Air gushes out of my lungs. I roll onto my side, groaning as a dull ache spreads through my body from the impact.

When I force my eyes open, they fix on Gabriel's loafers.

He grabs my hair and drags me over the floor. My scalp is on fire where he's pulling, hurting more the harder I fight.

The bed squeaks when he throws me down, and I scream in panic. I try to roll off, but he slaps me so hard I see stars. There's a violent yank on my arm, the rough kiss of a rope, and then I'm bound.

Like he's done this a thousand times before.

I start sobbing with frustration, fear, desperation. "P-please!"

"That's it," he says, voice menacingly low. "Keep begging. That's just how he liked it."

What. The. *Fuck?*

I kick and lash out, but it's as if Gabriel is made of steel. He doesn't even blink when I rake my nails through his skin hard enough to draw blood.

"Help!" The yell burns my throat.

I was right about the soundproofing. Gabriel doesn't give a fuck. He grabs my foot and lashes it to the bedpost.

My toes catch his chin, sending his head snapping to the side. There's a hush, a pause as he straightens his head.

His brown eyes resemble those of an animal head hanging above some redneck's fireplace.

There empty. Dead.

He grabs my other foot, lashes it down. I try and untie the knot on my left hand while he's busy, but it's so tight I don't make any progress by the time he's done.

And then he climbs on top of me, straddling my stomach.

Terror pours ice through my limbs. I go stiff, panting as tears leak from the corners of my eyes.

He grabs my chin, his fingertips biting cruelly into my jaw. Then he snaps my head to the side like he can't bear looking at me anymore.

A giant sob wracks me as he ties off my last wrist. He settles back, crushing my stomach with his weight, and studies me.

My head is still to the side, and I don't dare look at him. Instead I squeeze my eyes shut and start praying.

Our father, which art in heaven,
Hallowed be thy—

"Look at me."

—name. Thy kingdom come.
Thy will be done, on earth as—

"Look at me!" he roars.

His fingers wrench my head to face him, but I keep my eyes squeezed closed. It's stupid, it's fucking juvenile, but it's the only way I can defy him now.

I'm not going to lie here and take this.

"Trinity." His voice is soft now, sinister. "Open your eyes."

"Fuck you."

A slap sends white spots dashing through the black behind my eyes.

"You like it, don't you?" he rasps. "The fight. The struggle. The *pain.* Got that from your whore mother."

My eyes fly open. I stare up at him in shock. "How dare—"

He slaps me again. "Is this the only way you'll let me in? Is this what it will take? Because I've done worse." His voice catches. "I've done so much worse for so much less."

My heart thunders in my chest. What the hell is he talking about? His shoulders move back, hand raised for another slap.

"No! Stop! Please!"

He pauses, but his hand stays up.

"I don't know what you mean. Please..." A sob cuts in, I force it down best I can. "Just...just talk to me, Gabriel."

Pathetic, trying to reason with a mad man. But my head aches, and my cheek's on fire, and I can't take anymore. I'm so close to surrender, I can already feel his hands on me.

His chest rises and falls, exaggerated. His hand drops, but barely an inch.

"Please. Just talk to me. Tell me..." I have to swallow hard before I speak again. "Tell me what you want."

"What I want," he repeats woodenly.

His hand falls to his side. His eyes move off me, staring at nothing. Or maybe only something he can see.

"Yeah," I manage. My voice rebels, but I push out the words anyway. "Let's talk, Gabe. Just you and me."

His eyes slide back to mine.

I squirm under him before I can control myself because that blank face of his ratchets up my fear a thousand notches.

"So you can use me like he did?" he murmurs. Shakes his head. His voice drops to barely a whisper. "My fault. I let him use me. I let him control me..."

The hand he'd been about to hit me with curls into a fist. But instead of slamming into my face, he leans on it, putting his head close to mine.

He stares into my eyes from an inch away. I can feel his breath on my face, still a little too hard, too hot, from our struggle. My flesh writhes beneath my skin like I have a thousand worms burrowing through my body.

"It was his idea." Gabriel laughs, sending a puff of warm breath over my lips. "But no one will ever believe me. Know why?"

His eyes skitter over mine, searching. I keep my face neutral. Try and keep my eyes locked on his.

"Why?" I manage.

He draws back a little, and then his eyes fall to my lips. "Because he's a clever fuck, that's why."

Gabriel taps my temple hard with a finger. "Always ten steps ahead of me."

My entire body vibrates how hard my heart's beating. "I'm sorry," I murmur. "He shouldn't have used you."

"No!" he agrees, breath painting my lips again. His eyes are locked on mine now, so intense I can almost feel his pain. "No, he shouldn't have. Not if he loved me like he claimed he did. But you know what, Trinity? I realized something a few years ago." He glances away for barely a second before his eyes are back on mine again. "Still can't believe it took me so long, but I realized, of *course* he didn't love me. He's not capable of love. He'd just pretend. Just like he'd pretend to be normal."

He grabs my chin, shakes my head. But not violently this time. Almost gently.

"Had everyone fooled, didn't he?" He smiles, bitterly, cruelly. "Me. You. Everyone."

My head sinks into the dirty mattress when he pushes back to sit. He drags his hands down his face and then slowly climbs off me.

Relief floods me with heat, then cold. I don't know what to

say. I feel like I'm walking a tightrope, and one wrong word could send me plummeting to my death.

Literally.

But I don't need to. He's gone off on a tangent, and I'm merely his audience.

"I was such a fool back then," Gabriel purses his lips. "I was so infatuated with him, his plan sounded...logical. If his urges, his *compulsions*, only became worse when he repressed them then he had to find an outlet for them."

My skin grows cold. I swallow hard, and then force myself not to fixate on Gabriel, or the words spilling out of his mouth. Instead, I tug surreptitiously at the knots lashing me to the bed, trying to find a little give in them. Something. Fucking anything.

"We tried everything, Monica and I. Sick things. Things you couldn't wrap your head around. But it was never enough. The two of us? We were never enough for him."

He points at the bed, and I freeze. But he's so far lost in the past, I doubt he even sees me anymore.

"I'd strap her down for him. *Hurt* her for him. Ropes, whips, knives. We'd fuck her raw, but it was never enough for him."

My guts twist as I glance down at the mattress I'm lying on.

Lord, don't let this be the same one they—

My eyes flutter closed as I will my nausea to settle down.

"It became a game, in the end." Gabriel walks up to the bed, stares down at me. When he reaches out and grabs a lock of my hair, curling it around his finger, I do my best not to pull away or puke. "But Keith always won."

My body sags.

I'm not getting out of these knots. I doubt I'm even getting out of this basement. Not after I see the look in Gabriel's eyes.

Defeat.

He knows there's no coming back from this. You can't tie up your daughter in a basement and still expect her to love you.

If that's even what he was after. It's night and day with him. Like a faulty switch that keeps dimming and brightening a light even when you're not touching it.

"You're crazy," I say quietly. Not with malice. Just stating a fact, that's all.

Gabriel smiles as he huffs out a breath through his nose. "Yes." He agrees through a sigh. "I am." Then he releases my hair. "But not always. Not at first." He points at himself. "He made me like this. With his tricks and his games."

He's nodding over and over again, like he's stuck. "*They* did this to me."

"You can't keep blaming him. He's dead."

At this, he throws back his head and laughs.

The sound is more terrifying than when he was on top of me, slapping me into submission.

"Oh, God." A last laugh. "Yes." Another sigh. "They both are. They are so very fucking dead." He dips his head a little. "God answers our prayers in his own way," he says, placing a hand over his heart. "It only took a few thousand of them before he answered mine."

I grit my teeth at him. "It's karma. It's what happens if you're a bad person."

His face turns to stone, but he doesn't try and stop me.

"Think you'll get away with it? You won't." I lift my head, pushing my chin out at him. "And I hope God punishes you. I hope you die a slow and horrible death. Because that's more than what you deserve for what you did to those boys, you sick fuck!"

The silence that comes after my pronouncement seems much too quiet, like the walls in here are still soaking up every stray sound wave.

Gabriel tilts his head to the side. Takes a step closer. "You still don't get it, do you?"

I cringe away the closer he comes, but there's nowhere for me to go. Tied spread-eagled to this bed, I can't do anything to protect myself.

"I had nothing to do with those kids. Nothing!" He points a finger to the side, then stabs it into his chest. "He blamed everything on me. He set me up when I told him I'd take you away from him. And he couldn't have that, could he? Oh no."

Gabriel gives his head a furious shake.

"You were the only reason Monica stayed. You were the glue that held your dysfunctional family together. Monica wouldn't leave him, because he told her he would hurt you if she tried."

My ears are singing. Not hymns, but dirges filled with despair.

Gabriel lets out another bitter laugh. "And that was my fault." He lunges forward, grabs the front of my shirt in a fist. "I'm the reason you're alive. I'm the reason he had something he could use to control her with. To control *us* with."

His other hand cups my cheek. "He used you to turn her against me. And when I threatened to expose him, he made it look like *I* was the one who arranged everything. All those boys, for all those sick men? Me!"

My mouth is open. My eyes wide. But I can't digest the information flooding my mind.

"He found a film of a young boy." Gabriel's eyes are wide, his face sickly pale. "He made us watch it. Me and Monica. Told us *that* was what he needed. *That* was the only cure for his sickness. Just one boy. One boy, and he wouldn't prey on anyone else again."

"N-No, pl-ease," I manage, but sobs cut up the words.

"Who do you think it was, found that first boy for him? Hmm?" He leans close again, twisting the fabric of my shirt. Pushing me hard into the mattress. His fingertips dig into the side of my face as he forces me to look at him.

"Who do you think brought him down here, to the dark?"

"N-No…"

"Wasn't me," Gabriel whispers furiously. "I refused. I told her I'd have no part in it."

"Please."

"But she loved him so fucking much. More than life itself. More than that boy's life."

He shakes my head. Twists. The fabric is cutting into my flesh. It feels like it's compressing my lungs.

Or maybe that's fear.

Panic.

Denial.

"He didn't last very long down here in the dark. Keith said it was because he didn't have any friends to play with."

I close my eyes.

Our father, which art in heaven.

"But there wasn't enough room down here, was there? Monica tried to reason with him. Not enough room for another boy, Keith. Where would he sleep?"

Give us this day, our daily bread.

"So they had to find somewhere else. A bigger house. Someplace out of the way."

And forgive us our trespassers, as we forgive those who trespass against us.

"And they did. They found a lovely, big old house out in the country. A place no one would suspect. And they had to, because Keith had found himself some friends. Believers of his cure."

And deliver us from evil.

"Nice big house. With a nice big basement. And then the boys could have friends to play with. And there was more than enough space to put them, when they were dead."

"You're lying," I whisper. "Mom had nothing to do with this. She couldn't have. She's not—"

"Oh, you'd be amazed, child. You'd be fucking amazed."

Gabriel releases my shirt and absently smooths the fabric down over my chest as he stares into my eyes.

"Who do you think washed all that filthy money they earned?"

"No. They didn't have money. We weren't rich. You're lying!"

Gabriel's lips quirk up in a smile. "No, you weren't rich. Monica was clever. She made sure not to raise any suspicions. But as soon as you were eighteen, they were going to disappear."

He stands, leaving behind the ache where his fingers had been gripping my face.

"But then God struck them down. Now they're in hell, Trinity. Right where they belong."

"And what about his friends?" I ask, my voice hoarse, broken. "What about the boys?"

"Dead. They hid them well. His followers…?" Gabriel shrugs as he purses his lips and glances away. "They'll find other cures." Then his eyes are back on me, fiery and determined. "But God will seek them out, one by one, and he will strike them down."

"How can you be so sure?"

"Because I've been praying, Trinity." A smile crawls onto his face. "I've been praying for each and every one of them."

15

RUBE

"This is it?" Cass says through a mouthful of smoke. He tips back his head and then shakes it as he flicks away the butt end of his cigarette. "What a dump."

"Still can't believe this didn't come up before," Apollo says. He's got his hands in his pockets as if it's cold outside, but the sun is shining and I'm in short sleeves.

Could be the damp. It must have rained here last night, because the ground is still soggy in some places.

"Too close to home," I tell Apollo. "He made sure nothing led back here."

I head for the church, leaving them standing on the sidewalk.

Cass strays away down the road and Apollo hurries after him. Maybe Cass is worried he'll run into a priest. His hatred of the clergy borders on psychosis.

I let myself in and wander down the aisle toward the chancel. The nave is empty, which is no surprise for a Friday morning.

There's a sister near the altar, replacing some of the gutted-out candles. She turns when she hears my footsteps and does a double take.

"Can I help you?" she calls out, hugging herself and grabbing hold of the blatant crucifix around her neck. Seems this is one of the dioceses that don't require sisters to wear habits. But the big cross was still a dead giveaway.

"Morning, sister…?" I stop a few feet away, keeping my distance and hoping it'll help ease her mind.

"Vicky," she says reluctantly, giving me a small nod.

This isn't the greatest neighborhood, but why is she so spooked?

"Reuben." I lift a hand to shake, but she ignores it, instead watching me with wide eyes as if willing me to get to the point.

Chances were slim to none that anyone would hand over baptism records to a non-relative.

We'd stopped off at the mall on the way here and picked up fresh clothes for me. Not really something we could afford, but we all looked like a bunch of degenerates in our Salvation Army getups.

I bought a pair of dark jeans. Thankfully, it's warm outside, so I didn't have to get a jacket. Instead, I'm wearing a branded athletic shirt that looks a lot more expensive than it was, thanks to their 50% off sale. A little deodorant to mask the smell of new clothes, and I was set.

Ask, and ye shall receive.

"I'm sorry to drop in unannounced like this, but I only just got the address and, well…" I throw her a sheepish look. "I just couldn't wait to see it."

"See what?" Vicky asks, but at least she's not holding herself rigid anymore.

"The chapel." I glance around. "She wasn't lying. It is beautiful. And I think we'll just about be able to fit everyone in."

"Excuse me?"

I glance at her from the corner of my eye. "The wedding

party?" I wave at the rows of pews. "I think we'd just about be able to fit everyone in."

"Wedding? Here?" Vicky's eyebrows dart up. "When?" She shakes her head.

"Our wedding." I let my voice get a little deeper.

Vicky takes a step back.

I immediately hold out a hand. "I'm so sorry, but are you sure you're booked here?" I look at the ground, my jaw bunching. "I knew that wedding planner was full of—" I cut off, and hurriedly make the sign of the cross, ending off by lifting the metal crucifix around my neck and kissing it.

Another purchase, since Cass said the black crucifix Zach got me was 'too intense.'

I turn back to Vicky, who's wide-eyed now.

"I'm sorry. My fiancée tossed out the last wedding planner we had, so we have a new one, and I didn't like her from the get-go but…" I lift my hands, shrug. "You don't want to mess with a bride-to-be."

Vicky shakes her head. "When is the wedding?"

"In three weeks," I tell her. "Wedding planner was supposed to call. I just stopped by because I was convinced from the way Trinity described this place that it might be too small for all the guests."

Vicky holds up her hands. "Trinity?"

"Malone." I move my chin to the side. "Daughter of Keith and Monica?"

Vicky puts a hand over her mouth. "Oh my…I…" She shakes her head. "I didn't even know she was old enough too—" But then her jaw clicks shut. "I'm going to check the register straight away."

I let her walk a few paces before following. She leads me back through the nave, to a small office beside the foyer.

"If we decide not to get married here, would you send her

baptismal records over to Father Kennedy? I'll give you his email address."

"Oh, we don't keep electronic records," Vicky says. "But I can always fax the certificate through to him."

I take my phone out, put down her details as a new contact even though the certificate is useless to me. I need the record the parish keeps where they note the parents' names and, usually, an address. It's a long shot, but right now it's all we have.

She motions to a chair, and we sit in stuffy silence as she opens a big ledger and makes a note of the impending wedding in three weeks.

"Where were you baptized?" she asks, peering at me over her glasses.

Some things you don't lie about. "I wasn't."

The temperature inside the room drops a few degrees.

"Do you have any of the documents with you?"

The sudden chill in the air spreads right to my lungs. "Documents? Like my social security number?" I reach for my wallet, but she shakes her head.

Ticking off on her fingers, she starts up, "I need your Freedom to Marry letter, your dispensation form, your civil marriage license, and the information for marriage form."

Christ.

I almost cross myself again hearing that list.

"Guess I have another wedding planner to fire," I murmur, as if to myself. "Is there still time for me to get those, or do we have to postpone? I hope not. I've already lost the deposit on a cake because the previous planner had the dates wrong. And don't even get me started on the flowers. Did you know that, apparently, peonies are only beautiful if they haven't opened all the way?"

I'm not an actor like Cass. Hell, even Apollo could have done a better job convincing this woman that I'm a groom in a pickle.

But I got the gig because any sister of the cloth would be too shocked Cass didn't catch flame when he walked into the chapel to deal with him, and Apollo...well...he gets distracted sometimes.

Also, I had sisters. Which apparently makes me the closest thing to a wedding expert we have.

Thankfully some of my frustration comes through because, even though I'm not Catholic, Vicky softens a little to my plight. "No dear. If you go down to the courthouse today, you should have everything you need in a week or so."

"Can you..." I stop for a second, make it look like I'm calming myself. "Can you please just check if you *do* have Trinity's records? With my luck, I've come to the wrong church."

"Oh, you're in the right place," Vicky says, mothering mode now fully engaged. "But it's a good thing you ask, because some of our records were destroyed in a fire a few months ago."

And there it is. That's why she was so uneasy seeing a stranger in the chapel. There's a shadow in Vicky's eyes that wasn't there before.

She goes over to a metal filing cabinet and opens it, her back to me. "What is her date of birth?"

I check on my phone, give it to Vicky.

I'll be pushing it if I ask, but it's burning me up. No pun intended. "A fire?"

At first I don't think she's going to answer, but then she lets out a sigh and closes the cabinet. I already have my suspicions before she starts talking, and when she's done, they're confirmed.

"Terrible thing," she murmurs. I can't help but notice she's empty-handed as she adjusts her glasses and takes a seat. "The police ruled it as a botched robbery or something." Vicky purses her lips. "Father Quinn was here that night. He often stayed late. Said he liked the quiet in the chapel. He lived close to the railway tracks, so I understand why."

"Father Quinn?" I say. "Trinity never mentioned him." The next almost sticks in my throat, but I force out the words as smoothly as I can. "She only ever spoke about Father Gabriel."

Vicky lights up like a billboard. "Oh, Gabriel." She nods a few times, a smile deeply etched on her face now. "Yes, they were close. He loved the Malones." The smile fades a little. "But no, he'd left years before that. Father Quinn took over the flock from him. Good man, if a little...studious."

An introverted priest? Downright unnatural.

"So Father Quinn was here when they broke in?" I nudge her, seeing as she's no doubt still daydreaming about Gabriel. I get it, the guy's good looking. But if she knew a shred of what his rotten heart was capable of, she'd be shitting herself right now.

"Yes." She drops her gaze, takes off her glasses. "They came in, shot him, searched the place, and then..." She shrugs. "They said it wasn't arson. The police. Said a candle had fallen on some papers. But this isn't the eighteenth century." She laughs a little, but it's sad and hollow. "It's not like Father Quinn sat here reading by candlelight."

I let a little silence pass. But I have to be on my way, because her empty hands mean I was right.

"So...those records?"

She looks up and blinks like she forgot I was sitting here. "Oh. Sorry. No." Shakes her head. "They must have been—"

"Destroyed." I cut in. "In the fire." I rub my eyelids as I let out a heavy sigh that's not nearly as much acting as it should be.

"It's okay," she says. "I know Trinity. We can recreate the records. Most of the congregation still lives around these parts. Miss Langley was there. I know that for a fact. She comes to all the baptisms and first communions."

"Miss Langley," I reply, nestling that bit of information in my head. I'm not exactly planning on canvassing the town, but who knows what a name could—

"She babysat for Trinity," Vicky says, beaming as she gets lost in a past that I'm guessing was much more bearable than the present. "Not often, of course. Just when her parents went out of town."

My hackles rise up like a motherfucking rebellion.

"Out of town?"

"Oh, Trinity didn't tell you?" Vicky cocks her head a little.

"She…doesn't talk about them very much." And thank fuck I can even think clearly at all with how my mind is scrambling.

"Yes, of course." Vicky's brow creases. "Terrible thing, that."

A lot of terrible things happen around these parts. If I didn't know any better, I'd tell her to go looking for the Indian burial ground this town was built on.

I mentally plead with Vicky to carry on talking.

For once, the Universe is on my side.

"Her father was a missionary," Vicky says. "Her mother went on one or two missions with him, but then she stayed at home after that. The missionary life isn't for everyone."

Oh no, it most definitely isn't.

"And Miss Langley sat for them?"

"She did. If I can get another two or three witnesses, then I can have those records ready by next week." Vicky looks proud of herself, and I almost feel sorry that her hard work will be for naught.

"Well, I do hope you find her."

"Won't be that hard," Vicky says with a laugh. "She's Trinity's next-door neighbor."

I have to stop myself from jogging back to the car. Cass and Apollo are already inside, Cass at the wheel.

What the hell were they expecting? That I'd come running out with a file under my arm like they're the getaway car?

I slam the truck's door, turn to Apollo. "Find Maude Street." Then to Cass. "I have the address to her old house."

Cass puts the car in gear, staring at Apollo in the rear-view mirror.

I don't know why we're all so strung out, but I can feel the seconds streaming by as Apollo searches.

"Turn around," Apollo says. "Then take the first left."

Cass stomps on the gas and throws the car into a wide arc that leaves tire marks on the road. I squeeze my eyes shut, wishing I'd told him not to rush. But maybe it's a good thing. If Vicky calls the police and sends them to Maude street, they might get there before we do.

I don't know what we'll find there, but something's telling me we have to hurry.

"Faster," I tell Cass.

He doesn't say anything, but he skips the next light regardless of the fact that it's been red since it came in sight.

I guess it's a good thing this is a quiet part of town and there weren't any cars on the road. The only one in sight, in fact, is a white Hyundai.

But I don't think it would have mattered.

We're on a mission from God.

16
TRINITY

The urge to start feeling sorry for myself is back, and twice as strong as before. Honest to God, I don't know how the Brotherhood did it. I've been tied to a rusty bed in my family's basement for what feels like days, and I'm about ready to lose my mind.

The rats don't help. I can't see them, only hear them, and that makes it worse somehow.

Gabriel turned the lights off before he left. Something about the dark helping me find the light I was so desperately seeking.

I should have known he had me figured out. I mean, he'd told me so himself. I'd never considered myself an optimist, so I guess I'm just naive then. A hopeless romantic—

Gah!

I cut off the thought with a grimace. That's what he'd said when he'd been talking about my parents. And God he'd even sounded a little lovesick.

Which makes *me* feel sick.

I test the ropes again, rattling the metal bed frame, but they're as tight and unyielding as the previous thousand times.

All this time I was living right above this room, and I had no idea.

Rattle. Squeak.

He's coming back. And soon. He doesn't have to—I'm sure he thinks I'm pretty secure—but it was the way he said those words.

You should pray, Trinity. Pray to God for forgiveness.

Forgiveness? How fucking *dare* he? I don't believe for a second he wasn't a key player in this whole thing. Of course he'd try and shift the blame—he'll die a horrible death in prison. And it's not like my parents can testify against him.

Rattle, rattle, SQUEAK.

I stop moving. That last squeak sounded different. Like something was giving.

Rattle, rattle, rattle, rattle, rattle—

The part of the bed frame designed to hold the mattress collapses under me. Pain dashes through my wrists and ankles as I'm suddenly suspended limb from limb in the air. I gasp, let out a breath, inhale deep. When I squirm, my butt barely brushes the mattress under me.

Fuck.

My wrists ache and burn where the ropes are cutting into me. My left hand especially—there's a dull, thumping ache coming from the base of my thumb, as if the sudden tensing on the ropes did some serious damage.

As soon as I can breathe through the pain, I start shifting again, tugging at the ropes.

I'm loathe to try with my left because it already hurts so much. I go around again. Right hand, right foot, left foot. Nothing. The bed's posts are still rooted to the spot. Nothing seems to have changed except the fact that I might have a dislocated thumb.

My left hand aches even more, as if thinking about it aggravates the injury.

Huh. Houdini would pull off a famous escape like this in the blink of an eye. But those were all tricks. Wasn't he double-jointed or something? He could put his shoulder out of its socket and—

My eyes swivel to my left hand. In the dark, I can't see anything.

Oh God.

No.

Can I?

It's already hurting so much…

But what if I managed to dislocate my thumb? Then I could slip my hand out of that rope, right?

I squeeze my eyes shut, trying to build up some courage.

My thumb is probably already pretty malleable. All I need to do is pull it through the noose. It'll hurt, duh, but maybe not as much as earlier. And the pain is—

Pretty fucking unbearable. And the agonizing ache is only getting worse the longer I linger on this stupid plan.

But it *is* a plan.

And it might even work.

And then I'd be free, no longer hanging here on my strings waiting for the puppet master to return.

I don't even know what he went to go and do. Is he trashing another room? Oiling himself up? Lying in my parents' bed and—

Fuck! Those thoughts are not in the least helpful.

Breathe.

You can do this.

Oh Lord, I hope I can do this.

I grit my teeth.

I hold my breath.

And I slowly start pulling on my left hand.

The pain in my thumb immediately intensifies a million-fold. I start shaking internally, my body fighting with me to stop the torture, but I can't.

I won't.

I keep picturing the Brotherhood. Determination gleaming in their eyes. The things they'd say to me right now if they knew I was considering defeat.

But the pain gets worse, and the rope isn't budging. Pain wells, and with it comes a wave of frustration. I pull harder, the tears that brim and then leak down my face not even blurring my vision. Or maybe they do, I can't tell in the dark.

"Ah!" The yell doesn't echo. This small chamber is too well insulated.

But as I yell, I jerk on my arm as hard as I can.

Agony bursts into my hand. For a second, I'm convinced I've torn off my thumb.

I scream twice, first at that jolt of pain, and then again when my hand drops onto the mattress below me. I drag my hand onto my chest, cradling it against my chin as I let out a ragged sob. I start panting through my mouth as I try to get a handle on the pain.

That hurt more than the lashes I got from Miriam combined with Zachary's spanking.

I force my breathing to slow. Imagine the pain leaving my body with every exhale.

My hand's hot and throbbing, but eventually the pain recedes enough that I can think past it.

With the restraint freed, my shoulder is on the mattress now.

I laugh when I realize I have to try and untie the knot around my right hand with a hand that now sports a dislocated thumb.

Oh Lord, how I laugh.

But then I stop. And I grit my teeth.

And I push through the pain.

Somehow, using my other fingers, tearing off nails, wailing through the pain, I manage to loosen the knot.

My face is wet with tears. I think I've chewed a hole in the side of my cheek, but after what feels like eons of struggling and trying to ignore the red-hot pain in my hand, both shoulders thump onto the mattress.

Time's slipping away, but I allow myself a few minutes to just lie there. Regaining my strength. Trying to get back my composure.

When I sit up and start working on my legs, there's a burning conviction inside me.

I don't care what it takes—Gabriel's going to pay for this.

17

CASS

"I got a bad feeling about this," Rube murmurs. "Something isn't right."

"Like the fact we're still in the fucking car when we should be in there?" I say, rapping on the window with a knuckle. "Yeah, bud, I feel you. All sorts of fucking wrong."

Rube throws me a glare. "We can't just barge in there—"

"Guys, come on. This isn't helping." Apollo grabs my headrest and pulls himself closer, nestling between the sedan's front seats.

We swapped out the liquor store's truck for a silver VW someone left unlocked in a driveway. That was about an hour ago—whether it's been reported stolen yet is anyone's guess.

"What's not helping is us sitting here like fucking spectators. I'm getting out."

"Wait. Just fucking *wait*." Rube opens his door and climbs out of the car. It's a testament to how big he is when the shocks let out a creak of relief.

I'm relieved too, because I was itching on the inside like a fucking junkie.

My love affair with heroin is an on-again-off-again thing. I've always been careful with my dosages after getting out of the basement—I started chipping straight away without even knowing it was a thing—but I've been through stages in my life where I've used religiously enough to get strung out.

That's how I feel right now.

Strung out.

Long overdue.

Except my drug of choice isn't black tar.

It's her.

Trinity fucking Malone.

And she's in that house. I can feel it. Right there, close enough to see if she was standing at a window, while we're over here in this piece of shit car, sitting around like we're scoping out the place for a fucking home invasion sometime next week.

I've been patient. We went with Rube's plan at the church when I was all for locking whatever nun was creeping around the place in the bathroom while we rooted around in their files.

From what Rube tells us, that would have been futile. No trace of Trinity was left in that place.

But now?

Now we're sitting here with our thumbs up our asses while Mr. Cautiously Careful out there triple-checks God knows what.

I climb out the car, ignoring Apollo's bleated, "Wait, Cass!"

He climbs out a second later anyway, so what the fuck?

"Counting the tiles on the fucking roof?" I ask Reuben.

He doesn't even bother to scowl at me. "He knows we're here."

"Impossible."

"He could have seen the car."

"Then he would be out the back door already, no pun intended."

"That wasn't a pun."

I grind my teeth at Mr. Cautiously Careful AKA Sir Correct-me-if-I'm-Wrong. Which I never could, because he never was.

"That thing you're feeling?" I tell him. "It's the earth revolving on its fucking axis. She could be—"

I stop.

I'd been about to say dead, and I don't know why. Gabriel wouldn't kill her—she's too valuable. She's what led us here in the first place. And he had to have known that, right?

That's why he took her. Why he's using her. Maybe that shit about him being her father was purposefully planted on his laptop for us to find. He knew we'd assume the worst.

But fuck. You start going down that rabbit hole, and you end up as knotted as a pair of horny dogs.

"We do this now, or we don't," I say, glancing at Apollo. "The longer we stand out here, the—"

"You're right," Rube says.

And thank fuck for that, because I was close to smacking him upside the head. I start forward, but his voice stops me. "Get back in the car. We'll circle the block. Maybe we get in the back way, or through a window."

I turn to him and stare him down. He's about the same height as me, but I know I'll be the first to kiss dirt in a fight.

But that doesn't matter.

Because he's *wrong*. We can't wait anymore.

She's in there, and she's in danger. Fuck, Trinity being within a foot of Gabriel is more than I can stand thinking about. Even if she is his daughter, I know a perverted prick like him wouldn't think twice about sticking it in her.

They've been alone so long already, I'm sure he's done it a couple of times.

Usually I can control myself. I don't get angry, I get snarky.

But this? The thought that right now he could be—?

"Fuck this," I snarl.

"Cass. Please."

I stop, but only because it's Apollo and the poor guy honestly wants to help. It kinda sucks that he's always so nice about it. Always seeing every side of the argument. He should have been born a few years earlier where he could have run free with his hippie friends, protesting the Vietnam war and getting fucked on acid all the time.

"Just...wait. Would you?"

So I wait.

I wait for hours, days. A fucking eternity.

I wait while Reuben and Apollo start discussing what they'd do if they couldn't find an open window. Should they break it, hope no one hears?

Oh wait, Rube thinks he saw someone. What's that? Another person walking down a street in Suburbia? The fucking horror. But no, he was mistaken, it was just some old lady pruning her rose bush.

And then I wait some more, because now they've moved onto conflict resolution. What if Gabriel has a gun? Nah, Rube doesn't think so. Not all bad guys have guns or some shit. But Apollo's not sure. Now *he's* Mr. Fucking Careful.

I can't.

I can't take it.

This waiting. This supposing and assuming and fuck ton of maybes. Not while Gabriel's doing God only knows what to my blasphemous little slut.

This time I don't warn them. I just turn and walk away.

Apollo makes to grab me, but I dodge him. And then I storm the fucking castle gates like I have an army at my back.

Because I do.

They'll come. Rube and Apollo will be right behind me.

And we're going to rip Gabriel a new asshole. And then shove foreign objects up it until he bleeds. And then give him a blood transfusion so he can cling to life...only to suffocate him with a pillow made from his own skin.

Yeah, I've been thinking about it. A lot.

Maybe I'm not that calm after all.

But fuck me, I'm good at hiding it.

I stalk up to the door, and I lift a hand to try the handle.

A grin tugs at my mouth when it turns and the door swings open.

But that smile dissolves a second later when I see Trinity standing in front of me. Wide-eyed, face bruised, clothes rumpled, hair disheveled, mouth peeling open like she's about to scream.

And that's all I see.

Just her.

Because fucked up as she is, *ruined* as she is, she's so fucking beautiful I can't believe I've been without her for so long.

My *drug*?

Fuck that shit.

She's the blood in my veins. She's what makes my heart pump, and my organs work, and my skin glow.

And she's right in front of me. Like a prayer God answered without me having to even get on my knees and utter a single word.

I'm swelling. Bursting with happiness.

Fuck that—with joy.

And here I thought that was only possible when I was high.

We found her.

She's ours.

The world is suddenly a better place. A place I might decide to live in a little longer than I'd planned.

But then Trinity's gone.

Someone's tackling me from the side.

And I realize it was all a trick.

Gabriel used her as bait.

And I fell for it.

My shoulder hits the ground first, and then the rest of my body, the force of the impact driving the air from my lungs and spittle from my lips.

Ha, *literally*.

So excuse the pun.

4201. *Beep.*
    4202. *Beep.*
  4203. *Beep.*

I blink sweat out of my eyes and take a second to work my neck with my good hand. I don't know what's worse—hoping that I'll hit the right combination before Gabriel comes back, or wondering if I even have the first two numbers correct to begin with.

Nope! Can't think about that. Negativity need not apply.

4204. *Beep.*

4205. *Beep.*

Thump.

I freeze. If my heart wasn't pounding so hard in my chest, I might have been able to make out if that sound had been my imagination or not.

Thump.

No. It's not. Gabriel is back.

4206. *Beep.*

4207. *Beep.*

4208. *BEEP.*

My hand cramps up. Not from pressing numbers, but I'm guessing from the ropes and from the tugging. My left hand aches relentlessly at my side, but I ignore it as much as I can.

4209. *Beep.*

Thump.

Oh Lord, he's coming.

4210. *Beep.*

My heart's in my fucking throat. Every time I try to swallow, it bobs around like an ice cube in a glass of lemonade.

Fuck, why the hell did I have to think about that when I'm so thirsty?

Thump.

My hand shakes so much, I can barely punch the right numbers.

4221 *Beep.*

Damn it! I have to remember I've already tried that one.

Thump, thump, thump.

He's right beside me. Which room is that? I'm trying to picture the layout of my own house, but I can't.

4211.

Click.

Is it the dining room? The living room?

42—

Wait.

I focus on the light above the panel. It's flashing green now. Was it doing that before? Why do I remember it being solid red?

I grab the handle, and open the door.

It swings inward and bathes me in gray light. As I step outside and turn into the hallway, I figure out what room he's in.

Dad's study.

The room right above the portion of the basement I was just in.

No wonder I never heard anything. Dad kept that door locked.

I'm a fucking idiot. I thought my Dad was a God-fearing man with a fully functioning moral compass.

How could I have been so wrong?

The thought makes me nauseous, so I hurriedly stop trying to figure anything out. Instead, I focus on creeping down the hall as quietly as possible.

Quietly…but quickly.

The hall takes a turn and reveals the front door. It's only about two yards away. My heart kicks into overdrive again, and then I'm running.

It's fucking idiotic, but I can't help it. I can't stop. It's too close, and I'm too scared.

So I run.

And then I slam into the wood as I'm fumbling for the lock. It turns, the tumblers clicking loudly as they slide back into the door.

I twist the handle. Step back so the door can open.

Behind me, someone starts running.

Thud, thud, thud, thud, THUD!

The door is open.

But I can't go through because someone's standing there.

Cass is standing there.

What the hell is Cass doing here?

He opens his mouth as if he's about to say something. But he never gets the chance. Someone crashes into him, sends him tumbling over the rose bushes lining the front drive.

Cass becomes Zach. Tall, grim, panting.

A second of frozen time. Then I surge forward, delirious with thoughts of escape. Hardly believing my luck.

He'll save me.

Wrap me in his arms.

Hold me tight.

But none of that happens. He doesn't drag me out of harm's way.

Zach surges forward, and then shoves me. Hard.

I crash into the door. My scream is little more than a choked gasp of pain as my injured hand is trapped between my body and the door.

Zach pushes past me. My head slams against the wood. Sparks flash and pop in front of me as I sink to the ground.

And then he's gone.

My conscious mind drifts, losing track in a deluge of pain and confusion.

There's a loud clap in the living room, like a car backfiring. There was a young couple down the road who lived here a few years back. Their car would do that sometimes. Always scared the shit out of me.

Grunts and roars from the living room. Then another clap, this one louder than before.

Then legs swarm past me. I tip my head back despite the pain.

Reuben. Cass. Apollo.

They all look down at me, but only as they pass. Then they move on, deeper into my house.

It's weird having them here.

Weird being back.

I should show them around. But I have to clean my room first. What'll they think of the basement? Maybe I shouldn't show them that. They wouldn't like it.

I'll show them the picture of the unicorn. It'll make them laugh.

Awsum.

"Hey, pretty thang."

I force my eyes open, catch sight of Apollo's face. He's pale, eyes jittery. "Everything's just fine, hear me? You're safe now."

And I believed him.

Lord, I *believed* him.

19

ZACH

Christ, where are my brothers going in such a hurry? I'm too far away to see who's driving—all I know is that Reuben was inside the Redford Missions of Love church for a few minutes, and then came out empty-handed but with a speed to his steps I haven't seen in a while. Not full out running—I guess he didn't want to draw unwanted attention, but it was obvious he was on the move.

When they slam on the gas and throw the car into a U-turn, I almost think it's because they spotted me.

But I doubt it.

It seems they have other things on their mind.

I give them a lead before following.

We drive for a few minutes, headed downtown. Our route takes us past a mall, and then almost back the way we came before heading downtown again.

Are they being paranoid? Retracing their steps?

Or are they struggling to find their way in a strange town? Ha, if Apollo's the one navigating, then we're all in for a few more U-turns.

Eventually, we venture into the suburbs. Perfect little houses on their perfect little lawns. Two and three bedrooms, mostly. Some double stories here and there.

Where are we headed, boys? I can't for a second believe Gabriel would live in a place like this.

Trinity.

I start looking around a little harder. Driving a little slower.

Is this her old neighborhood? There was no address on the intake form at Saint Amos. I guess, by then, she was officially a ward of the state.

Or someone had fucked with her records.

My brothers turn down a side street. I park on the sidewalk, tracking them on my phone's app, because I have a feeling this is their last turn.

Seconds later they stop.

Then I'm out of the car and jogging down the opposite side of the road. Thank God I had the foresight to pack a hoody. I keep the hood pulled up as I jog. Paired with sunglasses, I'm hoping I'd look like another guy out on a jog, but I know it'll only take one longer-than-normal glance in my direction for my brothers to recognize me.

The people around here like their trees and shrubs. And not so much fences between properties. As long as no one looks out their window and spots me jogging over their freshly manicured lawn, I should be good.

My brothers' silver car is parked a few drives down, opposite side of the road. I slow down, slip behind a bushy shrub, and stretch like I've got a cramp. But all the while peeking at them through a gap in the foliage.

A minute later they get out of the car. Reuben first, his head turning all directions as if he's scouting for danger.

Then Cass.

Then Apollo.

But they just stand there, talking. Watching.

I peer down my side of the road. There are a few trees and shrubs I could use as cover, but I have no idea which house they're targeting. I could end up jogging right into their line of sight.

Reuben turns and looks straight at me.

I throw myself back, stumble over a fucking garden gnome, and land flat on my ass.

As I'm about to get up, I hear a door open behind me. I look back as an old lady walks out onto her porch. She scans her lawn, and despite her thick glasses—or perhaps because of them —sees me.

Shit.

I get up, trying not to bolt, and then stop when I feel a tug on my pants leg.

Christ, I've gotten my jeans hooked in a thorn.

The old lady's garden isn't quite as well kept as the others around here. Her roses, for instance, are the kind you'd expect growing wild around a mansion where neighborhood kids dare each other to knock on the door.

I yank at my pants, and that shakes the entire row of fucking roses.

If Reuben is still looking this way, it would look mighty suspicious.

So I fall into a crouch and do my best to unhook my jeans without rustling as much as a single leaf.

"Everything all right, dearie?" a thin, wobbly voice wants to know.

I glance up into a pair of watery blue eyes, and give the old woman the most charming smile I have. "Got a little stuck on your roses," I tell her through my teeth.

"They are magnificent, aren't they?" she wheezes, clasping her hands at her breast as if she's offering up a prayer to God for her killer botanicals.

Another subtle yank, and finally my jeans are free. But I don't stand yet, because that would put my head and shoulders above the rose bush. I don't want to reveal myself until I know what the hell they're up to. And the last thing they need is a distraction.

I glance around. I could head back the way I came, but Mrs. Nosy's yard is wide open but for this thorny hedge.

"Are you with the church?" Mrs. Nosy wants to know.

I stare up at her with a frown. Dressed in a hoody? In what world could I possibly—

But then her eyes move down my chest, fix on something there a second, and fly back to my eyes. Her smile brightens a little.

I look down too, to see what she finds so fascinating.

Trinity's crucifix. Blood red against my gray hoody. Impossible to miss. It must have come out while I was jogging, or when I landed on my ass beside her roses.

Mrs. Nosy beckons me with a frail hand. "Why don't you come inside, dear? I'll fix you a glass of lemonade."

I feel like I've stepped through a portal back to the eighties where old ladies go around offering cold beverages to any sweaty teen that happens to come within yelling distance of their whitewashed porches.

But my options are limited. If I break cover, my brothers could see me. If I go inside with the nice lady and let her pour me a drink, I could wait them out. Keep track of them on my phone. Fuck, I might even give them a call and see if they pick up.

Don't know what I'd even say if they did, but I'd think of something.

The old woman's name is Langley, and she's a Mizzz because her husband died a long time ago.

I'm starting to think she had ulterior motives for the lemonade, especially when she puts down a plate of cookies too. I ignore them—I haven't touched refined sugar for many years. I don't plan on falling off that wagon any time soon, so I only take imaginary sips from the glass of lemonade.

"Are you one of the new missionary boys they told us about on Sunday?" Miss Langley asks.

I would have choked on my cold drink if I'd actually been drinking it. "Missionary boy?"

"For the mission to Ghana." Langley beams, which happens anytime she mentions the church.

Now I'm convinced this is Trinity's old haunt. It could just be this one biddy, but I have a feeling everyone around here is really serious about finding Jesus.

A priest like Gabriel really brings that out in a person.

I figure I don't have much to lose except having the cookies withdrawn—God willing—so I say, "Ghana." I look introspective. "God willing, Miss Langley, we'll be changing hundreds of lives in that village."

She clasps her hands again, her lips trembling. "Oh, you must be so excited."

"I am." I shift in my seat, nod my head a little. "But if it wasn't for Father Gabriel, I wouldn't even be here."

"Father..." Langley sags in her chair. "I miss him so much. He was such a good influence on you young ones."

Fuck, if she only knew. But I nod along, try and look as Catholic as possible, and even go as far as to toy with Trinity's crucifix.

"Actually, I've never met him."

Langley's eyes widen behind her thick glasses. "You haven't?"

"No. It was Trinity." I pick up a cookie, break off a piece. "She told me all about Father Gabriel."

"Trinity!" Langley lets out a long sigh as she sinks back in her chair. "How is she, the little lamb?"

"Oh, she's doing wonderfully."

"I'm so glad." Langley shakes her head as she looks out the kitchen window with its lacy curtains. "I was so upset to hear what happened. And right here, so close to home."

"The accident happened here?"

"Oh no, that was somewhere in town." Langley waves a dismissive hand. "I mean, for such a gifted child to lose her parents. So young."

"Gifted?" I sound incredulous, and Langley doesn't like that one bit.

Her eyes are narrowed when she turns back to look at me. "Father Gabriel always said she was a gift from God. Her mother couldn't conceive for many years." Langley shakes her head, clucks like a mother hen. "But then Keith and Monica found God, and He blessed them with a child."

Seems everyone knows everyone in this place. Hell on earth.

I don't know how to react to what she said, so I don't. Instead I finally take a small sip of lemonade and try not to think about how much sugar it has in it.

"Such a wonderful family," Langley says. She stares out the window again, a fond look on her face. "That child was always so sweet. A true blessing. Never once when I looked after her did she as much as make a fuss."

Looked after?

"Now I remember," I say, nodding and toying with another piece of cookie. "I was wondering where I'd heard your name. Trinity mentioned you."

"Oh, she did?" The old lady blinks rapidly. Dear God, is she fogging up? "How kind of her."

"Said you were her favorite babysitter."

Langley's eyes start brimming. She hurriedly looks away, and then seems to come to. "Oh, uh, you'll be needing that donation." She stands before I have a chance to ask her what the hell she's on about.

She disappears down the hall, and I take my drink and pour it down the sink. When she comes back in, I'm in my seat again, just putting the glass back on the table. Her already wide smile grows when she spots my empty glass. "Would you like another?"

"Oh no," I tell her, patting my stomach like we've just finished Thanksgiving dinner together. "Folks around here are too kind."

She giggles a little at this and starts writing out a check.

Like taking donations from the congregation.

She hands it to me, but doesn't let go. "Where is your little… the clipboard? With the—" she gestures vaguely "—with the place for me to sign?"

I pat my pockets theatrically. "You know, Miss Langley, I think I left it next door."

Her eyes almost goggle out of their sockets. With surprising speed for such an aging gal, she's on her feet, her head whipping to that same kitchen window as before. "Father Gabriel is back?"

And then it's as if her lemonade was spiked with fucking amphetamines. I'm standing a second later, ruthlessly suppressing the urge to run.

"What do you mean?" My voice comes from far away.

"Gabriel!" She turns to me, clasps her hands again. This time like she's begging. "Oh, I thought… I thought you just came from him. I was hoping he'd come back."

I want to shake her until her teeth rattle. "Back where? I don't—"

"Didn't Trinity tell you?"

My heart bangs into my breastbone as if to try and get me moving. "Tell me what?" I'm grimacing at her through my teeth, but she doesn't seem to notice.

"Father Gabriel. He moved into their old house. I guess the estate put it up for sale, but I never saw a board outside. And I'd have noticed—they're going up all over the place! Why, we had a young couple move in right across the road. Big house for just the two of them. You'd think they're planning to fill it, but I don't know. The woman looks closer to forty than thirty." Langley shrugs, as if the fact that she's rambling isn't having any effect on me.

It is.

I'm about to have a heart attack if she doesn't tell me what I need to know. "Gabriel is living next door?"

"Yes, yes he is. But he's hardly ever here. Still, so much better than living next door to a stranger, wouldn't you say?"

I don't say anything.

I turn and I run the fuck out of that house like the devil himself is breathing down my fucking neck.

They're here for Trinity, not Gabriel. Somehow, they got the address for her old house. That's why they parked down the street.

But if Gabriel bought the property, who the fuck knows what kind of traps he laid out for unwanted guests?

I run, and I don't stop.

I plow right through Langley's roses, ignoring the thorns that prick at my skin, and I race across the next-door neighbor's lawn.

But I'm too late.

Cass is up front, about to try and open the door. Fuck, maybe he's even going to try knocking first.

Reuben and Apollo? They're straggling behind, fuck knows why.

I'm closer to Cass than they are, but I'm still too far away.

All I can say is, thank God for Miss Langley's lemonade.

When I grit my teeth and push, I go a little faster. I clear the hedge separating me from Cass like an Olympic hurdler.

I crash into him just as the door opens.

Just in time to see Trinity's shocked face.

Just in time to see the shadow deeper in the house.

A man, lifting a gun.

Because of course he has a fucking gun. Why wouldn't he?

Cass and I go over another rose bush. He's yelling. I scramble up, dart back to the door.

Trinity is still standing there, blocking me. She doesn't seem to realize she's about to die.

It's better, not knowing.

As soon as I shove her out of the way, that gun is on me. Pointing at *me*. I know I'm already dead.

And the knowledge sits there like heartburn in my brain. It tries to overwhelm me, to render me useless through fear, but I shove it away even harder than I shoved her away.

I sprint down the passage. Three steps, and I'm there. Staring into a pair of brown eyes that should recognize me, but don't.

When I slam into Gabriel, the gun goes off.

But it's fine, because it doesn't hurt. I'm still moving, still fighting.

I herd him backward through momentum and rage. Pushing, pushing.

We end up in the living room a second later. His teeth are bared like a wild animal's. I'm snarling like a beast. We tackle each other, end up on the carpet. I get a blow to his head. He gets a knee to my groin.

And then the gun goes off again.

And this time…

This time there *is* pain.

It's vast and it's endless and fucking magnificent in its abundance.

But that's not fine, because now I can't fight anymore. And Gabriel…he's on his feet. He's running.

Thank you Jesus.

He's not running toward the front door. Toward Trinity or my brothers.

The cowardly fuck is running away.

Thank Christ.

I try to cross myself, but my body just lies there.

Body and mind. Two different things entirely.

I'm still here. I'm still conscious. But all I can do is watch and observe—paralyzed as, all around me, the world dissolves into chaos.

20
RUBE

I've never felt so torn in my life. My body is being sent in two different directions by a mind suddenly unable to prioritize. But I'm rooted to the spot because this is where Zachary is lying.

We're in Trinity's living room, judging from the couches and the dusty television set. But Trinity's not here. She's still in the passage by the front door.

That's where I want to be.

I caught a glimpse of Gabriel a second before he turned a corner and disappeared toward the back of the house. No doubt escaping through the back door we would have been covering if Cass hadn't been so fucking impulsive.

That's where I want to be too.

Instead I'm standing here, watching Zachary's blood soak into the carpet.

And then Trinity screams, and it's as if everyone's minds come back from wherever they'd wandered off to.

"He's getting away!" Cass says, but he's running toward Trinity, not Gabriel.

Apollo falls to his knees beside me, inadvertently soaking his jeans in blood. "Is he dead?"

I don't know.

I just don't fucking know.

"Call an ambulance," I tell Apollo.

But now his hands are full of blood because he was trying to stop it running out of the two holes in Zachary's torso, and that's freaking him out and he's gone and frozen up.

"Apollo!"

Brown eyes snap to me. "Yes?"

He can't be here. Not around all this blood. Like a fucking candle in a snow storm.

And I can't let Gabriel get away either.

It shouldn't be this easy to make crucial decisions, but it's as if there's no choice to make at all.

"Don't let him get away!" My voice is too loud—it booms back to us—but maybe that's what gets Apollo on his feet. I stab a finger down the passage. "Follow him!"

Apollo turns and runs.

"*Just* follow him!" I yell after Apollo's retreating back, with no clue if he heard me or not.

Then it's back to Zach because a glance behind me shows Cass is examining Trinity like he just got his Ph.D.

Guess neither of them is phoning the ambulance.

I fish my phone out of my pocket. There's a part of me that's sitting back and watching me operate, and it's gobsmacked that I'm still functioning. That I'm lucid. That my voice is legible when the 911 operator on the other end of the line answers my call.

But that's because they need me right now. My brothers. Trinity. They need me to be strong. I can freak out later, or not at all. I don't need to add fuel to this fucking inferno.

"I need an ambulance."

And then I go blank, because I guess a part of me isn't all that focused right now.

"2192 Maude Street," comes Trinity's voice. It's faint, but it's steady.

That's my girl.

The operator starts talking me through emergency procedures. Applying pressure to Zachary's wounds to stop the bleeding. And I try. Fuck, I try. But his blood keeps seeping through my fingers. And it's eating into the carpet and heading for my knees.

I shift back like it's contagious.

Cass appears on the other side of Zach's limp body. He moves away one of my hands, using both of his to stop the flow of blood from the wound.

I mimic him.

And slowly the blood stops trickling through my fingers. I like to think I did that. That I somehow stemmed the flow.

But it could be that Zach's heart has stopped pumping.

21

APOLLO

Leaves and low-hanging branches whip against my face. Holy shit, did Gabriel run track or something? I'm struggling to keep up. He had less than a minute head start on me.

We're weaving our way through the dividing line sandwiched between properties. Not all of the houses have fences, but most of them do have trees and shrubs for privacy.

Gabriel obviously knows this area very well. He's pulling all the moves—throwing trash cans between us, rousing dogs who must have been distant offspring of Cujo.

All I can do is try and keep him in sight. Lucky for me, he's leaving behind a path of devastation. Broken branches, rustling shrubs, gates thrown open.

I chase him over a road, and then down a cement embankment.

And then I lose him.

I'm panting, bloody hands on my bloody knees as I scan left and right. The embankment led down to a storm drain, but there's no fucking way I'm going into that black hole.

I'm not an idiot.

I know he's waiting in there for me.

Shit!

I could go over the top. But if he's watching then he'll know what I'm trying to do. So should I stay, or should I—

Something slams into the back of my head.

I land on hands and knees, fire scraping over my palms as I skid over the cement floor.

Before I can scramble up, a foot hits me square in the stomach.

God! Again? Fuck!

I kick out, manage to catch Gabriel's shin. Not that it fucking helps—I could have been kicking a tree stump.

He takes a step back, and then surges forward again. Grabs the back of my neck. Hauls me to my feet.

I catch the crook of his arm when he goes to punch me, and that he wasn't expecting. But he recovers so fast, I don't even have time for some kind of counter strike.

He rips his arm free and shoves me like we're a pair of bullies marking turf in the schoolyard.

I slam into the side of the storm drain's massive mouth, banging my head.

There go the last of my fond childhood memories.

And that's when Gabriel whips out his gun. Which is round about the same time I put my hands up.

Oh God, the blood. I squeeze my eyes closed and try my best to remain fixed to the earth.

"Okay! I yield!"

And he laughs. The fucker actually laughs. There's a click from the gun, which I assume is him taking off the safety.

I'm supposed to know about these things, but I was so high when Zach took us for practice shooting. I can't remember a damn thing.

Instead of yielding, like I asked him so damn nicely, Gabriel grabs my shirt and rams me into the concrete wall again. Then he drags me around the corner. It's an overcast day, so there's no sharp line in the limbo between shadow and light. Just a dark haze.

All the better to rape you in, my dear.

Jesus, fuck, no.

I tilt forward to try and push him out of the way. The icy nozzle of a gun burrows into my forehead, urging my head back and back and back until it presses against the uneven wall behind me.

Christ.

I lift my hands, close my eyes. "Just make it quick, okay? And if it's all the same to you, I'd prefer it if you rape me after I'm dead."

There's another click, and that confuses the fuck out of me, because I know some guns have a hammer, but this one doesn't.

I open one eye, then the other.

Gabriel's lowering the gun.

But the moment I open my mouth to thank him, it's up again.

"Stay where you are," he says.

He wasn't going to kill me? Fuck me? Why? I mean, I'm grateful obviously, but confused. But there's no way in hell I'm going to antagonize him into shooting me. What good would that do anyone?

"Sure, yeah. I'll stay right here."

My hands are still up, and it's taking quite a lot of my concentration to ignore the smell of copper in the air. I should be fine, long as I don't dwell. Long as I don't look at my hands.

Gabriel trains the gun on me as he steps back.

Follow him.

Aw, fuck, Rube. I wanna, but he's going to kill me if I try.

Follow him.

"Hey, uh…"

Gabriel pauses. The hand around the gun tightens.

"I just want to know one thing."

He frowns at me. "Quiet."

I curl the fingers of one hand until just my index is up. "Just one. Please? Humor me? It's the least you can do."

Gabriel shakes his head like he's wondering which of the two of us have lost our minds.

Probably both.

"What?" he snaps, taking another step back.

"Why'd you do it?"

He stops. "Do what?"

"The basement. The kids. Us." I point at myself with my finger. "I mean…that wasn't cool, man. Seriously. Are you a psychopath? Because you're lacking all sorts of empathy."

Gabriel's lips lift into a snarl, and it looks like he's reconsidering letting me live. But fuck it. I mean…

"That's why you're following me?" Gabriel moves the gun a little closer as if he's pointing with it. "Talk to Trinity. I told her everything."

"Like how you chose us? Did you tell her that? Because I've always wondered about that. I mean, compared to Cass and Rube, even Zach, I'm not much of a looker."

Gabriel shakes his head as if he's got something in his ear. "I don't know why she chose you."

"She? She who?" Was it Zachary's mom? I never met the woman, but—

"Monica chose. She…she drew less attention than Keith. No one thought twice about her sitting in the park, reading a book."

Wait…*Monica?* As in Trinity's *mom?* But there's a look in Gabriel's eyes as if he's waiting to see my reaction. Playing me.

"Yeah, okay. Blame it on a dead girl." I nod a few times. "Clever. No one can prove you wrong."

Another snarl. "You want proof?" He steps closer and jams the gun against my chest.

If I'd been paying closer attention at that shooting range, I might have remembered how to take a gun off someone. I mean, I'm pretty sure that's something they cover.

But I didn't.

So I can't.

I don't dare try. Because his finger is curled around the trigger, and I have a feeling the smallest jolt will send a bullet straight into my heart. Ain't no coming back from that, not unless you're the Son of God. And I'm pretty sure he's come and gone.

"Yeah, proof would be nice," I tell him, barely moving my lips in case he sees it as a threat. "But only if it's no trouble. Don't want you going out of your way to prove your innocence or anything."

He narrows his eyes at me. His lips move. "Apollo."

"You got me." It's hard to be cheery when there's a gun digging a hole in your pec, but I fucking try.

"You worked in the laundry at Saint Amos." His voice is soft now, his eyes unfocused.

"It was the kitchen, actually. But you knew that already."

"Why would I?"

And it's fucking weird, in that second, I believe him. But I'm probably biased because my cause of death is so close I can lick it.

"Everything you're looking for is on Keith's hard drive."

If I had ears like a dog, they'd be pricking up right now. "Yeah? Where's that? Gomorrah? Sodom?" I can't help it. I kid around when I'm nervous.

The way Gabriel's jaw ticks, he's not amused.

"In the study. In the safe. Same combination."

"What, the study door and the safe?"

He makes an angry sound and steps back, shaking his head. "I don't care how he made it look. I didn't do it. None of it." Another step. He's brighter now, lit up by the faint gray light of the overcast sky.

But before he turns to leave, I say, "And what about that file on your hard drive? The archive you hid in the system files? Same combination?" I know it isn't. My password cracking program already went through the numeral-only phase.

"Archive?" He turns back to me. "It's one file."

My heart legit skips a fucking beat. "Same combination though, right?" I ask. "That also going to prove you're innocent?"

"It's password protected." He looks at the ground. "If you can open it, show it to Trinity." When he looks up, his eyes have a dark shadow over them that has nothing to do with the rain that's on the way. "Then maybe she'll change her mind about me. About them. About everything."

Un-fucking-likely.

"So what's the password?"

Gabriel's face turns to stone. "I don't know, child. I've spent years trying to figure it out." Then he shrugs and starts walking away. He glances back at me. "Promise me you'll show her."

Anyone with a shred of sense in their heads will tell you to never make a deal with the devil. But they've never faced a devil like Gabriel.

I guess he's had years to practice his poker face, because fuck knows I can't tell if he's bluffing.

And it's kind of a stupid request. I mean, why wouldn't I show Trinity? She's as much involved in this as any one of us.

"Promise me." He's stopped walking. Somewhere along the line, he put the gun back in his pocket.

I drag my fingers through my hair before I remember about

the blood, but luckily it's dried already. It's still gross though, still makes me light-headed even thinking about it.

Gabriel's face collapses. "Please."

"Yeah, fuck. Whatever."

He grimaces, perhaps for my language, perhaps for my vagueness, but it's as good as he's going to get. And I guess he realizes that, because he turns and walks away.

Follow him.

But instead I slide my back down the concrete wall and sit on my ass, trying to process why the fuck I let Gabriel get away.

"…but I can't blame you. *I'm* pissed off at me."

Consciousness ebbs and flows, bringing with it a familiar voice. Who's Apollo talking to? He seems agitated.

"You weren't there. You didn't see the look on his face. How he spoke about you."

"Who?" I try to say, but nothing comes out. My lips don't even move. I feel like I'm caught on the edge of sleep. My brain is certainly foggy enough. And all I want to do is slip away again.

Apollo drops his voice, makes it raspy. "Promise me you'll show her."

My fingers twitch. My lips move. "Apollo."

But he's so caught up in what he's discussing with the other person in the room, he doesn't notice.

"If I can just figure out that password. But what the hell is it? He said the combination was the same for the study and the safe, right? But the study didn't have a lock. The basement had a lock…but we'd have to get back inside the house to check it out.

And now that it's a crime scene, the fuck that's going to happen, right?"

Lord, maybe I should go back to sleep. I can't understand a word he's saying.

But then someone's holding my hand. "Trin, listen. I know you're in there somewhere. Can you wake the fuck up and explain this to me, please? Maybe you can decode the Gabriel Chronicles, and that would be swell, because Cass and Reuben are pretty pissed off with me. I need a win."

Mmm. Sleep. That does sound good.

"Come on, Trin."

How can I say no?

I force my eyelids open. They're heavy, fluttering like a downed butterfly. Too-bright light spears into my head. "Ow." I choke out hoarsely, squeezing my eyes shut again.

"Hey! You're back!" Another squeeze to my hand. "Fuck yeah." Something brushes my cheek. "Okay, so let me fill you in, right? I was chasing after Gabriel, and—"

"Apollo, enough." A shiver chases through me when I recognize that deliciously low and rumbly voice.

Reuben.

I force my eyes open to slits and move my head to try and find him.

He's standing opposite Apollo, on the other side of my hospital bed. As I catch sight of him, he wraps his hand around mine. So warm and tight.

"Welcome back," he says quietly. "I hope you had pleasant dreams."

"Course she did," another voice says, the speaker out of sight. "Because she was dreaming about us. Weren't you, darlin'?"

I have to tip my head forward to see Cass. He's lounging in a chair pushed to one wall, but he stands and comes closer when we lock eyes.

"What happened?"

The last thing I remember is taking Gabriel to the bell tower. How he found the photo. And then…him shoving me against the wall. I hit it hard—is that why I'm here? I shiver violently, and Apollo immediately tugs the thin hospital blanket at my feet all the way up to my chin.

"Body warmth will work better," Cass says, giving me a lopsided grin.

"Cut it out," Rube demands, throwing him a faint scowl. Then his eyes are back on me. "How are you feeling?"

"Heavy."

"Anesthesia," Apollo says. "It'll wear off."

Rube squeezes my hand. "They said you can come home tomorrow."

"Home?" My mind flashes back to that tiny, cramped room at Saint Amos. To the Brotherhood's lair where Zach shoved a knife between my legs and told me he'd fuck me with it if I showed my face again. I squeeze my eyes shut. "I don't want to go back there."

"Not *your* house," Apollo says through a chuckle, making no sense. "*Our* house!"

"He means our hotel room," Rube says dryly, but looking at Apollo, not me.

"It's where we live," he says, shrugging. "What else am I supposed to call it?"

"It's not home. Not even close." Cass runs his fingers over the top of my foot. "But it'll be a far sight better with you in it, that's for sure."

Anywhere's better than that horrible school. I smile at Cass. At Rube. At Apollo. I get another peck on my cheek from Apollo, and Rube starts massaging my hand. I lift my left hand, and stare at the mass of bandages over it. When Rube catches my puzzled look, he shakes his head and gives me a faint smile. "Dislocated thumb. But it'll heal just fine."

When did that happen?

He ducks down, presses his lips to my forehead. Whispers, "You'll heal just fine, Trinity."

I let out a happy sigh, but that beautiful moment only lasts a second. I wriggle a little to sit up taller, and crane to look around the room.

Someone's missing. Did Zach stay away on purpose? He's made it clear he hates me, so I wouldn't be surprised. But that hasn't stopped him hanging around with me before. Honestly, I'd have thought he'd have enjoyed being here, especially if there was a chance to see me in pain. That's what he gets off on, right? Pain?

But now that I'm looking, I notice an edge to the brothers. A grimness to their smiles. Shadows under their eyes. It's not the kind of concern you get from someone who bumped their head against a wall.

What aren't they telling me?

"Where's Zach?"

When their eyes drop in unison, so does my stomach. Right to the fucking floor.

It makes no sense. He hates me, and I'm terrified of him. But the thought that something's happened to him, it scares me more than that knife up my skirt ever could.

Because I know he'd hurt me...but never more than I could take.

Knowing that, I shouldn't have run off that morning and gone to Gabriel, but I'd thought Zachary would change. I thought being with him, with all of them, would make things different. Like I was sprinkling magic pixie dust on them.

I'm worse than a hopeless romantic. I'm a fucking *fool*.

No one's going to change just like that. And these men?

Probably never. The damage done to them is too deep. It may have scarred over, but those scars are permanent.

Instead of trying to change them, I should accept them for who they are.

But something tells me my epiphany came too late.

"Where is he?"

"Let's not..." Apollo trails off.

Cass steps back, waving a hand. "You know what, we can chat about that later. You need to rest."

I turn wide eyes to Reuben, who's looking from Apollo to Cass with a blank expression. "Reuben? Reuben!"

He looks down at me. Strokes my eyebrow with his thumb. "It's too early to tell," he murmurs.

"What is? What do you mean?"

"You don't remember?" Apollo asks.

I stare at him, my voice rising to a shout. "Remember what? Tell me what's going on!" The last I direct to Cass.

He's watching me through his lashes. And then he blinks, like he's snapping out of a spell. "He took two gunshots to the chest. One barely missed his heart. The other...didn't."

Someone *shot* Zachary? My body goes ice-cold. "Oh my God."

Reuben squeezes my hand. "It's too early to tell if he'll pull through, Trinity, but the doctors are doing everything they—"

I pull out of his grip, grab the edge of the sheet, and do my best to get out of the hospital bed. "Is someone going to help me?" I demand through gritted teeth.

Apollo rushes around the bed, but Rube puts out a hand to stop him. I scowl up at Reuben with as much ferocity as I can muster, but before I can open my mouth to cuss him out, he bends and scoops me up off the hospital bed.

Now I'm floating through the air like an aerial dancer. Cass comes over, grabbing the IV stand and wheeling it after us as Rube heads out my hospital room behind Apollo.

I've never been in a hospital before, but I have a feeling I'm in one of the private wards because I was the only one inside the room and there's tasteful artwork on the walls we pass.

We go down an elevator, and when we exit, there's suddenly too much excitement and activity. I burrow back against Reuben, and as if they sense my sudden panic, Cass and Apollo walk in front of us like a shield.

I hear voices murmuring up ahead when we stop. And then Cass says, "Does it look like I give a fuck about visiting hours?"

Rube grumbles something I don't catch, and then we're on the move again. He takes me through two more doors, and then the air is filled with the mechanical beep of machinery and the whoosh of life support systems.

Apollo and Cass part, their faces grim.

Rube takes me right up to the bed as if he won't even entertain the thought of my feet touching the ground.

Zachary's chest lifts and falls in time with the massive machine on the other side of the bed.

He's pale and drawn, his cheekbones poking at his skin. Lips bloodless. Deep shadows under his sunken eyes.

My vision blurs. I blink hard, freeing my tears so I can see him again.

Apollo is talking to someone in the background. A nurse? A doctor? Their soft murmurs don't sound positive.

"Put me down," I say.

"We should get you back—" Rube begins, but I lift my unbandaged hand and lay it on his chest. Still not looking at him. Still focused on Zachary. "Please. Put me down."

I have so many questions, but that's not important right now. Right now, I'm trying to understand why it feels like the world is breaking down around me.

There's no way I could have imagined the things he did and said, but now it feels like it was all a bad dream. The man lying in this bed isn't capable of such violence, of such spite.

It's impossible, but I know it's true, and those conflicting thoughts make me feel dizzy and on edge. I want to shove away those thoughts and focus on my anger, but when I glance around the room, I see I'm not the only one struggling emotionally.

How can I be angry with him when he's dying? We can sort out our shit later.

I slide out of Reuben's arms and land on wobbly legs. He grabs me around the waist, keeping me steady as I lean forward and take Zachary's hand in mine.

"Hey," I whisper, and then clear my throat. "It's me. Trinity. You remember me, right? The little girl who annoyed you so much?"

But nothing changes. There's no quirk of his mouth, no twitch in his fingers.

I glance behind me and tilt my head back to look up at Rube. "Can he hear me?"

Reuben nods, his grim expression softening. "Of course he can."

I turn back to the bed. Move a little closer. I stroke my fingers down the back of Zachary's hand, careful not to nudge the IV drip. "Hey, so, the guys and I were wondering when the hell you're coming back." I try to laugh, but it doesn't come out right. "It's kinda lonely without you." My voice catches on "without you" and when I try and speak again, I realize I've gone mute.

Cass appears at my side. He slides an arm around my waist, just below Rube's, and squeezes me. "Yeah, you fucker. I mean, I get taking a vacation and shit, but this is costing us some serious dough." He laughs too, and it sounds so forced that my heart shrivels up like a dying flower. "Well, guess it's costing *you*."

Apollo walks around the bed, and he hesitates before reaching out and stroking Zachary's head. "You know we still have asses to kick, right? Can't do that if you're lying on yours."

There's quiet. Cass, Apollo, me...waiting.

Rube clears his throat. He hands me to Cass, and I miss his arms the second they leave my body.

When he stands over Zachary's bed, it's as if someone puts a stake through my chest and twists it.

Compared to Rube's strong, broad body, Zachary's looks so...fragile. Broken.

"What you did..." Reuben begins. "It wasn't right. You know that. We all know that. But I'm hoping it was one of those times you couldn't help it."

I turn a puzzled frown to Cass, but he closes his eyes and gives his head a shake, as if telling me he'll explain later.

Rube clears his throat again. Then he reaches out and lifts Zachary's hand before lacing their fingers together.

"But then you did something so brave, so selfless...we'd be dicks not to forgive you." His voice goes thick. "So if you don't want to come back because of what I said, just know that I was full of shit. I do forgive you, Zach."

"I forgive you too," Apollo says. He gives Zachary's head another stroke. "And I need you, man."

"I forgive you." Cass grabs his leg. "And you know I fucking need you."

Then they all turn to me.

But the words stick in my throat. And when I shake my head, tears spill out of my eyes and race down my cheeks.

They don't know what he did with the knife.

They didn't hear how he threatened me.

I can forget about what he did, but I don't know if I can ever forgive him.

"He saved your life," Apollo murmurs. "Doesn't that mean anything?"

"Apollo." Rube's voice is firm, his frown deep.

I glance at Apollo, then back and up at Rube. "What is he talking about?"

Rube points at Zachary's chest. At the two sets of bandages plastered over his skin. "One of those bullets were meant for you, Trinity."

"And one was meant for me," Cass says beside me.

And then it comes rushing back.

My old house.

Gabriel trying to drown me in the bath.

The basement.

Gabriel chasing me down the hall.

Cass at the front door.

When I look down at Zachary again, it feels like someone is wrapping barbed wire around my heart.

"I...forgot." I swallow hard and put my hands over my face. "How could I—"

"Concussion," Apollo supplies, and then shrugs when I look up at him with slitted eyes. "What? You asked."

I lick my lips. He saved my life. Possibly in exchange for his.

Only a cold-hearted bitch would hold a grudge against someone who sacrificed themselves for her.

"I forgive you, Zachary. And I need you too." I look up at his three brothers, and my next words come easy, because I've never spoken truer ones in my life.

"We all need you."

23

TRINITY

SIX MONTHS LATER

Water laps against the side of the infinity pool, merging seamlessly with the nearby ocean. It splashes against my body as I slap my arms down on the cool tiles beside the pool. I shiver at the contrast between warm and cold, and almost slip back into the heated water when a pair of bare feet pad into view.

I tilt my head back, blinking water from my eyes as I stare up at Cass.

"Water's perfect," I tell him.

But he just keeps standing there, watching me. If it was any other guy, it would have been creepy as all hell. But it's Cass, and with those stunning blue eyes staring at me, it just makes me feel like I'm melting inside.

"Are you getting in, or you just going to keep gawking?"

"Rube wants to see you," he says.

I stop paddling my feet, sinking a little lower into the water as a chill races through me. "Now? But—"

"No buts." He crouches beside the pool, his swimming shorts hiking up his legs. He's put on muscle in the last few months.

Everyone except Apollo has, who flat out refuses to use our mansion's built-in gym for anything more than some light cardio when it rains longer than a day. "You promised."

"Yeah, bu—" I cut off, pressing my lips together. "God. *Now*?"

"Now, my blasphemous little slut," he says with a rueful grin.

I give him a half-smile, and let him haul me out of the water. His eyes rake over my body, taking in every curve. In the past, I'd have wanted to snatch up a towel and cover myself.

But the Brotherhood have taught me a lot of things. Being proud of my body is one of them.

How can I hate something they worship?

Cass leads me back inside the house, but not before we both glance back at the view. The crests of the waves are barely visible —fluffy white lines that chase each other across the pale shore. At night, the ocean sighs like a sleeping beast, and I've fallen in love with it as much as I have with them.

All of them.

The ground floor of the mansion is built for entertaining, but we've never had any guests. What we have is too special. Too unique. People would ask too many questions. Or they wouldn't understand, and try to become part of something they're not.

Cass veers off into the kitchen, and I pause at the foot of the broad, open stairs that sweep up to the first floor. "What are you doing?"

He comes back a second later with strawberries and a bottle of champagne. "Hungry," he lies.

"Bribing me won't work," I tell him, grabbing a strawberry off the tray and popping it in my mouth as we start up. "But I do commend your efforts."

He chuckles at that, but not as enthusiastically as he usually would.

My steps become slower the higher we go up. And then almost stop when I can see over the landing.

They're all there. Congregating. Waiting for me.

The second floor is reserved for the bedrooms, and the mini-theater with its massive TV and an assortment of day beds and recliners. My men spend a lot of time up here, watching movies, sports, reality shows. Soaking up the world they missed the last decade and a half.

Sometimes I join them. But most of the time I'm curled up on the window seat nearby, working through the pile of books beside it.

I missed out on a lot too. Tolkien. Dickens. Rowling. Harlequin. My men don't tell me what I can and can't read. Don't tell me how I can and can't dress.

For the first time in my life, I'm free.

Truly free.

Rube turns to face me, arms crossed over his chest. He's wearing a dark, short-sleeved shirt that looks painted on to his beautiful sculpted torso, and a pair of baggy sweatpants.

Those dark clothes, paired with his black eyebrows and black hair, make his green eyes pop.

I'll never forget the morning I woke up beside him, turned around, and saw his real eyes open for the first time.

I guess just like it's taken me forever to get used to Cass's longer hair. It's not as long as Apollo's but when he's in the mood Cass ties it up in a man bun that makes me start panting.

"Enjoy your swim?" Rube asks, but there's an edge to his voice like he's already planned how much I'm going to regret stalling.

Apollo sits forward on one of the day beds, an unlit cigarette dangling between his fingers. I don't let them smoke inside the house, and I guess he hasn't gotten around to heading outside to have it yet.

He's wearing three-quarter shorts and a too-big vest that shows most of his ribs and chest through the armholes. Cass's favorite pastime—besides watching celebrity cooking shows—is to make fun of his style. He doesn't seem to realize Apollo doesn't have a style—Apollo wears the clothes that are in his cupboard, usually whatever's on top of the pile he sees first.

As if thinking his name summons him, Cass steps up behind me, proffering the tray of strawberries as he presses a kiss to my ear.

"Ma'am."

I wave him away dismissively, but only after I've snagged another strawberry off the tray.

"Fine," I say through a sigh. "Where is he?" I ask, sticking out my hip and trying for all the world to sound like a cocky bitch.

Rube's head tilts and then he steps to the side, revealing the only non-reclining armchair in this space.

Zachary is perched on the edge of the seat. He's wearing a Gucci T-shirt that probably cost more than the couch, and a pair of tattered jeans.

He looks the same as he always has.

Weeks after we left Virginia and came to live in Dana Point in this mansion Zachary bought us, the others started transforming. Like butterflies fresh out of their cocoons.

Cass grew out his hair.

Reuben stopped wearing his colored contacts.

Apollo...okay, he hasn't transformed much. But he does spend a lot less time by himself than he used to. He and Cass go surfing together in the morning where in the past, according to Rube, he'd have gone alone.

But Zach?

Put him in a cable-knit sweater and a pair of loafers, and he's Brother Rutherford.

Which is one of the reasons why it's been six months, and Zachary and I still haven't spoken more than two words to each other.

Because *he hasn't changed.*

Not on the outside.

Not on the inside.

"I did enjoy my swim, thank you for asking," I tell Rube, now blatantly ignoring Zachary. "In fact, I think I'll go have a lie-down. All that splashing around tired me out."

I turn my back, slip past Cass, and head for the master bedroom.

"Trinity." Zach's voice stops me in my tracks. And fuck, I hate that he still has that kind of power over me. "Please."

The taste of strawberries goes sour in my mouth. "No." My back is still turned. "I'm not…" I want to say ready, but that's not the right word.

I hear fabric rustle. Zachary getting to his feet. I hear his bare feet on the floor as he comes closer. The moment his hands touch my shoulders, I spin around and shove him away.

There's a sudden tension in the room, like every one of his brothers is holding his breath.

"I said no." The words are barely a whisper.

Zach watches me, and then nods. He takes a step back, drops his eyes. "Okay."

I blink hard, and look away making sure I don't catch anyone else's eye.

No, he hasn't changed. He might act it, and his brothers might insist he has, but I know he's the same angry, spiteful person he was six months ago.

Sure, he's been going to therapy. But from what Cass tells me —which isn't a lot—he's only just started on a very long journey.

And in the meantime? He's pumping himself full of drugs so he'll be the kind of man we all want him to be.

Calm.

Peaceful.

But what happens when he stops taking his drugs? Will he be holding a knife up my skirt and telling me to fuck off again?

Yes, I'm grateful he saved my life. But he's the whole reason I was in that house to begin with. It's because of *him* that I told Gabriel everything I knew. He's the one that made me question everything I thought I knew. And when I had no answers, I turned to the only man I thought could provide them.

Gabriel.

His brothers think he's earned my forgiveness.

He hasn't.

Not even close.

But every time I try to explain it to them, I get tangled up in words and emotions. So I told them I wasn't ready. That I had things to work through before I'd let Zachary be a larger part of our lives than he is now. Because I can't deny them anything, but I'll be damned if I'll let him anywhere near my heart.

The sound of my damp feet is barely audible over my pounding heart as I head to the top floor. The entire level is reserved for the main suite. Bedroom. En suite bathroom. Massive walk-in closet. A small lounge. A wrap-around balcony with a hot tub.

I lied about going to sleep. I'm too wired for that to even be an option. But at least I can rinse my hair and get into some comfy clothes. My skin's pebbling after being in that warm pool.

When I step inside the black, gold-veined marble shower, it turns on automatically.

Apollo rigged the whole house with stuff like that. At night, my way is lighted with barely-visible downlights all the way down to the kitchen for a glass of water. When I step into the pool, the lights turn on.

I lose myself under the shower's rain setting, trying not to think about the looming argument.

It always comes when I say no.

Then my men spend days trying to change my mind. We fight. We make up. And the whole thing's forgotten for a week or two.

Then the cycle begins again.

I'm considering telling them Zachary has to leave.

But he provides for us. Everything we have, it's because of him. And they've moved on already. They truly forgave him in that hospital room.

It's just me.

Fingers skate down my spine. I spin around, gasping, for some reason expecting it to be Zachary.

But it's Reuben. Naked. Wet.

My eyes trail over his pecs. His washboard stomach. The thick cock in its bed of dark curls.

"What—"

He grabs my shoulders and presses me against the cool marble wall. Then he swipes hair out of my face, cupping my head in his massive hands.

I think he's going to say something, but instead he ducks his head and kisses me.

My arms are around his neck a second later. I press my body against his, savoring the feel of his naked skin against mine. He forces his tongue into my mouth, fighting me back when I resist him.

I know what he's doing. He's softening me up. Hoping I'll change my mind about Zach.

And since I like this game, I'll allow him to play it.

He slides his hand down my stomach and caresses my clit with the tips of his fingers. On cue, I spread my legs, inviting him lower.

But tonight he teases me. The only thing he deepens is his kiss, his fingertips feather soft as they stroke me.

Hot tingles spread through my core. I'm already becoming wet from his touch, and as if he's reading my mind, he takes away his hand and instead grabs the back of my neck.

I could kiss him for an eternity, but now that he's stoked a fire inside me, it's not enough. I need him inside me, filling me, ending the ache he forced on me.

But when I push him away, breaking our kiss, and I stare up into his mesmerizing green eyes, I already know what's going to happen before I open my mouth.

"Fuck me," I command him.

His eyes narrow. "Haven't you learned any manners yet?"

My men are big on manners lately. I can be as demanding as I want in bed, but I have to be polite about it.

But I was set up—again—and that makes me feel rebellious.

I'm ready with another demand, but Rube darts forward and catches my lips with a kiss.

This time he doesn't hold back.

It's fierce and it's controlling and it makes my legs weak.

And he uses that against me. When I sink down, expecting him to grab my ass and haul me up against the wall, he instead breaks our kiss and pushes me to my knees.

"What are you—" is all I get out before he presses his thumb and forefinger into my cheeks, opening my jaw.

And then his cock is sliding into my mouth, already hard, already salty with precum.

He grabs a fistful of my hair and moves my lips up and down his dick.

I would have resisted more, but God I love the sound he makes when I'm sucking him off. I look up at him, and a tremor races through me at the intensity in his eyes. How his jaw bunches like he's barely able to hold himself back.

But thank the Lord he does, because otherwise I would suffocate. As it is, I can barely fit more than half his cock in my mouth.

"We've given you more than enough time," he says, his voice as tight as the seal of my lips around his dick. "So why won't you listen to him? Why won't you even hear him out?"

I hate the fact that they're taking his side. I guess I haven't known them as long as they've known each other, but you'd think they'd demand he pay for what he did to me.

Slamming my hands into his thighs, I push away from him. Rube relinquishes the grip on my hair just enough so that I can choke out his cock.

"He's never even said he's sorry," I blurt out. "But you want me to forgive him?"

Rube's eyes narrow. "He's tried, Trinity. More than once."

I start to argue, but then Rube shoves his cock back in my mouth.

"Every time he wants to talk, you walk away. Or tell him to go fuck himself. Or decide you need a nap."

Oh my God. He makes me sound like a spoiled brat. But with each reprimand, his cock is being shoved into my mouth, so I have no choice but to shut up and listen.

"So when I'm done with you," Rube says, his voice dropping an octave lower, "You'll go out there, and you'll listen."

He tightens his fist in my hair.

It's taken him a long time to even dare to do anything that might bring me the slightest pain. He's refused to sleep with me ever since we arrived at this mansion. He keeps saying he doesn't want to hurt me again. It doesn't matter what I tell him. What his brothers tell him.

And I'm starting to think it has something to do with Zach. I know Rube's not childish enough to bribe me, but...It's as if he needs me to forgive his brother before he can even think of making love to me.

I'm not happy with the fact that I could be the one sabotaging my happiness.

Another twist. Sharp pain brings tears to my eyes that the shower's rain setting patters away.

"Do you hear me?" he asks. His voice is gruff, tight. He's getting close.

I nod, and even bat my eyelashes at him. Then I swirl my tongue as best I can around the tip of his cock, my core clenching at the salty taste of him.

He lets out a deep groan, and then thrusts hard into my mouth as if he wishes he was fucking me instead.

Don't we both?

When he comes a second later, I swallow what I can, but some of his load trickles out the side of my mouth while I'm choking it down.

He pulls out, his cock bobbing an inch away from my lips as he uses his thumb to scoop up the cum dribbling down my chin.

"Don't waste," he murmurs. I dart forward, drawing his thumb into my mouth and sucking it clean.

"Good girl." He strokes my wet hair, and for a second I think he's going to put his cock back in my mouth for another round.

I guess I deserve it.

As much as I hate to admit it, he's right. Ever since he came back from the hospital, I've been avoiding Zach. I refuse to listen to him, dodging every request he's made.

Honestly, I'm surprised it's taken this long for my men to call me to task for it.

Rube crouches, grabs my hips, and helps me to my feet. Then he smooths back the hair straggling over my face and kisses my forehead.

"When?" I murmur, closing my eyes. I'm pretty sure I can

reschedule any date I set. More importantly, I'm hoping that if I do set a date, he'll finally do the one thing I've been begging him to for months now.

Make love to me.

He trails his fingers down my body, slides his hand between my legs, and tests me with a crook of his middle finger.

His breath is warm and sweet on my face when I look up at him, waiting for his reply.

But he's wearing a grim expression I don't like one bit.

"Now."

24

ZACH

As soon as I realize my leg's bouncing, I lean forward and rest my elbows on my thighs, lacing my fingers together. I've got nothing to fidget with, so I toy with my fingers, meshing them together then moving them apart, as I wait in the small den adjacent to the main bedroom.

Our bedrooms are on the second level, but Trinity sleeps on the top floor, and everyone usually joins her up there.

Except me.

I was banished the moment I set foot in my own house.

My leg starts jittering again until I push away that negative thought.

A cigarette would have helped. A joint would have been even better.

Trinity doesn't like us smoking cigarettes inside the mansion. Despite the fact we outnumber her four-to-one, my brothers treat her word like law.

I don't understand it. Not one fucking iota.

There's no sane reason for us to bend the knee to a girl. Especially one as little as her.

But she's got everyone wrapped around her little finger.

Including me.

Not that I'm complaining. Trinity fascinates me. Despite everything she went through she only holds one grudge.

I've heard her admit to my brothers that she's forgiven Gabriel. Her parents.

But not me.

What gives?

Tonight is her last chance. If she won't hear me out, if she won't pass that same forgiveness onto me...then there's nothing left for me to do but leave. It would kill me to go, to abandon my brothers again, but I'll have no choice.

Maybe I'll still get the kids on weekends, who knows?

I drop my head, letting out a rueful huff as I watch my fingers work against each other.

Then come the footsteps.

When I look up and see her standing a few feet away dressed in a silk robe that does nothing to hide her exquisite curves, my heart pulses in my chest. I put a hand over it, wincing before I can stop myself. Ever since the surgery, it's been doing some strange things inside my chest.

My doctor says I'm imagining it.

I think he bought his degree.

Trinity's eyes dart to my hand, then back to my eyes. Her face is steel, her body rigid.

Rube comes up behind her, a towel wrapped around his waist. I'd have assumed they fucked in the shower, but from what the guys tell me, that belt cinching her waist might as well be a chastity belt. There's been nothing serious between the four of them since that day in the library back at Saint Amos.

Guess we all still have some issues to work through.

"Well?" she says, quirking her eyebrow at me. "I'm listening."

My hackles rise at her tone, but then Rube sticks out a hand, palm down. I force myself to take a breath, and then I stand, urging myself to stay calm.

"Where do you want to—" I begin.

"Right here. Right now." Trinity plants her ass on the couch opposite to the one I was sitting on, putting a small coffee table between us. Then she spends a few seconds rearranging her robe, as if she doesn't dare let me get a peek at her legs.

"Fine." I sit again, run my palms down my thighs, and wish my heart didn't feel like it missed every other beat.

And then Rube leaves. I stare at his retreating back, my eyebrows shooting up to my hairline.

So much for moral support.

"Can we hurry this up?" Trinity says.

I turn back to her, my lips thinning. But then I remember what Rube said before he went into the bathroom to talk to her.

Don't let her get in your head.

He doesn't know she's been in there since day one. Wasn't able to get her out back then, sure as fuck won't be happening now.

I start off the only way I know how. "I'm sorry."

She sniffs, crosses her legs, and stares out the window at the black ocean. There's a moon out tonight, so the beach glows under its pale light, but I'm sure she's watching the waves. They're hypnotic at night.

But nothing compares to her.

With her eyes off me, I have a rare opportunity to study her. Her dark curls, heavy with water, cling to the side of her neck. I want nothing more than to peel it away and lick up the beads of water it will leave behind.

With the apology out of the way, I can get onto the good stuff.

"I'm not going to defend what I did. Or try and reason with

you. It was wrong. Dead wrong. And I shouldn't have done it. But I can't go back. I can't change what I did."

But she says nothing. Just keeps staring out the window.

"Trinity."

I bite my tongue, keeping back another prompt.

When she finally turns to me, her amber eyes are fucking luminescent. "That's it?" she murmurs. "I was wrong, I shouldn't have done it. *That's* your apology?"

I open my mouth, but she doesn't give me a chance to speak.

"You're right, Zach. You can't change the past. But what's stopping you from doing it again? Leaving them again?"

"I just said—"

Wait... *Them?*

That's what this is about? She's pissed because I left my brothers behind?

I frown at her, stand, hesitate. And she tips back her head to stare at me, as if daring me to walk away from the conversation.

Because that will be the end of it. Then I might as well keep walking until I'm out the fucking door.

I move around the coffee table, slow so she doesn't bolt. And she lets me sit next to her, which is the closest I've been since I shoved her out of the way of Gabriel's bullet.

"I was protecting them," I tell her. I reach for her, but she pulls back, eyes slitting warily. "I'd..." I trail off, and then it's my turn to look away because I'm not sure I can bring myself to tell her the next part. Not if I'm still trying to get her to trust me.

"You what? Thought they'd be better off without you? That they'd just go on with their lives?" She twists, facing me, her knees knocking against mine. Then she stabs a finger into my chest, ruthless, no concern for the scar less than an inch away.

"If that's the case, then you should never have come back because it's obvious you don't give a fuck about them."

I open my mouth. She cuts me off.

"If you did, you wouldn't have left them when they needed you the most. They almost got killed, and that's on *you*."

I can't take another stab in my chest, so I grab her wrist. But as gently as I can, only tightening my grip when she tries to tug her arm free.

"*You* almost got killed too," I tell her. "Or did you forget?"

My brothers told me she had a bout of amnesia when she came out of the anesthesia. According to them, her memories all came back. But she's acting like she has no fucking clue what almost happened back then.

If she had died...

Her pulse throbs under my thumb. Quick, strong. She's angry, but she's keeping it under control. I guess we've both learned some tricks the past few months.

Her eyes flick left, right. "We're alone now," she whispers fiercely, leaning in close enough to kiss. "You can drop the act."

My heart slams into my rib cage. Before I can stop myself, I'm grinding her wrist bones together.

She winces, and then a spark of victory lights up her eyes. "They'll believe anything you tell them, Zach, but you showed me your true colors. And I can't unsee that."

And then it hits me.

She's talking about the knife. What I said when I told her to leave.

I drop my head, huff. "Fuck," I murmur.

She huffs too. "Yeah, fuck." Then she pulls her hand out of my grip and gets to her feet. "I won't ever let you hurt them again. Not now, not ever. And if that means you'll always hate me, then you'd better strap in, because it's gonna be a bumpy fucking ride."

Trinity moves to walk past me, but then I'm standing, my body a wall she can't pass. She rears back, glaring up at me, mouth opening.

I don't give her a chance to speak.

She makes an angry sound when I grab her wrist and force her hand against my heart, pushing her palm flush against the thick scar left behind by my surgery.

"You're wrong about a lot of things," I tell her.

"Am I?" she mutters, trying to pull her hand away.

"You were wrong to forgive Gabriel."

She ducks her head, laughs bitterly. "Oh my God."

"You were wrong to forgive your parents."

Her head snaps back, her plump mouth distorting into a snarl. I don't try and stop when she slaps my face with her free hand, but then I grab it too, press that against my chest.

"And you're wrong not to forgive me."

"You don't get to decide who—"

"You want the truth? I told you to leave that morning because I couldn't stand the sight of you anymore."

She gapes at me, indignant, but far from incredulous. How she saw this coming, I don't know. I guess I got my point across better than I thought the morning Gabriel snatched her from Saint Amos.

"You make me sick, Trinity."

Hurt flashes in her eyes.

That tiny spark of pain reminds me of the beast I harbor inside my mind. The one that seeks out violence and chaos…and vulnerability.

That's all it takes.

Just one spark.

And I'm done.

I can never hurt her again. Never bring her pain again. Not like this. I wasn't going to carry on talking. I was going to leave her with those bitter words. But for the first time in my fucking life, I want to ease her pain. Even if it denies me the thing I've always craved so deeply.

But she has to understand.

I slam her hand into my chest. "Every time I looked at you, my heart would twist. Every time you came close, my skin would go cold." I manipulate her hand, bringing it up to my cheek. Not the one she slapped—that one's still stinging, but the other.

I press her knuckles to my flesh and will her to feel that chill.

"Every time we were together, the five of us, I felt like I was dying."

Slow realization turns her bronze-dark eyes to bright amber.

"So yeah, I told you to leave. I shouldn't have, it was selfish as fuck, but when I thought about how I felt around you...a sadist like me...I couldn't even imagine how you made *them* feel."

I glance past her, to where my brothers said they'd wait.

"So I made you leave. And I told myself I was doing the right thing." I shake my head, let go of her hands. "That we'd be better off if you were gone."

Her hands drop to her sides. The hurt is back in her eyes, but it's different. It doesn't fuel me like it should.

I clear my throat. Rake fingers through my hair.

"When I realized how wrong I was...that's when I came back. And it was wrong. I shouldn't have pushed you away from them, Trinity. It wasn't my decision to make."

She stares up at me, silent, barely blinking. Her chest rises as she takes a deep breath, but she exhales without saying anything.

"And what I've been trying to tell you..." I look down, reach for her hands.

I wait for her to pull away so I can turn and leave.

She doesn't.

Trinity lets me take her hands again. Does nothing as I lace my fingers with hers. As I pull her a little closer.

I clear my throat again.

"I'm waiting," she says.

I start to growl at her impatience, but I check myself immediately.

Swallow. Fucking breathe.

"I don't forgive you, Trinity Malone. I don't think I ever can."

Her eyes go wide. Her fingers tighten around mine. "What?" she says, but it's barely a whisper.

"I was broken before I met you. Broken, and selfish. And I was happy not giving a fuck about anyone but myself." I tug her the last bit, until her body's pressed against mine. "Then you came along, and you fixed me. You made me *feel* again. I'd promised myself I'd never be scared again. And then I met you."

I shake loose one of my hands, then the other. I finally get to peel the strands of wet hair from her throat, and run my thumbs down the side of her neck.

"And now I'm terrified all the fucking time."

She puts her hands over mine, her lips parting. "Zach, I didn't—"

"I love you, Trinity. But I don't think I can ever forgive you."

Her eyes are limpid, glowing.

I duck my head. Aim for her lips. And they part oh so fucking invitingly.

But then a finger presses against my mouth, hard enough to push my head back. My eyes fly open, and I glare down at her as she puts her head to the side.

"No."

A most familiar frustration rises inside me. "No?"

"I don't accept your apology." She shrugs. "That was a good start," she says, and then clears her fucking throat. "But it's not enough."

"Christ, woman, what the hell—" I start.

She puts her finger back on my mouth. "Nuh-uh."

I pull away. Bite down on my lip and pretend it's hers instead.

It doesn't work.

I want to rip her to shreds...and then plaster her back together with kisses. I'm trembling from the force of stopping myself lunging at her.

She puts that same finger to her own lips, purses them. Cocks her head again. Taps her lips once, twice, three times.

"What?" I growl, when she stays silent.

"You must be tired," she says.

I shake my head. "Not even a little."

"You should rest."

She takes my hands, laces our fingers, and leads us toward the bedroom. And then my heart does that thing I hate so much —twisting in place before thumping around like a tooth in a loose socket.

"Why didn't you just say you wanted to fuck?" I tell her as I leer at her ass through the silk robe she's wearing.

She stops dead in her tracks, and turns to frown at me. "Who said that's what I want?"

I blink, exhale hard. "What?"

She points at the bed. It's a king-size, covered with pillows and furry blankets. A girl's bed. "Sit."

I don't like the mischievous light in her eyes. "Or what?"

"Or you can leave, Zach." She quirks an eyebrow. "Forever."

At first I think she's dead calm about it, her face not even twitching...but then I see her hands. They're in fists at her side.

So I go over to the bed.

I sit.

And she smiles at me like I deserve a fucking treat.

Trinity turns her head without taking her eyes off me, and calls out, "Guys? I need a hand." And then, with a twist of her mouth, adds a reluctant, "Please."

"Shut it, would you?" I whisper, waving a hand behind me. "I can't hear if you two keep yakking like that."

"You shouldn't be eavesdropping in the first place," Rube says.

"Aw, leave the kid alone," Cass says.

I turn and scowl at Cass over my shoulder. "Kid?" I'm almost two years older than him.

He smirks at me from where he's lounging in the hot tub. He practically lives in the thing. I'm surprised he hasn't sprouted scales yet.

I put my ear back to the crack in the sliding door. Rube pulled it closed when he came back a few minutes ago, and then scolded me when I tried to open it.

Zach and Trinity are talking so quietly, I can barely make out more than a word or two. It's driving me nuts.

"Apollo, chill," Cass calls out.

"Shh!" I hiss.

There's a splash, and the slap of wet feet on the deck. The balcony is covered in slats of wood that stretch all the way to the eight-seat hot tub. A yard away, the balcony ends with a glass railing so you can soak up the bubbles while staring out at the ocean.

I fucking love this house.

I've never loved anything as much in my life…

Okay, that's a lie.

"…forgive you, Trinity Malone. I don't think…"

I strain to hear more.

Screw this.

I grab the sliding door. "I need the—" I begin.

Rube lets out a low, "Not a chance," a second before Cass grabs the door and slides it closed all the way.

Right in my face.

"Come on, man. I won't bug them."

"Let them talk," Rube says. He's standing by the railing, leaning on crossed arms as he stares out at the ocean. He faces forward again as Cass splashes back into the hot tub.

"Come and get in," Cass says. "Knowing those two, this could take hours."

Hours?

I sigh, and stand for a few more seconds by the door. I guess Zach will tell us everything anyway when they're done…but how am I supposed to wait that long?

As I'm about to turn around, I hear something.

I'm right up against the door a second later.

"What?" Cass demands behind me. "What is it?"

I love you. But I won't ever…

I turn wide eyes to Cass, then to Rube, who's facing me now.

I creep away from the door like Zach and Trinity are the ones listening to us, and beckon Rube over when I reach the hot tub.

He frowns, but walks over anyway.

Cass glances up at him and then shields his eyes with a flat hand. "Dude, can you put on some shorts or something?"

Rube is still wearing the towel he came out of the bathroom with. "How about you stop looking?"

Cass rolls his eyes, and then trains them on me. "What did you hear?"

"He said he loves her." I step back, clapping my hands together in front of me as I wait for their response.

Cass rolls his eyes again and mutters, "Christ, finally."

Rube looks like he turned to marble. "He said that? You're sure?"

I nod feverishly. "I know what I heard."

Rube shakes his head. "You must have—"

"Jesus, Rube, don't put on that act. We all fucking knew it."

Rube's one eyebrow cocks up. "We did?" he says dryly.

"Fucking obvious from day one. She pushes his buttons just right, and he loves that shit."

And Rube doesn't argue, because I guess he did know. We all did, just like Cass said.

Zach's mental, but under all that repressed rage, and hate... he's just a guy. It's been brutal for us, even after we got out of that basement, and it fucked us up in different ways. Zach went on the offensive. He'd push people away the moment he saw them as a threat. To himself, to us—it didn't matter, because to him, we're one and the same.

I'm so fucking glad he was the one who said it first. Because holy crap, I've been wanting to tell her that for a while now.

Zach's not our leader anymore. We don't need that kind of structure. But maybe it was some kind of respect.

Unspoken, but unanimous.

I love that about us.

We have an unbreakable bond, the four of us. With Trinity...

I don't know if she'll ever be on the same level as us—

mentally, emotionally—but we have the rest of our lives to figure it out. And I'm not going anywhere.

Now that Zach's told her how he feels…I'm pretty sure he's not going anywhere either.

"So you think she'll let him upstairs?" I ask them.

Cass rolls onto his back and sticks his toes out of the water, not bothering to humor me with a reply.

"Don't know," Rube says. He comes closer, grabs my shoulder, squeezes. "But that's her decision, not—"

"Guys!"

All three of us spin around to face the door. And I'm sure my heart isn't the only one that goes *thump* at the sound of Trinity's voice.

"I need a hand."

Cass lets out such a delighted chuckle, the hair on my arms stands up. He jumps out of the hot tub, streaming water over the deck as he races for the door. We shove and push at each other, jostling for pole position, but all it takes is a disapproving rumble from Reuben to make us stop.

We look back at him. Cass shrugs, mouthing, "What?"

Rube holds up a finger.

And then Trinity lets out a sulky, "Please."

Rube nods his head.

All it takes is elbowing Cass in the stomach, then I'm the first through the door.

"You called," I say, walking up behind Trinity and sliding my hand onto her shoulder. The black robe she's wearing does all sorts of delicious things to my fingertips, especially when I trace her collarbones through the silky fabric.

Zach is sitting on the edge of her bed, looking mighty out of place against the pale pink bedspread.

Rube comes up behind me, but doesn't pass. I guess he's waiting to find out what she wants, just like me. Just like Apollo.

And, judging from the frustrated look in Zach's eyes, he doesn't have a fucking clue what this is about either.

"This is going to get a little tricky," Trinity says, but without taking her eyes off Zach. But she puts her hand over mine, molding my palm over her shoulder. "Where do you think he's going to sleep?"

Apollo's about to say something stupid, I can see it, so I cut in with a quick, "It's a king. There's enough room."

"Is there though?" Trinity muses. She glances up at me, pouting like she's legit having to think about it.

Fuck, I could eat her whole right now. But rather than wolf my way through a delicacy like her, I'd rather take my time and slowly nibble my way over every inch of her.

"So what are you saying?" Rube says.

She looks over at him, and starts stroking the back of my hand. "I don't think he'll fit."

Jesus Christ, she's doing this on purpose. I don't care how innocent she sounds, she's got to know every single word coming out of her mouth is a double entendre. I mean, the guy's sitting on her fucking bed. She's wearing nothing but a silk robe. And I can practically smell how desperate she is for a fuck.

We've spent many nights in that pastel pink bed of hers—me, Rube, Apollo. Nothing more than some light petting and some serious kissing though. She's constantly leaving us with blue balls, and then walking around like she doesn't have a fucking clue how close we came to holding her down and just taking what she seems so ready to give.

I know it has to do with Zach. And I know Rube has this fucked up notion that he'll rip her in half with his giant dick.

If I thought it would make even the slightest difference, I'd have told them all to spend some quality time on PornHub and see how many cunts get ripped apart on there.

We can't break her any more than we already have…and I didn't hear anyone complaining back then.

But after all the shit with Zach getting shot, Gabriel getting away, and our last chance at revenge decomposing in its own shallow grave…I guess we all suffered a bit of a setback.

Hopefully, that shit's all settled now.

"Fit where, my little slut?" I ask her, sliding my hand down the front of her body and cupping a breast.

Zach's eyes move to my hand, then up to my face. I grin at him.

He's the sadist in the house, sure, but that doesn't mean I don't like fucking with him.

"On the bed," she says, as if it's painfully obvious what she was referring to. I give her tit an extra hard squeeze for that, and she lets out an indignant little gasp.

"Then he sleeps on the floor," Rube says.

I barely stop a laugh, glancing at him from the corner of my eye. Rube walks up and comes to stand beside Trinity. He crosses his arms over his chest, and then cocks his head to the chaise lounge pushed against the glass wall opposite the bed. "Or the couch."

"Hmm," Trinity muses. "Maybe the couch."

There's a long, drawn out silence. Then Apollo ducks toward Zach and whispers, "I think she wants you to go over to—"

"Yeah, fuck," Zach growls, standing in a rush. He comes close as he walks past, and gives all three of us a scathing glare.

I almost fucking giggle. It must be eating him up, trying to keep his temper in check.

I've been there to pick him up after each therapy session, and shit gets fucking real in those first few minutes as we fuck off out of Dana Point.

When Zach ratted on me to his shrink, telling the guy I helped him control his urges, I was dragged in there for a session or two myself.

Ain't fuck all wrong with me, so I refused anything more permanent, but I was happy to help out Zach.

Except, now I can't. I'm not allowed to be his pin cushion anymore. We'll never get to finish the smiley face of cigarette burns on my stomach.

The shrink was horrified when I lifted up my shirt, which I found hilarious...which Zachary didn't.

That was my last co-session with them.

So when he walks past and throws us a glare, it feels like it lands harder on me. Like I'm the one who said he has issues he needs to sort out.

Well…he *did* abandon us. And he didn't do fuck all when Gabriel took our Trinity away.

So yeah.

Therapy is his punishment.

And he can glare at me all he wants for thinking I'm a hypocrite.

But I do feel for him. I can't imagine what it's like, having to deal with our shit on top of the maelstrom of pain and suffering churning around inside his head.

So I grin at him.

That makes him huff and turn his back on us. Big mistake.

Don't ever turn your back on a wild animal.

Rube grabs the back of Zachary's neck and shoves him forward, pinning him down on the bed.

Trinity gasps. Apollo shoots forward. I barely manage to grab the back of his shirt and haul him back before he can interfere. When he turns to give me an incredulous stare, I shake my head.

We all have shit to work out with Zach. Trinity, in essence, opened the flood gates.

"You really think he deserves to sleep up here?" Rube grates, looking back at Trinity.

I'm shocked—and a little amazed—that her voice is calm when she says, "Yes."

Rube lets him go.

Zach scrambles up, turns, and Rube's hand is around his neck again. Zach lifts his arms as if he wants to grab Rube's wrist, but then he looks over at Trinity, and his hands fall down beside him as he lowers himself onto the edge of the bed.

Now I'm wishing Apollo had heard more than Zach apparently confessing his love for Trinity, because the fact that

Zach's allowing this shit to happen? I'm guessing we missed some serious drama.

Although, "allowing" isn't quite accurate, judging from the expression on Zach's face. I'm guessing there's a hurricane brewing inside his head.

I feel sorry for him, I do. But it's about time he starts manning up.

"How about we use a reward system?" I say, and start stroking Trinity's shoulder again.

"I'm listening," she says.

Rube glances at me over his shoulder. "Reward for what?"

"If he's good, then he gets to sleep on the couch." I move my head beside Trinity's, like I'm the devil whispering into her ear. "If he's bad, he sleeps on the floor."

Zach clears his expression, and no wonder. I like whatever game Rube and Trinity are playing. I want in.

Who knows…tonight we could all be winners.

Apollo's lips tug into the wickedest smile I've ever seen on him.

Trinity steps forward, out of my grasp. And then over to Rube and Zach, gently moving Rube out of the way.

And the sonofabitch goes.

But I guess we'd be in just as much shit if *we* disobeyed Trinity right now.

She touches Zach's chest, and then points to the pink, padded headboard with its big rhinestone studs.

"Sit."

Zach's mouth twitches, but he manages to keep his expression neutral as he shifts back on the bed until his back is against the headboard. He grabs a handful of her pillows, and he's about to toss them over the side of the bed when Trinity clicks her tongue.

"Leave them alone."

He grits his teeth, but then he subsides, looking totally out of sorts amid the mountain of girly throw pillows. And then Trinity climbs onto the bed. And then she takes off her fucking robe.

"Hey," I call out.

She turns to look at me, eyebrows quirked up.

"What the fuck, woman?"

Now it's one eyebrow.

"Impatient, much?" Apollo mutters next to me.

"Yeah, obviously." I wave at Zachary. "How is this any kind of fair?"

Rube chuckles.

The motherfucker actually fucking *chuckles* at me.

"Do you want to sleep on the floor?" she asks.

I drop my gaze. Shake my head.

Trinity faces Zachary and slowly crawls over the bed toward him. He sits up a little taller, glancing over at us with a blank face before looking back at her. Like he thought he knew how this game would go, but now he's fucking clueless.

You and me both, buddy.

I feel like going off and having a sulk. I didn't sign up for a spectator sport. I love a good tennis match, but nothing beats actually holding the racket in your hands and slamming it into a fucking tennis ball.

But she doesn't care. Trinity knows we're all fucking salivating over her tight, curvy little body as it sways over to him.

She taps each of Zach's ankles, and he spreads his legs so she can kneel between them.

This is goddamn animal cruelty. Why the hell are *we* being punished?

She tugs at his belt, biting her bottom lip as she eases his pants off and down his legs. She doesn't even leave him with a pair of boxers.

I'm shocked he doesn't have a boner yet, because I'm already rocking a semi.

Oh, right. He's not wired like that.

That makes all of this even worse. This tease show won't work on him.

She retreats, taking his pants with her. Then she tosses them over the side of the bed.

"Apollo." She turns to look at the guy, and his face lights up like a Christmas tree.

He steps closer, and then pauses. "Yeah?"

Trinity lures him onto the bed with a crook of her finger, and then sits up on her knees when he gets closer. She looks up at him, for all the world like he's the sun and she's the head priestess of a sun-worshiping cult.

She runs her fingers through his hair.

Takes off his shirt. Helps him out of his pants. Then she pats his chest and turns to look at me. Beckons me.

I'm up on that bed so fast I get carpet burn from the fucking sheet. She doesn't have to help me out of my pants—they're off before I get within a foot of her.

Trinity looks down at my dick and then back up at me with rosy cheeks. For all the world like the fact that she's made me this hard is something she's struggling to come to terms with. Then she pats me on the chest.

But I dart forward and kiss her instead. Because fuck the rules—I'll go mad if I don't taste her right this second. She responds with a moan that makes my dick throb, and then pushes me away.

"Wait," she says through a laugh. "Just wait."

"Fuck, woman," I growl. "What do you think we've been doing the last six months?"

"Cass," Rube says, voice low.

My skin prickles in warning, and I sit back on my haunches

like the good little pet I am because that's how desperate I am to ensure she'll let me stay on the fucking bed.

I feel so fucking whipped right now.

And I couldn't give a shit.

Is this what love is? Because, fuck, I'd never have thought it felt this good.

She calls Rube up next. The bed gives a little creak when he gets on, and I know I'm not the only one who flinches.

Come to think of it…if any one of us could break her, it would be him.

She tugs the towel from his hips, and then kisses each of his pecs while she stares up into his eyes. But when he reaches for her, she leans out of the way, shaking her head.

She takes Apollo's hand and leads him to the middle of the bed. She positions Rube at her left, me on her right.

When she finally turns back to Zachary, he shifts a little like he's wondering what's going on in her pretty head.

And damn it, so am I.

Right now I wouldn't rule out a circle jerk.

Then she turns around and offers Apollo her deliciously plump ass.

"Oh," he says. "Fuck."

I roll my eyes and start shuffling over to him. If he doesn't know how to fuck our precious Trinity from behind, then I'm going to show him exactly how it's—

A hand slams into my chest, halting me. I glare across Trinity's back at Rube. "Man, come on."

He shakes his head, and I swear he's suppressing a smile. "Do you want to end up on the floor?" he asks.

Douche bag.

Meanwhile, Apollo's murmuring, "Um," and stroking Trinity's ass like he's never seen a woman in his life before.

I feel physical pain right now. And that's because my cock is rock hard and I have nothing to stick it into.

Trinity reaches around and hands Zachary's belt to Apollo.

I shiver. Hard.

I'd been staring so hard at her perky little tits, I hadn't even noticed when she took Zach's belt off his pants.

Which, I'm guessing, was her plan all along. Because judging from the groan Zachary lets out, Apollo's suddenly stiff body, and an inhale that gives Rube even bigger pecs, none of them noticed either.

"Oh, Trin, no..." Apollo protests weakly.

So she slaps him with the belt. Not hard—I mean, he barely even flinches—but it's enough to make him reconsider his position on BDSM.

He pats her with the belt.

Christ. I can't even.

"She's supposed to feel it, jack ass," I tell him.

Apollo looks up at me, cringes a little, and whacks her again. This time at least hard enough to leave a faint mark.

She lets out a little sigh, and promptly lays her head on Zach's thigh, an inch away from his dick.

Which isn't so flaccid anymore.

"Do you want him to hit me harder?" she whispers, looking up at Zachary.

All he does is groan, and then shift like he wants to get off the bed.

Rube and I move in unison. We each grab one of Zach's shoulders and slam him back into the headboard hard enough to rattle it against the wall.

He sends us both an angry scowl, but settles down when Trinity moves a little closer, nestling between his legs like a sleepy cat.

From the way her head's positioned, I'm sure Zach can feel every breath on his dick.

God, and here I thought she was torturing us? Zach's got the best fucking view in the house, but he can't touch her, can't move…and worst of all, he's not the one holding the belt.

A powerless sadist.

I fucking love it.

And maybe that means I have a touch of sadism in me too, because I'm getting hard from the tortured look on his face.

Apollo belts her again.

Trinity puffs out a sigh.

Zach groans and presses his eyes closed.

"Watch," Rube says, his other hand going around Zach's throat.

I wouldn't call Rube violent—not in the slightest—but he does have a thing with necks. I don't even want to go there, because I don't know if it's something related to his time in the basement, or a kink he picked up along the way.

It's also the only thing that Zach seems to respond to. And maybe that's the sole reason Rube does it.

Thwack.

I stare down at Trinity, at the look of rapture on her face, and I know she's not faking. The moment I set foot in her tiny room at Saint Amos, I knew she was a freak.

I bust in there, and she looked up at me like I'd opened God's bedroom window. But I get that a lot. And that's not what did it for me. I knew the second I threw her up against that closet door that she was hot for me.

Not like she was one step away from spreading her legs or anything. It was more…subtle than that. It was the way she looked at my mouth, how her breath turned into a little pant. Like she was terrified of what I was about to do to her…but she couldn't wait for me to start.

She loved what the four of us did to her the day we took her virginity. She flourished under our hands and our mouths and our cocks like a fern unfurling after the snow melts.

Now she's here, eyes fluttering as Apollo leaves stripes on her ass, and it's perfect.

Everything about this moment is perfect.

I don't know how long it will stay this way...but I'll be praying every night that it's forever.

27

RUBE

I t's like I snap out of a trance when Trinity murmurs, "Stop."
Apollo lets up immediately. I don't think he got in more
than eight or so shots, but every blow to Trinity's ass was torture
for me, so I can't imagine what he was going through.

I wanted to stop him. I wanted to grab her and wrap my
arms around her and then fuck up everyone who'd been
watching and not helping her escape that belt.

But she *wanted* this.

And I don't know how I'm supposed to feel about that.

Apollo's chest rises and falls as he looks up at us each in turn,
like he's also just waking up. He drops the belt and moves away,
eyes widening when he sees his own hard dick.

Why is he so surprised? No mortal man could have heard the
sounds Trinity made and not have a fucking hard-on. We're all
hard—even Zach.

I expect her to start sucking his cock. She was teasing him
the entire time anyway, she might as well. I'd be happy to watch.

But then she pushes up onto her hands and knees, and turns

to look at me. Her eyes are a dark bronze, her cheeks flushed, her lips gleaming. She licks them, and I quickly focus on her eyes again, like she'd caught me watching porn.

"Do you want to fuck me?" she asks, voice breathy, unsteady.

I can barely speak but I manage to get out a rough, "Yes."

"How badly?" Another slow lick of her pink tongue over her gleaming lips.

"Very fucking badly."

"Want to know how much I want you?" she murmurs.

In that moment, it's as if no one else exists. Everything— everyone—else fades away as she leans closer.

We are all barely more than a foot away from her and Zachary. I can feel the warmth of her body. Zach's.

I take my hand off his throat, and he coughs—just once. But I'm still holding him back, away from Trinity, because if he lunges at her I might kill him.

Which makes no sense, because I'm not a jealous man. But I guess I've just learned the extent of my patience.

It's most certainly run out.

"Rube?" she whispers.

"Yes," I say, after clearing my throat. "Tell me."

She shakes her head. Turns her shoulder to me. And then she lies back against Zachary.

I can't stop the growl. And Zachary looks over at me like he doesn't like the sound of it.

Trinity lifts her knees and kicks up on the bed, so her ass is on Zach's stomach. His head is beside hers now, which means he can easily kiss her if he wants, but at least his cock is far away from her pussy.

That should make me feel better, but it doesn't.

It's still closer than mine is.

She glances away from me, to Cass, putting her finger in her mouth and chewing on it like she's suddenly shy. Perhaps she is, because it's only when Cass slides a hand over her knee and urges her leg to the side that she opens them.

Apollo lets out a groan. Trinity looks at him, and cocks her head to the side. "Swap with Rube," she says.

For a second I almost feel sorry for him, especially when his face crumples with dismay. But he had a solid view of her ass and pussy while he was belting her.

My turn now.

I'm in front of her a second later.

Cass urges her leg open a little wider, and Apollo does the same with her other leg.

Revealing the light fuzz of hair on her mound and the dark pink slit between her legs I'm dying to shove my cock into.

"Fuck," I murmur.

And then Zach slides his hands down her stomach. My eyes fly to his, my teeth gritted. But I can't stop him. He can do what he wants, unless Trinity says otherwise.

And thank God, she does.

She clucks her tongue. Apollo and Cass grab his wrists and wrench his fingers off her belly. He moves under her, pressing his lips into a line as if he can't bear to have her on top of him anymore.

And that makes Trinity giggle.

I hope to hear that sound every day for the rest of my life.

She slides her hand down her stomach, locking eyes with me again as she strokes her fingers over her pussy. Even without touching her, I can see how wet she is.

How badly do I want to fuck her?

More than there are atoms in the universe.

She lifts her hand and presses it to Zachary's lips. "Lick," she commands him.

And the greedy bastard does just that. And then groans like he's sipped ambrosia.

"See?" she whispers, dragging her fingers through her soaked pussy again. "That's how badly I want you to fuck me."

My jaw bunches, and my cock throbs. I grab it at the base, trying to hold it still, trying to throttle it into submission. Trinity's eyes flutter down, and I feel her gaze on my dick as if she's stroking me.

"What the actual fuck are you waiting for?" Cass demands. "Because if you don't have your cock inside her in the next second, it'll be mine."

"I don't want to—"

"Hurt me?" she cuts in. "Do you think it'll hurt more than the belt?" She glances up at Apollo. "Would you like to belt me again?"

Zach lets out a soft, "Fuck," like he can't even handle the thought. And from the way his cock starts bobbing, I'm thinking he won't be able to control himself much longer.

So I shift up the bed. I wrench Zach's legs aside, splitting them open as wide as Trinity's so I can get closer to her.

I lean over her, my hands brushing Zachary's ribs, and press my mouth to hers.

I should be happy with our kiss. It's fierce and ravenous…but my dick falls against her stomach, and the feel of her satin skin against my dick fills me with an insatiable lust.

It's not enough.

It will never be.

"Make sure she's really wet though," Cass says. "Don't want to rip her in two."

There's a laugh in his voice. I lean back, and look down as he trails his fingers over Trinity's stomach.

Her belly flutters at that touch. She gasps when Cass

squeezes her clit, and then groans when he slides his fingers inside her.

My cock starts bobbing too, blood pumping furiously into the thick shaft. I grab it so it won't interfere, but when I see how Trinity's pussy starts dripping, I can't just sit here with my dick in my hands.

But before I can move, Apollo reaches over and smears her juices along her taint and over her back door. And the sound she makes at that has my cock throbbing in my hand like I'm seconds away from coming.

If she hadn't sucked me off in the shower, I'd probably be emptying my load all over her tits right now.

The torture is real, me sitting back and stroking my dick as Apollo and Cass finger fuck her inches away. And when they slide their free hands under her knees and drag her legs up alongside her chest, opening her up for me, it takes every fucking molecule of willpower I have not to thrust into her.

But she's so close.

Her body goes tight. Her eyes are closed, her mouth open. And when Zach's fingers glide around her ass, when he strokes her back door and then dips the tip of his pinkie finger inside her, Trinity comes.

With a growl I feel more than hear, I shove my hips forward. Not caring who or what I touch on the way, I force the crown of my dripping cock against her pussy, and then smear it through her slick, hot cunt lips.

She shudders, whimpers.

I look down, mesmerized how her pussy swallows the tip of my cock. Grabbing her ass, I lift her hips clean off Zachary's stomach.

She makes as if she wants to grab onto me, but then Apollo and Cass grab her hands and force her fingers around their dicks.

I'm not surprised when Zachary grabs hold of his own dick, taking advantage of the fact that no one is policing him anymore.

Cass happens to look over, and he sees what Zach's doing, but now it's like the four of us are sharing a secret. Because Trinity's head is thrown back on Zach's shoulder, and she doesn't seem to know what fucking planet she's on.

So we let Zach jerk himself off. And he and Cass and Apollo watch as I take my dick out of Trinity's pussy, smear it through her dripping folds, and then slap it over her clit.

She gasps, her body convulsing. "Oh God," she murmurs hoarsely.

Zachary groans, and then bites her ear. She turns to him, stares at him, openmouthed and lost as I slide my wet cock over her clit.

She's still stroking Cass and Apollo's cocks. And they're watching me tease her with my dick.

"Reuben," she moans, finally turning back to me. "Please." She whimpers, squirms in my hands. My fingertips sink into her ass as she wriggles around. "Please fuck me."

God, how am I supposed to say no?

I bite down on my lip, grab my cock, and guide it to her entrance.

"Christ," Cass murmurs. "Why the fuck is this so hot?"

"Because he's got a big dick," Apollo says breathlessly, "and her pussy's too fucking tight by half. He'll never get it in there."

I want to tell them to shut up, but I don't. Because every word ratchets up my own arousal a thousand-fold. Even the glimpse of Zachary's fingers moving over his own cock is making my balls ache.

"Is she wet enough?" Cass asks, and then swipes his fingers over her clit.

"She's fucking soaking my cock," I manage.

"Fuck, she is." Cass groans. "Beg him for his cock, my beautiful little slut," he says, reaching over and grabbing a fistful of her hair.

"Fuck me," Trinity says, turning to kiss the inside of Cass's wrist.

"Hard," Cass says.

"Fuck me hard," she says, her eyes shining with lust when she turns to look at me.

I force myself deeper inside her, her tight little pussy making every inch a struggle.

"Oh God, I'm so fucking close," Cass mutters through his teeth. He slaps away her hand and moves up the bed. "Open your fucking mouth, my little slut."

Trinity turns to him, eyes wide with shock. "What did you—"

He grabs her jaw, forces open her mouth, and rams his cock down her throat.

I squeeze her ass hard, and she yelps in pain, but the sound is muffled around Cass's cock. He fucks her mouth, a hand fisted in her hair, the other around her throat, pushing her into Zachary's chest.

Zachary groans, and I feel the aftershock of his body convulsing as it travels through Trinity's body right to my cock. Zach's cum hits her cunt, soaking my dick. I flinch at the unexpected heat, but it makes sliding into her a little easier. So I go in another inch while Cass forces his dick between her lips again and again.

Then she chokes. His load seeps out between her lips, but he doesn't take his dick out. He slams a fist into the headboard as his back arches, and rams another inch of himself down her throat.

She chokes again, and this time he pulls out. She splutters

and gasps, dragging a hand over her mouth and giving him a death glare. "You fucking asshole!"

He taps the side of her face. Laughs. "Oh, sweetheart, I'm only getting started."

He looks over at me, a strange smile lifting the corner of his mouth. "We're all only getting started."

28

TRINITY

I thought I was in control.

I'm not.

I thought they were just pawns in my game, that I could move them about and give them orders.

They're not.

And the most fucked up thing about all of this?

I'm loving it.

Every lewd, hedonistic second of it.

Because I don't want to control them. I want them to take what they want, when they want it. As rough and as savagely as they want, as they can.

Apollo wraps his hand around mine, forcing me to stroke him harder and then slower. From his face, he looks ready to come too. And when he looks up, rapturous, it's as if Cass knows too.

"Ever had your dick sucked, Apollo?" Cass asks.

He shakes his head, lips parting.

And then Rube starts pushing his dick into me again. Just the tip, and that already stretches me. I moan, rocking my hips to try and get him deeper inside me, but Apollo and Cass are still holding me down. Spreading my legs for Reuben and making sure my pussy is as wide open as it can go.

"Open your mouth again, my little slut. You have another dick to suck."

I glare at Cass, because now he's talking in rhymes and sounding so full of himself I want to slap him.

And fuck it, I do.

He looks back at me, mouth open, and puts his hand on the mark I left on his cheek.

"You didn't just do that," he murmurs.

Everyone stops.

"Cass, I'm—"

But then he ducks his head and I can't get another word out.

I lose myself in his kiss, feeling Apollo's dick throbbing in my hand as I hang on for dear life.

Zach starts stroking my back door again, and my body starts to tremble. Cass pulls back, pushes open my jaw, and turns my head.

Apollo doesn't quite make it inside my mouth. He shoots cum all over my lips and chin, and then tries to pull back, biting his bottom lip.

So I dart forward and close my lips over his cock, fitting as much of him as I can into my mouth, and licking him clean.

He lets out a low groan, his fingers sliding into my hair, tugging me down another inch.

Hands grab my breasts. Squeeze. It takes me a second to realize it's Reuben. He wants my attention now, and I have no choice but to give it to him.

Especially when he drags me off Zachary, lands on his back, and puts me down on top of him.

My legs go to either side of his hips, and I drop my head when I feel cool air over my pussy. I'm spread open, perfectly poised for Zach and Apollo and Cass when Rube shoves the first inch of his cock inside me.

A hand caresses my ass. Slaps me—hard. I turn around, expecting it to be Zach…but it's Apollo.

I lock eyes with Zach, and he moves around me on his knees.

Rube pulls his dick out and uses the crown to massage my clit. And then he grabs a fistful of my hair and drags me down for a kiss.

Which sticks my ass right into the air.

So no surprise someone licks me from pussy to ass and then sticks their tongue inside me. I whimper into Rube's kiss, and he pulls back my head as if wondering what's going on.

I can't even look back. I have no idea who's tongue fucking me. And when a second mouth joins the first, I have even less of a clue who's doing what back there. But when Zachary comes into my peripheral view stroking his dick…

Well, it could only be Apollo and Cass back there.

One of them shoves a pair of fingers inside me. Fuck, for all I know, they each have a finger in there.

My mouth falls open, bliss quivering through me as Rube keeps rubbing his dick over my clit.

"Fuck, I'm getting close," I warn him. Them.

They don't listen.

They don't fucking care.

Whoever's fucking me with their finger, they start picking up the pace. Their hand thumps into my pubic bone, sending a violent pulse through me with each impact.

There's a mouth on my clit now. A tongue that keeps lapping against my entrance. Another finger on my back door.

When Rube tightens his fist in my hair and shoves my head to the side, my mouth is already open for Zach's dick.

Not because I was expecting Rube to force me to suck him, but because I'm gasping for air.

Rube uses his grip to slide my mouth over Zach's cock, keeping up a steady rhythm. Then he grabs one of my hands, leaving me balancing like a tripod, and wraps my fingers around his dick.

I've never had to multi-task like this before. I don't even know if I'm doing anything right.

But when a mouth latches onto my clit and starts sucking as his tongue flicks that sensitive nub, my climax speeds closer.

A second mouth licks my pussy as the pair of fingers ramming inside me slow…slow…stop.

"Fuck!" I pant out. "No! Don't stop!"

But they do. Apollo and Cass pull back, leaving me a shaking, shivering wreck seconds away from a climax.

And then I realize why when Rube wraps his hand around my fingers, and helps me guide his cock to my entrance.

He uses the tip to push apart my lips, and slowly sinks the first inch into me.

Zach moves to the back.

Hands grab my ass and gently urge me to part even more.

And then a second cock brushes my pussy.

"No!" If I could have looked back, I would have, but Rube's still got his fist in my hair. "No, you won't fit!"

Zach lets out a dark chuckle. "Exactly what you said," he says.

Then he drags his dick up and pushes it against my backdoor.

"No! Fuck!" I start struggling.

There's no way I can handle this. It's too much. Who the fuck was I kidding?

Rube grabs my head, brings me down close. "If you can take me, then you take him too."

"No, please!" I'm still struggling, and Zach's dick slips away from its target.

"Hold her down," he growls.

Immediately, I have a hand on each thigh. Apollo and Cass force my legs open wider, and one of them even wraps an arm around my waist, holding me steady.

Someone starts teasing my clit with their fingertips. I hear someone spit, and feel wetness on my skin.

Zachary tests that too-tight opening again with his dick. "God, you're fucking beautiful."

Teeth nip my ass.

I'm done trying to figure out who's doing what. I'm drowning in ecstasy.

Fingers touch my pussy lips, drag me open.

The arm around my waist forces me down, and Rube's cock thrusts into me. Fingers stroke my backdoor the second Zach's dick slips away, but it's only to spread some lubrication. Because then he's back, and he's forcing himself inside me.

"No, God, please!" I'm sobbing. Choking.

I feel like I'm bursting, but there's no pain. Just so much fucking pleasure I don't know what to do with it.

I let out a hoarse scream when someone comes on my back with a groan.

And then Rube drags me down for a kiss. Filling my mouth with his tongue, as my pussy is forced down onto his cock.

When I come, the world stops.

I can't breathe.

My body locks up.

And then the agony of pure bliss hits me. Warm wetness slides out of me as Rube starts fucking me. As Zach eases his cock in and out of my backdoor.

"Fuck her harder," Cass commands behind me. "I want to hear her scream."

And they hold me down so Rube can do just that.

And I do scream.

And then I cry.

And then I come again while I'm still recovering from my last orgasm.

But when Rube's ready, and I see his face tightening, feel his dick throb, I grab his face and I kiss him as hard as I can.

Because I'm theirs. Wholly. Truly. To do with whatever they please. To admire, to worship, to satisfy, to fuck.

All they ask is that I accept the fact that they all need me. Each and every one of them.

And I do.

Because I need them just as much.

I've finally found my real family. They're kind and loving and genuine.

Everything a family should be.

I'm met with the aroma of baking bread, coffee, and bacon when I walk downstairs. My mouth is already watering by the time I reach the kitchen and see Cass at the cooker.

"Smells incredible," I tell him, sliding onto one of the bar stools in the breakfast nook so I can watch him while he cooks.

I never knew he was such a keen chef. But he's a hedonist like me, and food is one of our weaknesses.

He turns, bathing me with a gorgeous smile as he takes me in from head to toe. "Morning, my beautiful mess," he says.

I laugh, not even bothering to disagree.

My curls are all over the place, the shirt I found on the floor to cover up my nakedness before coming downstairs happens to be Apollo's too-big vest, and I'm pretty sure I have at least five hickeys on my neck.

Don't forget the fact that I barely had any sleep last night. I'm surprised I'm not walking with a limp.

"This beautiful mess needs coffee," I groan, but Cass puts up his spatula in warning when I attempt to climb off my bar stool.

"What did I say about setting foot in my kitchen when I'm

cooking?"

I quirk an eyebrow at him, but I stay where I am. I've had my ass pummeled with that spatula before, and I don't think I can handle that level of sheer eroticism so early in the morning.

Not without coffee.

Not while Cass is wearing my cooking apron.

He gives me an evil grin, as if he's reading my thoughts, and briefly abandons whatever heavenly dish he's cooking to make me a cup of coffee.

"Are you saying I'm not capable of pushing a button?" I ask dryly, as he sets down a cup in the espresso machine.

"You shouldn't have to," he shoots back. "Not after what we put you through last night."

I blush, and try to cover it up with my hands before he can notice. But he looks back just in time to see my cheeks turn red.

"Fuck, girl," he murmurs, "Don't make me come over there and give you something to blush about."

I barely stop a giggle from spilling out, instead focusing on the coffee Cass slides over the marble-top island toward me. He tosses the bacon and onions he was frying into a large bowl and starts stirring it as he sends me another lewd smile.

Oh God…is he making a frittata again? I take a quick sip of coffee to wash down the saliva flooding my mouth. And I'm not drooling over the food.

Cass looks like he just walked out of a photo shoot. I know he doesn't use product in his hair, so how can it look like he spent hours in front of the mirror teasing it into the perfect bed-head style?

Does it even matter that my apron has a pink unicorn on it?

No, it does not.

He rocks *awsum*.

"Now you let me get this in the oven, then I'm taking you upstairs and—" he begins.

"Breakfast will have to wait," Rube says from the stairs.

We both turn, Cass with spatula raised, me with my coffee cup by my lips.

As soon as Cass spots Rube, he switches off the oven and starts untying the apron. "What happened?"

Rube looks grimly at me, and then flicks his fingers. "Best if you see yourself."

My stomach lurches.

No.

No, no, no! I want to stamp my foot like a five-year-old. Can't I have a little bit of normal?

Cass and I follow Rube up the stairs to Apollo's room. It's kitted out with a double bed, and a computer station that—to me, anyway—looks like something out of the Swordfish movie.

The computer area is the only part of his room that's not chaotic. Everything else is partially submerged under magazines, surfing gear, or clothes.

"Do you ever let the maid in here?" Cass asks. He picks his way across the floor like he's walking through a minefield.

"She was in here yesterday," Apollo mumbles absently, and then pushes away from the table, pointing to one of three massive monitors.

Honestly, the only thing he's missing is a hologram projector.

"What is it?" I ask, standing in the doorway. I don't have a thing about untidiness...I don't like computers very much. The most time I've ever spent on one was when I was copying the files for them off Gabriel's laptop.

I guess maybe that's why I don't like them—they only remind me of bad things.

"It's an article posted a few days ago," Apollo says. "It's... uh..." he looks up at Rube, who nods. "It's about Gabriel."

I frown at him. "He made the news? Why would he do that? He's got to know the police are after him?"

He has Zachary's attempted homicide hanging over his head, a fact that I'm pretty sure was made clear when the police taped up my old house and then froze his accounts.

But it was like he disappeared into thin air after his discussion with Apollo. The police couldn't find a trace of him, and neither could we.

It's been months.

Secretly—*selfishly*—I'd hoped the guys had put everything behind them. That they were starting new lives and leaving their Ghosts and Guardians and all of that behind them.

Now this.

"He…kinda didn't have a say in the matter," Apollo says.

I roll my eyes. "What have I told you lot about being cryptic? It's just plain annoying."

Crossing my arms over my chest, I venture deeper into Apollo's room, until I'm standing beside Rube. He smooths a hand down my head, toying with a curl as I lean in to read what's on Apollo's screen.

VIRGINIA PRIEST FOUND DEAD IN TIJUANA

My skin goes cold. "No," I murmur. "Oh my God."

The article states Gabriel's body was discovered by hotel staff in his room in Tijuana, Mexico a day after he hung himself. What the hell he was doing there was anyone's guess.

I stop reading halfway through. Clear my throat. "Well…I guess that…ends it?" But when I look up at my men, they're all staring at me like they're waiting for the other shoe to drop.

"What is it?"

"You read that last bit, right?" Cass asks, pointing.

I decline to answer, instead I'm craning over Apollo's shoulder again.

The last line of the article sends a centipede crawling down my back.

The executor of Father Gabriel Blake's estate requests that any next of kin contact them urgently.

And then a phone number with a Virginia area code.

"Nope." I shake my head as I retreat. "Not interested."

"Trinity," Rube says, sliding his hand down my shoulder. But before he can grab me, I dodge away from his touch.

"Nope." I cross my arms even tighter. "Nope, nope, nope."

When I turn, fully intent on stalking out of the room, Zachary's barring my way.

God *damn* it! I hate it when they gang up on me outside of the bedroom.

"I'm not calling," I tell him, holding up my hands. "You can't make me."

"What if he left you something?" Apollo asks. "Don't you want to know what it is?"

"I couldn't care if he left me a private jet and some of Fort Knox's gold," I say, glaring at Apollo over my shoulder. "I don't want anything to do with him."

"He's your father, Trinity," Rube says.

"He's most *definitely* not."

"Whatever you don't claim goes to the state," Zachary says.

I turn away from all of them, instead staring out the window at the distant sea. It's idyllic out there which is bullshit, because nothing short of pre-hurricane weather will suit my mood right now.

"Including whatever's in that safe."

The sudden hush in the room after Zachary's statement isn't from us being quiet. It's the hush of breaths being held.

Shit.

I forgot about the safe.

But from their reactions to Zachary's statement, my men haven't. For all I know, Apollo's still been running his password cracking software every second of every day since they left Saint Amos. In fact, now I'm pretty sure they've *never* stopped searching for their Ghosts.

And I want to keep them from their truth because I'm too busy being happy?

I turn to Zachary. "Then go. You can take my social security card and claim whatever—" I wave at the computer "—it is."

Zachary shakes his head. "You have to be there in person."

"Yeah? And how would you know?" I have no right to be angry with him, but I need to channel this frustration—this fear —somehow.

"Because when I had to claim my inheritance after my parents died, I didn't want to be there either." He looks up, to the side. "But I'm glad I did, because at least we have a roof over our heads."

The bastard is guilt-tripping me.

And it's working.

I've contributed nothing to our home. I would have, obviously, but I don't have a penny to my name. No job. No inheritance.

But if Gabriel left me something…

"Fine," I snap. "Then let's go."

"What about breakfast?" Apollo calls out as we all stream out of his chaotic room.

"We'll get something on the way," Cass says over his shoulder.

"Aw, man. I was looking forward to that."

My stomach grumbles quietly to itself as I head upstairs to change.

Yeah, Apollo. You and me both.

30

TRINITY

I don't like this place. There's too much chrome and glass and expensive-looking art on the walls. Gabriel's executor—a middle-aged woman whose name I already forgot—has a habit of clicking her pen after every statement she makes, like a judge banging her gavel.

"And this is the last one. If you'll just sign here." She taps a line on the paperwork, as if I've been struck blind and can't notice the bright yellow post-it arrow stuck to the side of the page. And then clicks her pen.

Click.

I sign. Date. I slide the form over to Reuben. He signs as a witness. Dates.

The lawyer takes the paper back and then stands, going over to a cabinet with a keypad on the side. But not before she runs her gaze over my men.

I don't know how much she's figured out about our relationship, but the fact that all four of them accompanied me into the room probably gave her some clues. Then there were the hickeys I wasn't allowed to cover up with makeup. Four hickeys…four men…

She should know they're mine. And I swear, if she looks at them like they're a deep-dish pizza and she's just come off a fast, I'm gonna—

"Almost done," Rube says, sliding his hand onto my thigh.

I'm wearing a sunny empire-waist dress. I should feel like a doll, but I don't. Which is weird, because it definitely felt like Cass was playing dress up with me. He always insists on dressing me and anyone else who doesn't have enough willpower to turn him down before we leave the house.

My curls are scooped up on top of my head, but a few straggle down around my neck. I'm even wearing a touch of lipstick and a slick of mascara, which is usually all they allow me to wear, makeup-wise. I was also denied underwear, but that's a battle I lost a long time ago.

Thankfully I managed to get away with a pair of mules and not high heels like Cass almost always insists I wear.

It's not my problem they're all at least a foot taller than me.

The lawyer comes back with an envelope.

She's already handed me the keys to my old house, which is the only thing Gabriel left me in his will. Apparently, he only had a hundred dollars to his name. He didn't own a car, or any shares or anything. No overseas bank accounts. Nothing.

Just the house which, according to the lawyer, had been transferred into his name less than a year ago by my parents' estate.

"What's this?" I ask her.

And for the first time today, despite my barrage of questions, she shrugs. "It was found among his things. It's marked for your attention only."

"Maybe it's the password," Apollo says.

I don't have to look around to know his brothers are all glaring at him.

Best way to keep a secret? Don't tell Apollo.

"Password?" the lawyer repeats.

I wave my hand, and then toss a curl over my shoulder as I stand. "Private joke," I tell her. Then I stick out my hand, all formal like, and wait for her to shake.

She does, but reluctantly, as if she's waiting for me to open the envelope.

Don't hold your breath, lady.

I turn to leave, when Zachary says, "Did he leave a note?"

Freezing, I stare at the door. Only a few more steps, and we'd have been outside. Free.

But not yet.

"Um...yes. But I can't disclose—"

I turn on my heel, my voice snippy with how desperate I want to be out of here. "I'm next of kin. You can disclose it to me."

The woman looks at my men, then back at me. "I...have a copy."

"That's fine." I cross my arms, giving my boobs a little perk that doesn't go unnoticed. When I take the folded paper she hands me, and head for the door, my men follow me without a word.

Outside in the Range Rover, I'm nestled between Zachary and Reuben on the back seat, Cass driving and Apollo sitting shotgun.

Someone lights a joint, but I'm too busy staring at the envelope in my hands to see who it is.

They read Gabriel's suicide note in the elevator on the way down, handing it silently to each other. Rube wanted to give it to me, but I ignored him.

I don't want to know what Gabriel said.

Judging from their lack of conversation on the topic for the next five floors until we hit ground level, it wasn't important anyway.

"Aren't you going to open it?" Cass asks.

I look up, catching sight of his iridescent blue eyes in the rear-view mirror. "Maybe. Maybe not."

I slip the envelope into my purse, and tuck it between Zach and me. He looks over at the touch, and then grabs my wrist. He holds me for a beat, tight and fierce, and then smooths my hand over his thigh.

"Home then?" Cass asks.

"I'm hungry," Apollo says.

"You ate like an hour ago," Cass sighs.

"So?"

"Christ. Fine. And I'm guessing you want a fucking taco? Where's the closest—"

"Take me to Maude Street," I tell Cass.

Beside me, Rube shifts on his seat. I keep looking forward, willing him not to ask me if I'm okay.

Because I'm not.

But maybe I will be if I can finally burn my bridges.

I told the lawyer that I didn't want the house. That she could sell it. I signed some papers setting it all up.

But I know what my men want.

And now, maybe, I can finally give it to them.

"The safe?" Apollo asks, turning in his seat and grabbing the headrest. "We're going to look in the safe?"

"It's probably empty by now," Zachary says.

"Yeah, but maybe it's not." Apollo grins at me. "And we know the combination."

"Do you still remember it?" Rube asks me.

Of course I do. It came back along with everything else that happened that horrific day.

4211.

The same combination that opens the basement apparently opens the safe in the study. At least, that's what my men decided after deciphering what Gabriel said to Apollo.

I still can't believe Apollo let him go. Then again...I still can't believe a lot of the things that happened that day.

When we pull up to my old house on Maude Street, I almost wish I'd let Cass drive us to the nearest Mexican take-out instead. My stomach's in knots, and I know it'll only get worse when I'm inside.

I guess word got out about the shooting. Everyone who was home that day must have heard the gunshots. The screams. The ambulance arriving.

As we head for my house, I see a handful of For Lease and For Sale signs down the road. Even the one right across my house.

It's sad. I lived in this house for close to a decade, and the only neighbor I knew was my babysitter, Miss Langley.

I take the house key out of my purse. I stare at it for a second before inhaling deep, putting down my purse, and turning to Rube.

"Okay," I tell him. "I'm ready."

He climbs out of the car and helps me step off the Range Rover's running board.

Then all the other doors open, my men pouring out of the car and circling me like a bunch of secret service agents.

I hold up my hand. "I got this."

"You can't—"

I turn on Zachary. "I can't walk five yards without adult supervision?" I ask, sugar sweet.

His jaw bunches, but he doesn't say anything.

"Can't we just—" Rube says.

"Do you guys think it's booby-trapped or something? Is the

whole place going to explode the second I open the front door?"
I walk ahead a foot and then turn on them, arms on my hips.
"Seriously?"

They have the decency to look slightly embarrassed, but that
doesn't stop Cass from opening his mouth to argue.

"No." I lift a finger. "*No.* I'll be right over there." I point at
the house. "You'll be close enough to hear me scream."

Ooh, bad choice of words.

"Scream?" Apollo says, practically going to his toes. Rube's
hands curls into fists. Zachary's eyes narrow. And Cass isn't
lounging against the side of the car anymore. He's standing at the
ready.

"Just…" I let out an exasperated growl. "Just stay in the car,
would you? I'll be out in a minute."

I turn and head for the house, not bothering to find out if
they'll grant me my wish.

I get that they're concerned about my safety, but Gabriel's
dead. There's no bogeyman ready to snatch me anymore.

But when will they realize that?

My hand shakes when I try and put the key in the lock, so I
take a few long breaths before letting myself in.

I leave the door open, turn around, and give my boys a wave.

Only Apollo waves back.

Why do I have a feeling I'm going to pay for this when we
get home?

A faint smile toys around my lips.

I should do this more often.

The air inside my house smells stale. There's still blood on
the carpet where Zachary was shot. The furniture is still out of
place.

But Gabriel must have come back at least once, perhaps after
the investigation grew cold, because there's a hint of cigarette
smoke in the air.

I pause at the foot of the stairs, and then hurry up them to my room.

It's still in the catastrophic state Gabriel left it in. I turn and take the framed drawing of the *awsum* unicorn from the wall, stare around at the place I called home, and head downstairs with a knot in my throat.

My heart starts beating a little faster when I lift a hand to open the study door.

It's unlocked, but that's no surprise. I heard Gabriel moving around in the study when I was creeping out of the basement, and then he came running. Guessing there was no time for him to lock the door again.

I step inside my father's study and stare around. It's a mess. All the furniture's been shifted around. Books—mostly theological encyclopedias and leather-bound bibles—have been tossed off the bookshelf and lay scattered over the floor.

How the hell am I supposed to find anything in this mess?

And then I see it. It stands out like a beacon, and I don't understand how he couldn't have noticed it.

There's a large leather-bound bible still on the shelf, snuggled between two thick books. It's white, and I already know the letters on front will be embossed in shiny gold.

My mother's bible.

Except...it can't be. Because I took it from her reading corner the night I left my home forever. But when I pick it up, it has the same weight. The same gold-trimmed pages.

I open the cover. There's a letter-sized safe inside, perhaps two inches thick.

4-2-1-1

There's a soft beep.

I go to my knees, laying the book on the carpet so I can open the little safe's door so I can look inside.

A floorboard out in the hallway creaks.

I spin around, my heart climbing up my throat, and stare at the study door. But no one emerges from the hallway after a few ridiculously long seconds.

Jumping at ghosts. Or is it shadows?

I swear, if one of my men come in here because they think I can't look after myself for one second...

There will be hell to pay.

I shake my head and go back to the safe. Open the door.

A stack of hundred-dollar bills. Three sturdy envelopes.

The first envelope has a small thumb drive in it. I take it out, tuck it between my breasts.

Should have brought my purse, but I guess my bra will do for now.

The second envelope has a passport and some folded papers inside.

I open the passport.

Frederick Dalton.

I frown at the passport photo.

Who the hell is—

There's another creak, louder, right behind me. I whirl around, a hand to my chest. My cheeks flush with anger. "I told you to wait in the..."

But it's not Reuben. It's not Cass. It's not Zach, or Apollo.

It's a middle-aged woman I've never seen before, and she's smiling at me.

Which is fucked up, because there's nothing friendly about the gun she's pointing at my face.

31

TRINITY

Scream, Trinity, scream!

But my lungs are frozen with shock. I've never had a gun pointed at me before—not one I was aware of anyway. It's more chilling than I'd ever imagined. So malicious. So…impersonal.

The fact that it's a woman holding it doesn't matter. Her eyes are as cold and heartless as the gun's gleaming exterior.

She's dressed in jeans and a faded suede jacket, boots up to her knees. With her auburn hair pulled into a tight ponytail and a large handbag hanging from her shoulder, she could have been just another person walking past on the street.

Instantly forgettable.

When my lungs thaw enough for me to consider yelling out for the Brotherhood, three men walk into the study.

One has his gun aimed at me. The other two have theirs tucked in their belts.

"Get up," the woman says.

I obey reluctantly, my mind churning with useless options. No way I can run past them. And the study only has one window—and it's closed. Maybe if there'd been a gun in the safe...

"Shoes." The woman holds out her free hand and clicks her fingers.

"You...want my shoes?"

It's like there's a swarm of bees droning in my head. The woman tilts her head, as if daring me to say no, and I quickly slip off my shoes.

"Toss them."

I'm so fucking confused, but I throw them in front of the man wearing a black hoody. The other two are wearing dark sweaters, one with the collar of a polo shirt neatly arranged around the neckline.

Hoody picks up my shoes and tucks them under his arm. The man with the polo shirt sticking out of his sweater walks up to me.

I stiffen, my hands going into fists. But he walks right past, crouches, and picks up everything I've left on the floor—the passport, the money, the bible-safe. Then he goes over to the woman and puts everything inside her handbag while she holds it open, her eyes not leaving mine for a second.

"We're going for a walk. If you make a sound, I guarantee you'll need years of therapy to get over what they'll do to you." She cocks her head to the three men standing behind her. "Got it?"

My skin slowly starts crawling off my body. I nod, swallow hard.

I could still scream, of course. My men would be here in seconds. But they'd be walking into a gunfight with nothing but their fists. There's no way in hell I'm letting any of them take another bullet for me. Not when it was my decision to come in here alone.

And I'd joked the front door was booby trapped? Lord, the irony.

The woman makes a show of sliding her gun inside her handbag, still pointing it at me but circumspect about it now.

Hoody moves behind me and grabs the back of my neck. Pushes me forward.

I don't know what horrifies me more—the fact that his hand is cool and dry, or the considering look in his eyes when he passed me.

This can't be happening.

Who the hell are these people?

They're obviously here on a mission—they didn't act surprised to see me here, or at the stack of money. And judging from their weapons, they came prepared.

Did Gabriel send them to search for the safe? Does that mean he's not actually dead?

The thought sends an internal shiver through me.

I need to find out what's going on.

"Who are—"

Polo Shirt moves so fast, I don't have time to get my hands up to defend myself.

If Hoody hadn't still had a grip on the back of my neck, I'd be sprawled on the floor from the brutal backhand Polo gives me.

My eyes water from the pain, and I lift an icy hand to my cheek, trying to soothe the heat.

The woman is smiling now.

Finally, something I recognize.

It's the same smile Zachary wore the morning he told me to leave Saint Amos. When he had a knife up my skirt ready to slice and stab.

Enjoying my misery.

Just like she is.

32

ZACH

"She's taking too long," I tell Reuben. "She should have been out already."

"I think she's just saying goodbye," Apollo says. He looks like one of those birds who prance around in front of the mirrors their owners hang in their cages. Constantly ducking down and then lifting his head as if he's trying to check out his own reflection.

He's trying to spot movement in one of the windows, just like us. Trying to stare through that dark slit of the front door Trinity left ajar, down into the passage.

We're playing a game: the first one to spot Trinity wins.

"I'm going in." I grab the door handle, but all it takes is a sigh from Rube to stop me.

"We should give her space."

"Last time we did that, she got herself kidnapped," Cass mutters.

"No, last time Zach chased her away with a knife, she went crying to Gabriel, and *then* he kidnapped her," Apollo says. "Get your facts straight."

My eyebrows aren't the only ones to quirk up at that statement. Apollo's usually the last to challenge any of us, but I guess he's just as concerned.

"Time?"

"Five minutes, thirty-nine seconds since she set foot inside," Cass says, twisting in his seat and giving me a long-suffering stare. "Forty…Forty-one…"

I grimace at him, and he straightens with a faint grin on his face, but I see it slide off in the rear-view mirror a second later.

"So…I have to use the bathroom," Apollo announces. "I mean, when nature calls…?"

We're silent for all of a second before we pile out the car like a bunch of clowns exiting a VW bug. Except we're driving an SUV, none of us have a big red nose, and I doubt any clown has ever looked as grim as us.

I'm through the door first, expecting a whole shit show of things…but not the sudden paralysis that hits me.

My body grows heavy. Time slows. I'm filled with the visceral sensation of my heart pounding in my chest.

Rube grabs my elbow, steers me inside with him. But my eyes have already locked onto the stain on the living room carpet.

Blood.

Not something I'm ever affected by, not like Apollo. I'm not squeamish in the slightest. But this is different.

It's *my* blood.

And Christ, there's so much of it. How did I survive? But I almost didn't, and that's what's rooting my feet in place. I'm dimly aware of Cass and Apollo streaming past me, heading down a side passage that leads deeper into the house.

"No. Shit! She's gone!" comes Cass's voice from down the hall. "I fucking knew we shouldn't have let her come in alone."

"Check upstairs," Rube says, his voice tight, too loud.

All while my mind slowly disintegrates into white noise.

Rube shakes me, and then I'm up against the wall. He grabs my shoulders, his thumbs forcing my head up.

"No time for this," he tells me, and for once his words are fast, close together. "Need you to focus. Need you *here*. Not in the past. Got it?"

His voice centers me. Reigns me in. It gathers what's left of my mind and somehow contains it.

I lick my lips. Squeeze closed my eyes. "I'm here," I manage.

The pat he gives my cheek is more like a slap. Then he grabs the front of my shirt and hauls me after him. "We're checking the back!" he yells, aiming his voice up the stairs where I assume Cass and Apollo disappeared to.

Then he drags me after him.

The back door is standing open. We run through it. There's a wooden fence behind Trinity's house, but a section of it is gone. We go through it. We cut across someone's yard, dodging unruly bushes and low hanging tree branches, some of which are still swaying as if disturbed seconds before we arrived.

"There!" I slam a hand against Rube's chest as he turns to run in a different direction. I point.

His eyes go wide when he sees the van. But all he gets is a glimpse.

We run toward it, but we're too late.

The van pulls away with a screech of tires, and by the time we reach the road, it crests a small rise before vanishing behind it.

Unmarked.

No plates.

One in a million.

I already know we'll never find it.

Which means we'll never find Trinity again.

33
TRINITY

I flinch every time I hear a sound. Just for that second, I stop shivering. But then the cold leaks back, and I start trembling again.

Most of the sounds come from above.

Faint voices. Muffled footsteps. The scrape of furniture.

Hoody brought me down here, shoved me to my knees, and then abandoned me. I'm still wearing the gag he pushed between my lips the second the back door of the van closed behind us.

Right before he stroked my hair and told me what a pretty little girl I was.

I couldn't answer him, obviously. But I didn't want to. Because I think the woman left him in the back of the van with me on purpose. To remind me what would happen if I tried anything.

Now that I'm alone, now that my terror is starting to go stale, I can't keep kneeling here indefinitely.

I'm on a mattress placed on the floor. Its fabric is damp, and the air has a clingy chill to it.

There's a smell down here. One I don't like one bit. It's so foul that I start breathing around my gag instead of pulling air through my nose.

The sounds coming from upstairs aren't the only ones I hear. There are things in here with me. Small things. Scurrying things. Rats or mice. Their sharp little claws catch against the concrete floor.

It's hard to tell how long I've been down here. It feels like an hour or more, but I think I would have been a lot colder if that were the case.

Hoody tied my hands behind my back. When I fold down onto my heels, that puts my hands in reach of the knots around my ankles. I've already tried to undo the ropes around my wrists —they're much too tight. But if I got the ropes off my feet, I could at least walk around. Maybe find something sharp for the ropes around my wrists.

It feels like another quarter-hour goes by as I work at the knots. Blind, all I have to go on is a vague idea in my head. Eventually I start tugging as hard as I can on anything that feels like it might give way.

Sometimes I forget to breathe through my mouth, and then I have to fight down nausea when that smell hits my nose.

But finally—*finally*—something gives.

The knot loosens.

With a hard tug, I slip free. The soles of my feet prickle as blood rushes back into them. I have to fight back a sudden influx of thoughts about what would have happened if I'd sat here and waited until my feet turned blue, and then black.

I push up, swaying on the mattress, and then hurriedly step onto the floor. I test the knots around my wrists again, but they're still tight, and my hands are aching from untying my ankles.

I give one last violent tug, growling with frustration behind my gag, and somehow lose my balance.

If it hadn't been for the mattress, I'd have cracked my elbow against the concrete floor. But thankfully I land on something soft instead. I lie there for a second, wondering how the hell I ended up here, and then start to push up to my feet again.

But then I realize my hands are by my hips. Still bound, but...maybe, just maybe...

I roll onto my back, lift my knees to my chest, and loop my bound hands under my butt. It takes time—wriggling and swearing and sweating—but eventually I get my hands out in front of me.

I've chafed my wrists so much I smell blood in the air, but now that my hands are in front of me, I can take off my gag and my blindfold.

Shouldn't have wasted those precious seconds, though. It's so dark in here that it doesn't matter if I have a blindfold on or not. I can't even tell the difference between opening and closing my eyes.

But with the gag out, I have access to my teeth. And they can grip the nylon ropes a hell of a lot better than my fingers.

I'm shaking with cold by the time I get my hands free, but I'm so giddy with relief I barely notice.

I slowly turn around, blinking hard as I take in my surroundings. Maybe it's my imagination, but I think I'm starting to see faint shapes in the dark. Maybe there is a little bit of light down here after all.

I go slow at first as I start to explore. I don't want to bump my bare toes into anything, or knock over something that could make a noise.

But the more I explore, the more frantic my movements become.

Especially once I hit the first wall of the small basement I'm in.

"I need to get gas," Cass says.

I point. "Go down there."

"Oh my God, Rube, seriously. Do *you* want to push this thing? Because I—"

"Go down the fucking road."

An edgy silence fills the SUV's cabin. We're all staring out the windows, trying to spot a white van, a head of dark curls, the slightest thing out of place.

We've been driving around for almost an hour.

I don't want to call it—*refuse* to—but we all know she's gone.

Cass goes down the road I pointed out, but as soon as he reaches the next intersection he doubles back and heads for the gas station we passed about a mile back. He does it without a word, but making sure he doesn't catch my eye in the rear-view mirror either.

Guess I wouldn't be surprised if this got physical.

If the tension eating away at my insides is anything compared with my brothers, then there'll be nothing left of us come dusk.

We have to find her before then.

If the sun goes down before then, she'll be lost forever. That's all I can think. We have to find her before dark. Have to find her before dark.

I should be figuring out how to find her, not what will happen if we don't.

The moment Cass stops the car at a pump, I'm out of the door. I go inside the convenience store, buy a packet of cigarettes, a soda. Zach comes in behind me. He grabs some chips, a six-pack of ginger beer, and another packet of cigarettes. We don't look at each, don't speak. The clerk ringing us up keeps sending us a wary look through her lashes as if she's considering triggering the alarm behind the counter.

Cass is still pumping gas when we get back. Zach tosses his bag into the back seat and climbs up without missing a beat.

I head for a picnic table a few yards away, lighting a cigarette en route.

Grit crunches under shoes behind me, but I don't turn around. "It's Gabriel, isn't it?" Apollo says.

I grunt non-committally, and then turn to face him as I pass him my cigarette.

He shrugs before taking it. "I'm thinking he paid someone to put up that article online. Paid that lawyer chick to handle everything as if he was dead."

"No," I murmur, taking back the smoke. "It doesn't make any sense."

"He wanted her back. Couldn't find her. Knew this would get her attention. Seems pretty straightforward to me."

"Then he'd have taken her somewhere we couldn't find them in the first place."

Back then, when Zach was lying in that hospital bed with tubes sticking out of him, I was sure I'd lose it. So instead of fixating on how likely he was to die, I tried to put together the pieces of this fucked up jigsaw puzzle.

But too much of it didn't make sense.

Gabriel had evaded us for close to a decade. Then all of a sudden he pops up on our radar. All right, not *him*, per se, but a bread crumb. The first of many. An article anyone but us would have missed.

A missing child turned up five years after he'd been kidnapped walking home from school one day. Told reporters he'd been abducted by a priest. Turns out the guy was a bank manager, and little Stuart only thought he was a priest because he wore a crucifix and spoke about God a lot.

The kid's abductor made a run for it, and was never found, but that article sure as hell got our attention.

We visited the abandoned house where the kid had been kept. Then we broke in one night and took a look inside. Tried to figure out where Stuart had been held.

No surprise: it was the basement.

There were too many similarities in how it had been set up for it to have been a coincidence.

Mattresses, covered in dirty sheets, lying on the floor. Hooks dangling from the ceiling. Metal dog bowls for water and food. Metal sheets riveted in place over whatever windows there were.

And then there was the cold.

And the damp.

And rats.

That article, that *house*, eventually led to Father Gabriel. But before we could track him down, *he* came to us.

ORPHANAGE UNDER NEW ADMINISTRATION

A short piece. Barely news-worthy. But it made it into the paper, and it had his name in it, and that's how we located him.

We'd found the Guardian.

A man who moved around the country and set up basements

like the one we were kept in. Like the one little Stuart had been found in.

A man who kept his record clean. A man no one would suspect.

A priest.

And because we knew so many of our Ghosts were men of the cloth, there was no doubt in our minds that we'd found the orchestrator of the biggest child sex-trafficking ring of this century.

But how could a man who was so cunning, so fucking intelligent and well connected, be *so* stupid?

He could have taken Trinity anywhere, and we'd have lost them.

But he brought her here.

To her old house.

A house that was in his name.

That same day, Apollo told us everything Gabriel had said to him in the storm drain. But it had taken weeks of cajoling before Trinity told us her side of the story.

She believed Gabriel was lying. He'd become unstable, not sure if he wanted her as a daughter or a lover or a friend. And she decided she couldn't trust anything that came out of his mouth.

But what if Trinity was right? Maybe Gabriel *had* become unhinged. He'd realized he'd made a mistake taking her home. So he decided to try again. And this time, he would make her vanish without a trace.

"…think? Hey, Rube? Are you listening?"

I come back to the present with a big inhale, and then shake my head. "What?"

Apollo's eyes dim a little. "I said we should find an Internet cafe or something. I can download some of my code off the cloud and do some digging around. I mean, we've got the van."

I take a last pull of the cigarette before crushing it out under my foot. Then I head back to the SUV without answering him.

Cass and Zach are already inside. Zach is in the driver's seat now, and Cass is working his way through a ginger beer after deciding he'd rather sit in my seat than Zach's. I move around to the other side of the car and climb in, kicking shit over to his footwell to make room for my feet.

One of those things catches my eye.

Trinity's purse.

Cass and I both see it at the same time, but he gets to it first. Grabs it. Flicks it open.

His hand is shaking when he takes out the envelope, and I'm about to snatch it from him and tear it open how he's struggling to get the paper.

"It's a letter from Gabriel," he says.

His pupils shift left to right as he scans the page.

"Fuck." He looks up and locks eyes with me. "Guys...*fuck*."

TRINITY

I'm about halfway through my search of the basement when my foot hits something in the dark. With a metallic gong I'm sure could be heard a mile away, a dog bowl flies away with a *clang, clang, clang* before finally coming to rest.

My foot's wet.

I think there was water or something in there.

Now the smell's stronger. I gag and shake my leg, trying to get the water off.

Hell, I *hope* it's water. I'm not so sure anymore.

I hold my breath for a moment, wondering if anyone upstairs heard the ruckus. Then I start moving forward again, trying to remember which direction I was headed.

The smell is so much stronger now.

Stagnant water, is all.

My foot touches another mattress. Unless my imagined dimensions of this place are wrong, I'm close to another wall. I'm guessing this mattress is pushed up against it.

I lean forward, but I don't feel a wall where I should. So step onto the mattress and stretch—

Something bumps my foot.

If I hadn't clapped my hands over my mouth, I would have screamed. In fact, I do still scream, but the sound is muffled.

I jump back, my heart clanging in my chest almost as loud as that dog bowl.

What the hell was that?

I wait for something to happen. A sound that indicates movement, perhaps. More rat claws maybe.

But there's nothing.

So I crouch down and grope in the dark until I touch the edge of the mattress.

My fingers brush the surface as I move them reluctantly forward.

I'm almost sure I can make out the incredibly vague, pale outline of the mattress. But if so, then there must be a big stain in the center, because that area is dark.

God, I wish there was more light down here.

I swipe my fingers left to right over the mattress, with no idea where I'd felt the thing on my foot.

But there's nothing there.

Probably because I chased it away.

And I have no idea if I'm relieved or grossed out by the thought that I touched a live rat with my foot.

I'm just about to stand when my fingers snag something.

I freeze.

It takes me a few seconds to figure out what I'm touching.

Hair.

I leap back.

My scream echoes back to me, but I couldn't give a fuck if everyone above me heard. I scramble away, tripping on the edge of another mattress and falling hard on my ass. Then I'm on hands and knees, crawling. I hit another dog bowl but this one's dry and doesn't splash me.

I'm half-sobbing, half-choking by the time I get close to the other side of the basement—arms outstretched as I search out the wall I know is getting closer.

But instead of hitting the wall, something slams into my stomach. I fold in half, gasping in pain, sobbing with shock, and grab for something to hold onto.

I ran into a bar of steel.

A railing.

Stairs.

I'm up them a second later. Now my sobs are tearing me apart. Bile vaults up my throat, but I choke it down with a ragged gasp.

My hands bang against something.

A door.

I slam my fists onto it.

"Let me out! Please, please!" My throat burns as I shriek out a string of desperate pleas. "Let me out!"

As if someone on the other side of the door hears my prayers, it swings open.

I fall forward, stumble, catch myself, and go hurtling into the light. I can't see a thing—it's just white, and there's shouting and movement.

I run into someone.

They grab me.

Is it Hoody? The man with the polo shirt under his sweater? Or the woman with the gun?

I don't care.

I don't care.

I swipe my hands over my face, push hair out of my eyes.

The man in front of me, the one I ran into, he spreads his arms.

Smiles.

I recognize that smile.

But I don't know how.

Because the man staring at me is a stranger.

36

APOLLO

"Trinity's dad faked his own death?" I murmur.

I'm still staring at the letter Cass passed me. He read it out, but I'm reading it again. I was hoping I could get something—anything—by the font or type of paper he used.

But it's a standard font in Word printed on ordinary, cheap, letter-sized paper.

Even the signature just reads 'Gabriel' with an indecipherable flourish that could be anything.

Cass blows a plume of cigarette smoke out of the car window. "It would appear so."

We moved the car to the far side of the parking lot a few minutes ago. We should have started driving already, but we don't know where to go. Which means we could be heading in the wrong direction, moving further away from Trinity.

"What if he's lying?" Zach asks, twisting in his seat to scan our faces.

"Gabriel? Why would he?" Rube sits forward a little in his seat. "He's dead."

According to Gabriel's letter, Trinity's father—Keith Malone

—is still alive. And although he states it as a fact, he doesn't back it up with evidence.

"Then what about her mom? Is she alive too?"

"It doesn't say," Cass reminds me.

"Yeah…but…"

"Look, this isn't getting us any closer to finding them," Cass says. He flicks the butt of the cigarette out of the window.

"What will?" Rube asks.

Quiet settles down. I've been trying to figure that out the past ten minutes, and I'm sure everyone else has too. But we don't have any leads.

"We're assuming Gabriel took her, but what if it wasn't him?" Zach says quietly. And then puts his hand over Cass's so he'll stop tapping his nail. "He could have had someone else do it."

"But how would he know—" Rube begins, sighing as he speaks.

"The lawyer." Cass snatches his hand out from under Zach's and clicks his fingers. "She obviously called him when Trinity picked up the key."

"So? We weren't followed here," Rube says. "How would he know exactly when—"

Rube stops talking when Zach lifts a hand and points out his window.

We all turn to look.

"What?" I ask, peering at the house. The garden. The roof.

"There," Zach says.

And then I see it.

A For Sale sign.

But I don't get it.

"He's watching the house," Zach says. "Trinity's old babysitter said a young couple moved in across the road. No kids, but the house is big enough for a family of five."

"So they watch the house. Someone lets him know Trinity's

arrived. He comes and snatches her? And then what? Where does he go? And why?" Cass shakes his head. "What does he—"

"We have to go back," I say. "Back to her house."

Zach opens his mouth as if to argue, but then closes it again. Cass and Rube look at him, then at each other. Like there's a telepathic conversation going on.

It's fine, I'll wait them out.

"He's right," Cass murmurs. "Everything leads back to that house."

"But the safe is gone," Rube says. "What else could there be?"

There's a beat of silence. Then Zach says, "It's not much…"

I grin at him. "But it's a start."

37

RUBE

My first and only foster family had a study in their house. One wall was lined with bookshelves and old, musty books.

One day when my sisters were all at cheerleading practice and I'd been left alone for the first time in my new home, I was climbing up the walls from boredom. I tried watching television, but it didn't hold my interest.

So I explored the house, peeking into rooms I'd only caught a glimpse of before.

The study fascinated me. It felt stale and unused—when I opened the door, dust motes shifted through stray beams of light shining in from the window. I felt like I was walking into a crypt.

I went over to the bookshelf and worked my way through the titles. Some of the books stuck together when I tried pulling them out.

Those I left alone, scared I'd damage them and get crapped out.

But some came out a little easier. Titles I'd later learn to recognize, but which were alien to me back then.

Alice in Wonderland.

A Tale of Two Cities.

Casino Royale.

Great Expectations.

I'll never forget the smell of those books. Or how, when I turned the first page of Alice in Wonderland, I wondered why on earth an adult man would own a book like that.

Since then, I've always been drawn to books. My interest moved to bibles when I decided to play the part of a pious kid on his way to becoming a priest as a way to get closer to Father Gabriel without rousing suspicion.

Very little of that interest was feigned.

I found solace in the pages of any bible I read.

Cass is right—there's no safe in this room anymore. But there is a treasure.

Seems Trinity's parents collected bibles. Mostly King James, but there's a Geneva here too. I crack them open, hoping to find a clue, but they're as barren as the big white one Trinity came to Saint Amos with.

It makes sense—you'd destroy the value of the book by marking it—but a cheap mass-produced King James is just as empty.

I guess the church was just a front for Trinity's parents.

We split up to search the house. Apollo found a door we assume leads to the basement, but it has a keypad. That combination should be the same one for the safe we can't find. But Trinity never gave us the code. Apollo's gone to look around the house and see if there's another way inside the basement— maybe through a hurricane door or something. Cass and Zach went upstairs.

I said I'd search the study. But there's nothing in here. I crack open one more bible, but it hits the floor a second later when I hear a *rip* from upstairs.

Apollo must have just come back inside already—he and Cass are in the main bedroom when I arrive.

We watch, silent, as Zach digs his fingers into the edge of the carpet and yanks up another strip, baring the hardwood floor beneath.

"Hey, Zach?" Cass asks quietly. "Whatcha doing over there, buddy?"

Zach spins around in a crouch, staring at us with a lowered head. Eyes bright, wide. "You don't smell that?" he spits out. He waves a hand. "It's all over this fucking place."

I step forward, sweeping out and arm and using it to herd Cass and Apollo behind me, out of the way. "Smell what?" I ask.

Zach rushes to his feet. He charges toward me, and I almost back up when I see the ferocity on his face. But then he goes right past us, shoves a hand into a closet that's standing open, and drags out a sweater.

He brings it to me, shoves it under my nose. "This," he hisses.

I turn my head away, but he follows with the sweater until I take a reluctant sniff at the fabric.

When I snatch it from him and take another whiff, his shoulders sag. "It's him."

Zach's eyes slide past me, fix on Apollo, then Cass. "Our Ghost lives here."

The sound of ripping carpet fills the room. Cass joined Zach on the floor, and they've almost torn up everything. Apollo is by the closet, dragging everything out into a pile on the floor.

Zach has them believing they'll find another safe or something in here.

I'm sure someone with as many secrets as Keith Malone had tons of hidey holes...but even if they do find another secret place, I'm sure it will be empty.

I go through the nightstands. There's nothing of interest in there—bible, tissues, lip balm, lotion. A half-eaten candy bar still in its wrapper on what I assume is Monica's side, judging from the feminine scented lotions and creams, but it's turned white from age.

I almost don't pick up her bible. None of the ones I've found have proved useful yet—why would anything be different up here?

But just like some people can't walk past a rose bush without smelling the blooms...

The instant I lift Monica's bible out of the drawer, I know it's not like the others. For one, it's been read before. There are faint fingerprints on the cover, as if she handled it after putting on lotion or cuticle oil. When I turn the bible so the spine rests in my palm and focus on the gold-trimmed pages, there's a narrow section that's been rubbed off from use.

Behind me, Zach and Cass start discussing which side of the room they'll start tearing up the floorboards on.

I open the front cover. There's a short message in an elegant script.

The light shines in the darkness, and the darkness has not overcome it.

John 1:5

D*ear Monica,*
     Let this book be your light.
Love,

Gabe.

I let the bible fall open in my hands, hoping it will land where the spine was most often opened.

New Testament. The book of Mark.

No notes, no dog ears.

I start paging.

I reach the end of Mark. The faster I thumb through those near-transparent pages, the tighter my chest grows.

Then I skim ahead.

Luke.

The forty-second book of the bible.

I page furiously until I reach chapter eleven.

It starts a quarter of the way down the left page, in the first column.

Our father's prayer.

It's been underlined several times.

The word "forgiveness" was circled so hard it tore through the paper.

I snap the book closed. Turn.

My brothers are facing me. Zach is frowning, and as soon as his eyes dart down to the bible, he walks up to me.

"Luke eleven," I tell him, slamming the book into his chest.

And then I'm bolting out the room, down the stairs, through the passage.

4-2-1-1

The basement door unlocks. I shove it open, take a step.

But then the smell hits me.

I freeze.

I'm still standing there at the threshold, staring into a black void, when the others arrive.

"Fuck," Cass mutters somewhere behind me. "There a light or something?"

"Probably one down there," Apollo says. "But, like, you'd have to find it first."

"Anyone have a flashlight?" Zach's voice is tight.

"Got one on my phone," Cass replies absently.

But none of us move.

We just stand there, staring into the dark.

Which is absurd.

It's just a dark room.

A few stairs.

If Cass gives me his phone, there'll be light. Then I can go down there.

But it doesn't matter what logic my fucking brain throws at me, I override it every time with, "it's a fucking pitch-black basement."

Maybe I wouldn't have had an issue if Zach hadn't told me that this was where our Ghost lived.

Because then it would just have been a normal basement. A cavity at the bottom of a house. Nothing to it.

But it's not.

It's our fucking Ghost's basement, and that changes everything.

Apollo clears his throat. "So...uh...are we going down?"

"Yeah, course," Cass says, but as if he's lost in a dream.

"Why wouldn't we?" The words come out by themselves—I wasn't even aware I was going to speak.

My skin starts crawling. I take a step back. And as if that breaks the spell, Cass and Zach and Apollo all move back with me.

We press up against the wall, staring at the rectangle of night in front of us.

Cass fidgets in his pocket. Pulls out his phone. He turns on the light and shines it at the hole.

It's like it hits an invisible door someone painted black.

Fuck.

"Okay," Apollo whispers. "Look, it's just a room, right?"

He takes a step forward. Then another. I stare at him, taking in his long blond hair, his lean frame. He puts his arm out behind him. "Phone."

In that moment, I've never had greater respect for him.

And he doesn't even look back. Doesn't take even a second to see what we think. He just grabs the phone as soon as Cass puts it his palm, pushes back his shoulders, and heads for the darkness.

The second it swallows him, the three of us surge forward and cluster around the dark doorway.

"Apollo!" Cass calls out, like he's convinced Apollo's already been murdered.

"Yeah?" With the phone shining ahead, he's a starkly contrasted silhouette. The beam of light from the cell isn't as powerful as a flashlight, but it chases away the shadows long enough for Apollo to pick out a few shapes in the darkness.

Stairs.

Plastic flooring.

As soon as he reaches the ground, he points the light across the room.

"Mother of God," Zach murmurs.

"Nope," Cass says, sounding like he's about to get sick. "Try, Father of Hell."

APOLLO

I wonder if they can see how much I'm shaking? I'm holding Cass's phone as tight as I can, but there's nothing I can do about the way the light shimmies and shakes all over the place.

If my brothers weren't all standing there at the top of the stairs, I wouldn't even have thought about setting foot down here.

Yeah, it's just a basement, but come *on*.

It's as much a basement as we're a bunch of friends.

Every inch of this place is dripping sinister and oozing malevolence. I suddenly wish I had some kind of biblical training so I could exorcise this place and be done.

But instead I have to creep around and look for a damn light.

I find it, eventually. It takes me a lot longer than it should have, but that's because I can't stop looking at everything else in here.

The bed.

The teeny tiny little toilet.

The camera on its stand.

Especially the camera.

But I can't think electronics right now. This isn't the time to veer off on a tangent.

As soon as I spot the string for the light, I tug it.

Light blooms, but the way that swinging lightbulb makes the shadows dance and weave is giving me the heebie-jeebies.

"Okay, guys, it's safe!" I call up.

I don't dare turn my back, because I know how that ends. So I just back up a little as I wait for them to join me.

But they don't.

And when I finally have enough courage to look behind me, I see the terror on each of those three faces.

Crap.

Why the hell did I have to choose this moment to be so damn stupid?

"Really?" I purse my lips. "Just me then?"

"You're doing so well, buddy!" Cass calls out. "Just keep going."

I shake my head, throw them the finger, and go back to staring at the room. "What am I looking for?"

They don't answer, because I guess it's obvious.

A fucking clue, idiot.

But like…what?

Hair? DNA? Fingerprints?

Or stuff like whether the bed was chosen at random or for specific child molestation purposes?

The camera catches my eye again, and I realize why.

I know there won't be a tape or anything inside. I mean…*duh*.

But as soon as I make a beeline for it, Zach calls out, "Leave it alone, Apollo, the rest of the room is more—"

I throw him another zap. "You wanna micromanage me, then come down here and do it yourself," I yell up.

"There won't be a tape in there," Rube says.

"I know," I say, drawing out the last word. "But this is…"

I trail off, rolling my eyes. Every time I talk tech, my brothers' eyes start glazing over. Only Cass humors me every now and then, but I doubt even he would understand.

This camera is old. Like the eighties old. But it's in amazing condition, especially considering the fact that it's been in this damp basement for God knows how long.

I want to take it off its stand, but I'm sure there are all sorts of fingerprints on it. Luckily I'm wearing long sleeves today—I pull them over my hands and use them to pop open the cassette compartment.

"It's empty," I call out.

"Told you," Cass says.

But then I turn the camcorder around, and frown. Under the fat sans-serif type of the brand name, there's a slanted word in script. It has the eighties jagged feel to it, like ACDC's logo.

LIMITED EDITION

Right. Got it.

My brothers step aside so I can come out of the basement. Cass puts out a hand to stop me. "Where you off to in such a hurry?"

"Library. Or internet cafe, whichever comes first," I tell him. Then I hold up the camera for them to see. "Unlike the van, this thing is one in a million."

"How's that going to help us?" Rube asks as I start walking away.

"Don't know yet," I call back. "But I'll let you know soon as I figure it out."

Cass drives me to the local library while Rube and Zach stay behind in Trinity's old house. I'm not sure that's the best idea, seeing as how Zach flipped out earlier, but I guess if they do rip the whole place apart it might end up being all cathartic and shit.

I don't really care.

I'm too focused on how this camera is going to help us find Trinity.

It doesn't look like the kind of tech that's been in use since the eighties. It looks like a camera you buy on eBay at a ridiculous price because it's vintage, barely ever been used, and has some of its original packaging.

I'm hoping it's unique enough to have left a trace I can find quickly and easily.

And if it's not? Well at least I'm keeping myself sane and not constantly adding to my rather inventive list of things someone evil could be doing to a pretty girl like Trinity.

Cass watches me over my shoulder, but unlike Rube or Zach, he doesn't ask me what I'm doing every two seconds.

I'm grateful for that. I never mind explaining shit, but right now it would just slow me down.

Instead, he lets me get into the zone, and once I'm in…

"You should blink," comes his voice.

I sit back, shake my head, focus on him.

"What?"

He points at his eyes. "You have to blink every now and then. Keeps them moist." He stretches out his arms, jaw cracking with a yawn. "Let's get a coffee and a smoke."

"Dude, I was right…" I shove my palms over my eyes and massage my eyelids. "I was in the fucking zone."

"Yeah, well, you're going to develop a hunch if you keep

sitting like that. And I can't be seen hanging around with hunchbacks." He slaps my thigh. "Come on. Up and at 'em."

God.

I look back at the computer. I can't even remember what thread of a thought I was following before he so rudely interrupted me.

We've been here twenty minutes, and the only thing I've discovered so far is that this camcorder isn't as unique as I thought it was. They're all over eBay.

I follow Cass to a food truck, but I wave away his offer of a burrito with my coffee.

I need blood in my brain, not my stomach.

Cass is halfway done with his burrito and I'm halfway done with my cigarette when a cloud passes over the sun. I squint up, staring at the gray-tinged cloud and its now radiant halo of golden light.

"How did Rube figure out the code for the basement?" I ask Cass.

He shrugs. "Don't know. Said something about a bible verse."

"I know, I was there." I roll my eyes. "What does it say?"

"Fuck knows."

I pull out my phone. "Do you remember what it was?"

Cass stares into the distance, chewing ponderously. "Luke...something."

I give him a deadpan stare. "Really? Could you try harder?"

"Why?" Cass crumples up the burrito's packaging and overarm tosses it into a nearby trash can. "It worked."

"It's significant."

"Everything in that book's significant to bible belters," Cass says. "Literal needle in a haystack."

"That's not—" I cut off with a sigh. "Screw it."

I start searching.

inspiring bible verse luke...

Google autocompletes on that, so I give the first search term a try.

I tap on the first result, and it takes me to a bible website. I read the first verse of Luke chapter eleven.

It's a prayer. A common one because even I've heard it before.

I guess Luke's the forty-second book in the bible. Forty-two-eleven.

It was the combination to the safe, which is now missing, and the basement. What's the chance it's also the password used to encrypt the file on Gabriel's computer?

But it's not a pin number like the basement door...

"Library. Now." I call over my shoulder, already headed in that direction.

"I haven't had a smoke yet!"

"Save it!"

I have a feeling he's going to need one when we're done, anyway.

We race back to the library. I remote access my PC back in California and quickly add the entire prayer to my cracking program.

It takes milliseconds to parse.

The file pops open on the library's computer.

I'm wrong, though.

Cass won't need a smoke.

Neither of us will.

We need someone with a stronger stomach.

"You ever wish you could wipe out your memories?" Rube asks.

We're in our Ghost's bedroom. Neither of us would even consider sitting on the mattress, so we're squeezed in beside each other on the blanket box at the foot of the bed.

I don't even have to think about it. "No."

"Not at all?"

We're smoking a cigarette. It's our third in a row—we've been putting them out on the carpet in a blatant show of disrespect.

It should feel petty, but instead it feels amazing. Like we're extinguishing each and every one on the Ghost's bare skin.

"No, because then they'd get away with it. All of them."

"So revenge is better than forgiveness?"

I turn to him, narrowing my eyes. "I'm sorry, did I miss something? The last time I checked you were going to gouge out his eyeballs with your thumbs and then piss in the sockets."

He looks away. "If we hadn't come back here…"

I inhale deep.

Oh.

That's what this is about.

"Rube, it's not our fault. It's not *her* fault. It's theirs. Whoever took her. They initiated it, not us."

"Would have had a hard time initiating anything if—"

I bang my fist on his thigh. "We're going to find her. And we're going to kill whoever took her, like we should have Gabriel."

Rube is silent for more than a beat, so I look up at him. He's frowning. "You don't think it was Gabriel?"

I spread my hands like a prophet. "You really think it was?"

"Everything points to—"

"Exactly. Everything *always* points to him."

Rube's frown grows deeper. When he speaks, it's slowly and carefully. "Yes, because he was the Guardian, and—"

He cuts off when I shake my head. "You know what. You're right. Maybe it would be better if our memories were erased because we always storm in without thinking things through. We're so consumed with rage, and hate, and revenge, we don't ever stop to just…*think.*"

"You believe Gabriel was set up?"

I lay my hands in my lap, palms up, one on top of the other. I've been trying to meditate and shit—my therapist recommended it—but the only thing that happens when I close my eyes is that I'm immediately transported back to the basement.

It's always been the case.

Which is why I get so little sleep. It takes a lot of effort to convince myself that I won't wake up with some guy's hand down my fucking pants.

"I don't know what to believe anymore," I tell him. "And I don't know where Trinity is. And I don't know if we'll ever find her."

I see Rube's shoulders sag in my peripheral view.

"Maybe they'll find something," Rube says. "Apollo's good with that shit."

"It'll have to be a fucking miracle they find." I shake my head again. "I don't think anything less is going to cut it. Not this—"

There's a shriek of tires outside.

We're up in an instant, storming to the bedroom window. It looks out on the street, to our SUV that's just pulled up into the driveway.

Guess there's no reason to be circumspect anymore. If anything, I *hope* we draw someone's attention. If they come for us, at least then we'll know who took Trinity.

Apollo jumps out of the passenger door, Cass a beat behind him. They race up to the front door.

Rube and I meet them halfway down the stairs. It's crowded with the four of us, but that doesn't matter.

Apollo's holding out his phone. "Watch it," he wheezes. "One of you—"

Cass snatches it. "Christ, Apollo, get some fucking exercise." Then he looks at me, at Rube. "He figured out the password. He opened the file."

"The one from Gabriel?" Rube asks, reaching for the phone.

Cass pulls it out of reach.

For a second, just one *weird* fucking second, I think he's screwing around with Rube. That if he tried to go for it, Cass would pull it away again. Like driving away from someone before they can get in the car. But just a few feet. And then you apologize. And then do it again.

"Rube, my man," Cass says quietly. Then he shakes his head. Looks at me. "I...don't even know if we can."

"Can what?" Rube growls, going for the phone again. This time Cass lets him take it.

"Watch it," he says. Crosses his arms. He and Apollo share a look, and then drop their gazes. "We couldn't."

"It's a video?"

They nod, still looking down.

Christ.

There's a mess of noise from the phone. Rube turns it on its side, lifts his chin a little. But he's holding it. He's watching it.

I shift a little, peering over his arm at the screen.

Darkness. Then a flash of light. Pale blue carpet. Neat, clean. Suggestion of furniture which quickly resolves into a dark blue chest of drawers painted with big yellow stars. There's a red toy robot on top, and a random assortment of He-Man action figures.

Jesus Christ.

But Rube says nothing.

And we keep watching.

The view pans to a bed. There's a little boy sitting on the side. He has tear tracks down his face and his red Spiderman T-shirt is damp with spilled tears. He's still hiccupping, and as the person holding the camera phone goes closer, he lifts a little fist and wipes it over his eyes.

"Hey, Justin," someone croons softly. "Don't cry."

The boy frowns hard at the person holding the camera. "I wuh-want my muh-m-mommy."

"Oh, I know. I know. She said she'll be here any minute now."

I glance up at Cass and Apollo. They're staring at us now, both wide-eyed, like they're waiting for us to shout Uncle.

The kid's not even in a basement. Yeah, I couldn't go down into the dark earlier, but he's in a bright and sunny room.

Pussies.

But then I hear Rube swallowing. I look back at the screen.

It's gone black.

My stomach clenches.

Light returns. It shows a slim figure walking away from the

camera that resolves into a young, pretty woman.

Late twenties.

Dark, curly hair.

Bright blue eyes.

Freckles.

She goes to sit beside the little boy, and puts an arm around his shoulder. He cringes away, but she just ducks her head a little closer.

"Would you like some cookies and milk while you wait for Mommy?" she asks.

The little boy looks up at her, wary, and shakes his head.

"Are you sure?"

He drops his head a little. Sniffs.

She scoots closer. "I tell you what, Justin. Let's have a nap, me and you. And when we wake up, your mommy will be here."

Justin shakes his head. "I'm not tired."

"I know." She moves a lock of hair off his forehead, and looks straight at the camera. "But it will make the time go by so fast."

Rube clears his throat. "Is that Monica?" he asks, looking up at Apollo and Cass.

"Who else?" Cass says. Apollo nods.

Rube doesn't look at the camera again. "How does this help?"

Cass frowns. "Gabriel said Apollo should show this to Trinity. I'm guessing he told her Monica was involved, and she wouldn't believe him."

"Yeah, she didn't mention any of that to us," Apollo adds.

I'm looking at them too, but I can still hear what's going on. The rustle of fabric. The cooing sounds Monica makes.

Rube goes to turn off the cell phone, but I stop him. His head whips to look at me. "Really?" he murmurs. "You really want to watch?"

"It's not in a basement," I tell him.

"Does it matter?" His voice drops low and deep. "You know

what's going to happen. Why the fuck do you have to watch it?"

"Because it's not in a basement!"

Apollo leans back from my yell. I rake my fingers through my hair and snatch the phone from Rube's hand. I move my finger over the time bar.

There's a brief snatch of Monica's voice.

...show my husband what a handsome boy you are, Justin... doesn't that feel nice...don't cry now...

"This didn't happen in a basement. This boy isn't one of us."

"And that makes it okay?" Cass begins, indignation rife on his voice.

"Just fucking listen to me!" I pause the video, hesitate as I check the screen, then hold it up Cass. "There. See?"

Cass glances at it, and then immediately looks away. "Jesus Christ, you're a sick fuck," he mutters, and his face goes a shade whiter.

"Not...fuck..." I grit my teeth. "Look past the fucking bed. Behind it. There's a window. See? The curtains are open."

"Yeah, sure, I believe you," Cass says, but only looking at me out of the corner of his eye, not at the screen. "First prize, Zach."

"Wait...are you saying..." Apollo reaches for the phone, but then plucks his hand away. "Is there like a landmark or something?" he glances at Cass, bumps him with an elbow. "We could use it to triangulate the location of the house." And then his face falls. "But this must have been taken years ago. What's the point?"

"The point is, she didn't bother trying to hide anything. She didn't pull the curtains. She used the boy's real name." I tap my fingernail on the screen, but then hurriedly lock the phone when the video starts playing again.

Everyone goes rigid, jaws clenching, glaring at me.

"Sorry," I murmur.

They don't need to hear that.

Fuck, *I* didn't need to hear that.

"She felt comfortable enough to shoot a video on her phone and not worry about someone finding it."

"It was password protected," Rube says.

"Yeah." Apollo might have been trying to sound cheery, but his words just come out all wobbly. "Want to know what it was?"

Rube and I look at him. He drops his eyes. "Forgive us our sins," he says, sounding much less happy than before.

I push past them, unlocking the phone again. I turn down the volume and head into the living room, then hurriedly detour and go into the kitchen instead.

I don't need to be sitting next to a pool of my own blood trying to work this shit out, that's for sure.

Cass follows. He makes me a cup of black coffee and sits opposite me as I watch the whole video.

It makes me sick to my stomach to the point where I want to go puke up everything I ever ate…but near the end, Monica picks up the phone again and takes it over to the bed. As she's arranging it on the nightstand—bright blue like the dresser, with a night light shaped like Mickey Mouse—there's a clear shot of the window.

So clear, you can make out the horizon.

I freeze that frame, take a screenshot. It's got Monica's left eye in it, near the bottom. Her face is tilted down, but she's looking at the phone.

Probably imagining her husband's delight when she shows him the clip.

That eye sure is beautiful.

If you don't look too hard.

Because if you do, then you can see pure evil coiling in the darkness of her pupil.

Forgive us our sins?

Bitch, not now…not fucking *ever*.

40
TRINITY

Exodus, Matthew, and Ephesians say you must honor your father and your mother. They don't mention whether that still applies if your parents sold their souls to the devil.

"Who were they? Those boys you were with?" my father asks.

I guess I don't have to call him that anymore. I'm not his daughter. I should feel relieved, but instead I feel violated.

It wasn't my father who lived upstairs in that house with me and my mother.

It was an impostor.

A stranger.

But they made me call him Dad. And they made me obey him.

The impostor walks closer. Calm, collected.

My head snaps to the side when he backhands me. Pain blossoms on my cheek, and I see stars when my eyes squeeze shut involuntarily.

"Who were they?" he asks again, so quiet I can barely make out the words over the sound of blood roaring in my ears.

"No one," I manage, blinking back tears of pain and terror.

They tied me to a chair, Hoody and Polo, while the impostor and the woman watched. I'm in a den or a study. Plushly carpeted, thick drapes—drawn. It was gloomy inside until Hoody turned on a desk lamp.

There are lots of books on the wall here. A big desk. It looks a lot like the study Dad had at home.

No, not Dad.

The impostor.

He's standing in front of me, legs hip-distance apart. Casual, but ready.

For what? Does he expect me to be overcome by some feat of superhuman strength, shred these ropes, and make a go at him? I don't believe in miracles.

I thought I didn't believe in God either, but on some level I must have faith. Because I know the Devil's standing in front of me, and if there's a Devil, there must be a God.

"Trinity, child…" The impostor crouches in front of me. "There will only be more pain if you insist on being uncooperative. Do you understand?"

"They're just a bunch of boys," I tell him.

"What were you doing with them?"

"What does it matter?" I yell.

I glare up at him, but the second our eyes meet, I drop my head.

I'm not brave enough to stare Satan right in the eyes. Especially when those eyes belong to the man I thought of as my father for close to two decades.

The impostor sighs as he stands. He turns to Hoody, and they walk to the study door. Even though their voices are low, I can hear what they're saying.

"You got their plates?" Keith asks.

"Zachary Price. Dana Point, California."

My heart starts pounding.

Shit.

I guess it doesn't matter what I say, the impostor knows they're not just some random guys.

"Find them. Kill them." Keith looks at me over his shoulder. I wasn't expecting a look of fatherly adoration or anything—he's never looked at me like that.

My entire life, I don't think I ever did anything that made him proud, or gave him a reason to smile. I just always thought that was the kind of man he was—severe, chaste, Old Testament.

But now it's all starting to click into place.

It wasn't that he didn't love me.

He didn't have to, because I wasn't his. But I'm sure even the parents of adopted kids feel more for their children than he ever did—ever could have—for me.

Because there's not a trace of emotion in his voice when he says, "Kill her too."

And then he turns and leaves, not even bothering to look back.

My mouth falls open. The woman who brought me here comes in front of me and holds out her gun. But it doesn't have the same menacing effect as before.

Keith Malone just shredded my life to pieces.

And now I'm going to die.

Finally, the fear comes back. It shoots through me like needles of cold steel. My stomach twists, and I start dry swallowing like there's something stuck in my throat.

This can't be happening.

This can't fucking be happening.

I struggle, but the ropes are tight. I scream, but that just makes the woman frown.

She curls her finger around the trigger. I close my eyes, holding my breath as I wait for the inevitable.

"Jess, wait."

A hand lands on the woman's shoulder. She looks at it, glances behind her. "What?"

"I'll do it," Hoody says.

"Christ, Nick, there's no time for that shit." She shakes him off, points the gun.

"You go on ahead. I'll catch up." Nick wraps his fingers around the hand holding the gun. She twists it, snarling at him with irritation, and it goes off.

I scream.

My body's stiff as I wait for death or pain...but there's nothing. Just my pounding heart and the ice-cold flash of adrenaline pouring through my body.

"Fucking retard," Jess mutters, but her voice is moving away. "I'm leaving in ten, with or without you."

My eyes fly open. There's a hole about an inch away from my left foot. I manage a choking breath, and then there's a hand around the front of my throat.

Nick uses his thumb to prop my chin up, forcing my eyes to his. "How many times do you think I can come in ten minutes, Missy?"

I cringe when he licks his lips.

"Let's go find out."

I fall to my knees, but I'm up a second later, scrambling to get away. Behind me, Nick barks out a laugh and then shuts the door.

Locks it.

Pockets the key.

But I'm already on the other side of the room, grabbing the window sash and hauling it up.

The curtain wraps around my arm. I swat it away and lean out, lifting my leg—

The ground sways toward me.

But from a distance.

I hadn't realized it, but I'm on the third floor. And below me? A gravel path hugging the side of the house.

Oh Lord, I'll never survive that.

I spin around. Nick veers around the bed I clambered over, a filthy smile on his mouth. I look back at the drop. Swing my leg over the window ledge.

It'll hurt, but hopefully only a little. Then I'll be dead, right? No need for them to go after my men.

Except…I don't know if that's what will happen. Nick and Jess were given orders. Who am I to say they won't follow them to the letter?

Death by gravel is the coward's way out. And I'll be leaving my men clueless. For all I know, they'll walk into our house in Dana Point and Jess and her crew will already be waiting for them.

Bang.

Bang.

Bang.

Bang.

I can hear every future gunshot slamming home into one of my men's chests.

Just as Nick gets in arm's reach, I dodge to the side.

We're in a child's room, a boy judging from all the action figures and faded blue paint. Where is he now, the boy that used to live here?

I slam into the door, pluck at the handle. Yes, even though it's locked, because all I can hope for right now is a fucking miracle.

Locked.

Nick laughs again. I spin around, flattening myself against the wood. He's only got ten minutes with me. And I'm determined to keep playing this game as long as—

Nick lifts Jess's gun. Or maybe it's his own, who the fuck knows?

And then he shoots me.

41

RUBE

"Is this seriously the fastest you can go?" Apollo yells as he thumps the back of Cass's headrest. "I thought you said this was a muscle car?"

"Do you even have a dick?" Cass yells back. "This is a fucking SUV. The muscle car is that yellow Mustang we left back in California, you idiotic, dickless—" he cuts off with a growl that comes close to competing with the SUV's engine.

We're headed south down the highway at a ridiculous speed.

I've never been an adrenaline junkie. Going this fast makes me feel sick, not excited. But I grit my teeth and I bear it, because the faster Cass goes, the faster we get to Trinity.

She has to be there.

It's our only hope.

I mentally urge Cass to push the SUV as hard as he can without blowing the engine, and I hold onto the seat with claws for hands, and I will the contents of my stomach to remain where they are.

"How far, Apollo?" Zach asks.

Apollo briefly relents giving Cass shit, and checks his phone. "Another ten miles."

"Go faster," Zach says.

"Jesus fucking Christ," Cass mutters. "Do any of you even know what a speed limiter is? And that this car has one? And that, even if I *wanted*—"

"Shut up and drive," I bark.

Then there's silence.

And fuck, it comes just in time. Else I'd have told them to find me something to puke into.

"This is our turn off," Cass says just as we pass a sign for a shooting range a few miles up ahead. He slows the SUV and puts on the indicator. "Christ, they weren't fucking around when they decided to go remote, were they?" he mutters.

There isn't much to see—just another long road.

"We still don't know which house it is." Apollo holds up the printout from the Redford library and starts looking through the windows. "But it's got to be at least two or three stories."

"Sounds like we're looking for a mansion," Cass says dryly. He catches Zach's eye in the rearview mirror. "Sound familiar, Mason?"

Zachary narrows his eyes, but then his face relaxes again. He nods reluctantly. "Long drive, so the main house is far from the road. Lots of tree cover."

He's describing the house we were kept captive in. A place that used to be his home.

That silence comes again, but Cass breaks it this time after looking first at Zach, then at me.

"How about you burn this one down too when we're done?"

Just after the turnoff heading for the shooting range, signs start popping up for ranches and plots. We drive until we find the first house that fits our description, but since there are two kids playing in the front yard, we drive past.

A few minutes later, something more fitting comes into view. We park behind a small copse of pine trees—just far enough to keep in sight without being spotted.

It's a three-story house.

It's remote as fuck.

If there'd been more than one of its type in this area, we'd have to have searched them all...but there isn't. The only other houses are a few one-level ranch-style lots, most of them closer to the road.

Despite what Cass demanded, we didn't come with an arsenal. We all have Kevlar vests on under our shirts, but only Zach and Cass are carrying.

I never handle guns, and this is no exception.

Apollo also declined. I have a hunting knife on me, Apollo a switchblade. But we're only supposed to be backup for Cass and Zach, and we're merely going in to scope the place and see if this is where Trinity is being held.

"You sure you want to go in there unarmed?" Cass asks, twisting in his seat and grabbing the headrest. "I mean, you could just wave it around. It doesn't even have to be loaded."

I shake my head.

The last time I touched a gun, I almost killed two innocent girls, and traumatized an entire family.

If I'd had a sliver of doubt left that I wasn't a normal kid, that day changed everything.

It was a Saturday. Pissing with rain. My foster parents had a lunch date with friends, and their four daughters had decided to stay at home and watch sitcom reruns instead of going with.

I don't know who bought the bottle of booze, but it was almost empty by the time I walked past and saw them passing it around. I wasn't going to rat them out—I was just going to take it away. Our parents had made it pretty fucking clear how they felt about underage drinking. I mean, the youngest was thirteen. No one that young should be drinking anyway.

But when I tried to take it away, they ganged up on me. Thought it was a game. They were drunk, and I guess they'd been eyeing me for the past few weeks, because they tried to get me to kiss them.

They even started taking their shirts off.

A normal kid my age would have gone with it. But they were my sisters, and it was wrong, and the harder I resisted, the more intent they became.

My brothers think I'm a pussy because I never hit on any of them. I can't even imagine what they'd say if I told them the truth about what happened that day.

Because it wasn't just kissing.

They tried to get my pants off. And that shit triggered me worse than anything I'd experienced since we'd escaped the basement.

I snapped.

Lisa was the youngest.

She was so beautiful. Long blond hair, bright blue eyes.

I was just trying to keep her back, all of them. I shoved her too hard, and she took a tumble.

Ha. *Took a tumble.*

She slammed into a glass coffee table, face first. She almost lost an eye. I didn't see her again after that, but I have no doubt the accident disfigured her.

So much blood.

And then the screaming began.

I had to keep them quiet.

I know what happens when kids scream. Adults don't like it. Kids are meant to be seen, not heard.

I grabbed two of them, put my hands over their mouths. The third was unconscious on the floor. I don't even know how that had happened. If I'd done something.

Still don't.

And that's how they found us. My foster parents.

Me with an undone fly, their daughters half-unclothed, and I'm holding two of them tight so they can't scream anymore.

Blood.

Limp bodies.

The mother passed out.

Henry—my foster dad—was holding a gun. At first, I thought they'd just arrived. I couldn't understand why he'd carry a gun around with him.

But later, when the red haze receded and memories came flooding back, I realized they'd been there long enough to see what was happening and then Henry went to get his gun.

Because I was lost.

Out of my own body.

I didn't hear them begging with me to let their daughters go.

I just saw the gun. And then I tackled Henry to the ground. I pressed the gun to his head and pulled the trigger, but thank fuck the safety was on so nothing happened.

And I kept pulling that trigger until the police came and arrested me.

Zachary got everything sorted out, of course. Since no one actually died, and he'd offered to pay for Lisa's plastic surgery—and then some—the charges were eventually dropped.

"I'm sure," I tell Cass.

"Looks empty anyway," Apollo says. "Maybe we're too late."

We sit in silence for a moment, and then all flinch at the faint *pop* of gunfire.

"Shooting range," Zach says.

Me, Cass, and Apollo nod.

And as if that's the signal, we file out of the car and head for the house.

"Is that..." Cass points.

I nod my head. "A grave."

"Is there a..."

"We'll have to check later," I tell him. "Keep moving."

We're at the back of the property, headed for the patio doors. It's the first set of doors we found, and one of the sliding glass panels is standing open.

It's too quiet.

Surely there would be something. Voices, a radio playing, a television set. Unless, like Apollo said, we're too late.

Or this is a dead end.

Who's to say they even own this property anymore?

But the neatly dug grave out back gives me a shred of hope. We're too far away to see if it's empty or not, but there'll be plenty of time for that once we've gone through the house.

I hear a faint noise. Cass holds up a hand. We stop to listen, but hear nothing.

Could have been Zach and Apollo, going through the front.

But then I hear it again.

It's faint, but it's undeniably a gunshot. Me and Cass frown at each other, but we don't dare say anything.

"Shooting range," Cass murmurs.

I nod.

We keep moving.

Through an entertainment area. Down a hall. I see a shape, and tap Cass on the shoulder, pointing.

It resolves into Zachary, stalking down the other side of the passage like a cop in an action movie. We glance at each other, and then he nods and looks up.

Downstairs cleared.

Cass and I are closest, so we go up the stairs first. As soon as we turn to head down the hall, I hear a sound again.

A panicked sob. A choked breath. Fabric and clothes rustling urgently.

My heart's in my fucking throat, but Cass puts up his hand like he knows all I want to do is bolt forward.

I guess he also recognized the voice making those sounds.

Trinity.

42

TRINITY

The pain is so intense, I can't even scream. It's as if the bullet knocked every atom of air from my lungs. I drag in a horrible groaning gasp and slide to the floor.

I reach up, but I can't bear to touch the hole in my chest. Instead, my fingers shake in the air a few inches away.

Somehow, through the violent buzzing in my ears, I hear Nick chuckle.

Then I'm flying up, the pain intensifying as Nick twists the grip he has on the front of my blood-stained dress. "Hurts, don't it?" he says. "Should be thanking me on your hands and fucking knees, Missy, 'cos now you won't feel anything else."

He drags me to the bed. Tosses me on the mattress. I let out a low wail as I hit the firm surface, as that jolt sends a stabbing agony through me.

Liar.

The bullet hit me just below my right shoulder, but my entire torso feels like it's on fire. I can't move that arm, and my body is as limp as a rag doll.

Nick climbs onto me, pushes the muzzle of the gun so hard into my temple that I'm facing away from him, to a window.

The muzzle bites into my flesh, the cold metal spreading through me. Then he rips my dress up to my hips allowing the brisk air to caress my bare skin.

A wave of dizziness hits me. It feels like I'm on a boat, and the waves are tossing me around. Then like I'm drowning. Except I think I am, because when I try to breathe, there's shit in the way.

I cough. Retch.

Thick, warm liquid spills from my mouth.

The air smells like copper.

Am I dying? The pain is so immense, it's impossible to comprehend. I'm aware that I'm writhing with it, that he's fighting my limbs so he can wrench open my legs, but that's all distant and possibly happening to someone else now.

Or to my dying body.

Which is fine, because I'm not really there anymore.

I'm floating to the window. Heading for the bright afternoon sun beckoning me through the glass.

Not scared of falling anymore.

Because I'm weightless now.

I can just float away.

Up into the clouds.

And then the pain is back, a spear through my chest. I suck in a ragged breath, and turn my head.

Nick has his hand on my chest. He's leaning his weight on the bullet wound, grinning at me.

I reach up, numb fingers trying to pry his hand off my chest.

But then his body is between my legs, holding them open. And he's looking down.

There's still something cold touching my face, but it's

different now. I use my good hand, my left hand, to feel alongside my head.

It touches cool metal.

The gun.

Pain, but not in my chest anymore. Down there. Down where he's looking.

Let him look at my cunt, I don't care.

Because then he's not looking up. He's not seeing me fumble with the gun. Trying to pick it up.

He shifts, his hand digging harder into my torn flesh. I cry out, and he groans as if the sound gets him hard.

But I don't care, because now I'm holding the gun.

Pointing it.

It shakes.

Oh God, how it shakes.

It weighs thirty million tons.

I pull the trigger.

Where I expect him to go flying backward, he instead collapses on top of me. I cry out at the agony when his head slams into my chest. I try and push him off me, but I've only got one working arm and he's still wedged between my legs.

I let out a wail of frustrated agony, but thank God I'm taking a breath when I hear footsteps coming up the stairs.

It takes everything I have to lift the gun again. I sling my arm over Nick's back, gritting my teeth through the pain as I try and aim it at the door.

It's too quiet out there.

Is it Jess? She said she'd leave—how long was Nick busy with me for? And if she's gone, then who's coming up the stairs?

The impostor.

He's back.

I curl my finger around the trigger and blink sweat and blood out of my eyes.

The gun steadies.

Someone yanks at the handle. They rattle the door. Then a shot goes off.

Pop!

There's a thump, and the door gives in, handle distorted by the bullet.

A silhouette darkens the doorway.

I squeeze the trigger.

The clap of the gun is deafening. It falls from my hand onto the floor. The figure in the doorway leans to the side, and then slowly topples to the ground.

I killed him.

I killed my father!

Tears spring into my eyes, blurring my vision. I let out a choking sob and try to shift Nick off me. He won't budge, but then the bundle by the door starts moving.

A hand appears on the carpet. Thin. Delicate. Speckled with blood.

Jess.

I shot her.

But I didn't kill her.

"No, fuck," I whisper. My movements become urgent, but I still can't shift the fucking dead body off me.

A second hand joins the first. Jess drags the top half of her body into the room. She looks dazed—eyes wide and unfocused, lips slack—but as soon as she spots me on the bed, her eyes narrow.

Other than her hands, I can't see any more blood. But it's as if the bottom half of her body doesn't work anymore, because she doesn't stand, or crawl...she just keeps dragging herself over the floor.

I stick my hand in Nick's hoody pouch. Cigarettes, gum, a wallet. Useless shit.

I swallow hard, steel myself, and reach down.

My hand brushes smooth skin.

Lower.

I recoil when I touch his ass. If I could lift my head, I'd be able to see better, but there's a terrible lameness spreading through me.

The dizziness is back. It comes in waves, each higher than the last.

It would be so easy just to let one of those waves take me away. To let it consume me.

Because it promises no more pain. No more leaden terror.

Jess grabs onto the side of the bed. How did she get here so quickly? Or did I actually pass out for a second?

I reach down again, pushing away my disgust and horror at touching Nick's dead skin.

He must have pushed his pants down to his fucking knees, because I can't feel them. Even if he had anything useful in them, they're too far out of reach.

Jess grabs my right hand, tugs. Despite the dead body lying on top of me, she still shifts my arm enough to send a spike of pain through me. I sob, my breath catching. I wriggle furiously, even hoping that her grip might pull me out from under Nick.

She's grimacing at me, but her face is whiter than the walls. "F'kn 'tch," she says through her teeth. "F'kn kill you."

Metal drags over the fabric. She lifts Nick's gun, aims it point-blank at my face.

I don't even have time to close my eyes.

This bang isn't as loud as the first, but maybe that's because I'm already dying. I also expected this bullet to feel like the first. Like a blazing-hot punch, then a poker being shoved through my flesh.

But I just see red.

The side of my face is hot, then warm, then cold. And very wet.

I blink.

The world turns pink.

I blink again.

Jess slides to the floor.

Shapes move, too fast for me to make out. A weight is lifted. I hear voices, a yell.

Someone looms over me. My eyes are squeezed closed from the pain, so I don't know who.

For some reason, I'm sure it's Nick. That he's somehow still alive, and he's about to climb on me again. To finish what he started.

"No," I manage, slurring the word. "No."

Another wave of dizziness comes. The biggest yet. My face tingles furiously, my fingers ice-cold and numb.

I try to fight it, but I can't. It's too big, too powerful.

It lifts me up, so I'm flying, and then I come down the other side. But I just keep sinking and sinking.

And sinking.

43

CASS

When I step inside the upstairs bedroom, my mind balks at what I see. So while I'm still pointing my gun, I don't have a clue what I'm supposed to be shooting at.

Shock makes my brain slow as fuck as I try to work through it.

There's a thick trail of blood leading from the passage outside into the bedroom.

A *kid's* bedroom.

The one from the video. Even still has the same furniture, except some of it's been moved around and the paint is faded.

The blood leads to a woman propped up all awkward against the side of the bed like she's attempting an advanced yoga pose.

She's a suspect. Definitely.

Then there's the big dude on the bed. But he's taking a little nap. Fuck knows why he decided to take his dick out first, but I'm sure my brain will get to that in just a sec.

Then I see her.

My little Trinity.

And then the gun pointed at her beautiful face. My finger

squeezes the trigger without bothering to get me up to speed first.

Trinity recoils when the woman's head goes splat inches from her face.

The woman—kinda dead looking now, especially with the hole in the back of her head—slides down and sprawls on the carpet.

Trinity looks like she just got done auditioning for Carrie, and they made her do the scene with the bucket of pig's blood.

But then Rube's in front of me, and all I see is his back as he charges the bed.

He grabs the guy off of her and tosses him to the floor like a sack of rubbish. He goes to lift Trinity, but I manage to dart forward and catch his arm.

I shove my pistol against his chest.

If I could have spoken, I'd have told him to back off with his big fucking hulk hands so he doesn't break her. But my chest's all clogged up with panic.

Trinity's eyes flutter. Her blood is *everywhere*. But somehow, she's still got some left. It wells out of the crater in her chest, and then disappears into the already blood-soaked fabric of her dress.

I smooth her skirt down her legs as I study the wound.

I'm the furthest thing from a paramedic, but Apollo and I were the fixer-uppers back in the basement. I know a hole like that can't keep pissing out blood, or else Trinity's going to run dry.

The sudden high-pitched whine in my ears tries to compete with my pounding heart. And there's more noise on top of that. But I have no time to listen to any of that. I have to keep Trinity's blood *inside*.

I slap the flat of my hand over the wound and press.

Hard.

Her pained groan goes through me like a fork through the

heart. But I can't let up. When it starts seeping through my fingers, I grit my teeth and I put my knee on her.

Her whimper sounds exactly like the kind a kitten would make while I'm crushing it between my bare hands.

"Fuck," I whisper. "Rube, call an ambulance."

But he doesn't answer.

At first, I don't know why. And then I hear it.

Thud.

Thud.

Thud.

I drag my head around.

My eyes shut on their own.

Christ.

Jesus *fucking* Christ. That is not how you use a gun.

"Rube." I swallow down bile. "Rube!"

Thud.

. . . . . .

Thud.

I retch anyway. "Rube, Christ, call the fucking ambulance!"

Rube's knees creak as he stands. He lets out a blustery breath, sounding more animal than human. Something falls to the carpet, and I can only assume it's the gun he was using to cave in the man's skull.

I'm not going to be able to sleep for a week.

I keep my eyes closed until I'm facing Trinity again, and only then dare open them.

I think the bleeding has stopped.

Dear God, let the bleeding have stopped.

But she's passed out, and that's not good.

"Trin? Baby girl. Wake up."

"She's been shot," comes Rube's voice.

My skin goes cold. He's not even out of breath. He sounds…

Like he always does.

Maybe even a touch calmer than usual.

Shock, that's all. He's obviously in shock. Fuck, *I'm* in shock.

But I'm keeping her blood in, and that's all that matters.

Rube doesn't matter right now. What he was doing to the dead guy over there, that doesn't matter either.

My stomach convulses.

Nope. Keeping my puke *in*.

"I'm not sure of the address. Hold on." I only hear Rube's footsteps when he reaches the tiles out in the hall.

"Apollo!"

I jerk at his bellow.

"What's the address?"

2142 Maude Street, Trinity whispers.

My eyes fly open. But those white lips aren't moving.

Great. Just fucking great. Now I'm hallucinating?

Her chest isn't moving under my knee either.

What's worse? Suffocating, or bleeding out?

But no. Our girl's stronger than that. She can breathe with me on top of her, right?

I brush my fingers against her cheek, smearing around the blood on her face. Shit...I can't let the guys see her in this state. She looks like a medieval prostitute who applied her rouge by candlelight.

I snag the hem of my shirt. Wet it with saliva. Wipe it over her skin. That works. But God, there's a lot of blood on her face. I keep licking my shirt and wiping it off.

Her cheek is semi-clean. I move onto her forehead.

Is it just me, or is she slightly colder than a living person should be?

Nope.

Not a chance am I starting to think shit like that. She's just having a little siesta. Lot of work, fighting off a big guy like that. I'm not hundreds, but I think she shot him in the head too.

I have to take her to a shooting range sometime. She's a fucking natural. Okay, admittedly, it was as point-blank as you can get. I'm sure he's got powder burn. Ha, ha—we'll never know. Rube caved in his fucking skull with the gun.

"How'd you get so much blood on you, babe?" I ask her.

You shot the back of that bitch's head off, Trinity says.

"Whoa, easy on the snark there, little girl. Who's the one plugging you up? I believe it's me. You keep up that attitude, I'll let you bleed out."

Oh no, Cass, please don't do that. I love you so much. I want to live so I can thank you for saving my life, Trinity croons.

"That's more like it." I swipe my damp shirt over her nose. "And don't worry, you'll have plenty of time to thank me for saving your life. Rest of your life, come to think about it." Soon as her nose is clean, I press the tip of my finger to it. "*Boop!*"

"Cass," comes Apollo's voice from the doorway.

Christ. Can't he see I'm trying to keep our girl alive?

"What?"

"C-ass." This time, there's a hitch in Apollo's voice. I stop trying to clean Trinity's blood-splattered face and glance over my shoulder at the door.

"Get up," says the man behind Apollo as he walks them inside. Dark eyes scan the room, taking in the partially headless corpse on one side, then the other body on the floor by the bed.

He's a handsome man, but unnaturally so. His nose is just too narrow and shapely. His cheekbones slightly too pronounced. Like he was good looking to start with, and then went under the knife a few times just for shits and giggles.

"I said, get up." He presses the muzzle of his gun so hard against Apollo's ear that my brother's head tilts to the side.

"N-No," I manage. "If I do, then she'll die."

"If you don't, then *he* dies."

Apollo's holding tight to the arm slung around his upper

chest. His eyes are closed, but I really wish they were open so I could at least have a chance of communicating with him.

It's pointless, though.

He's not a fighter like us. He's the thinker. The philosopher. A true hippy who believes violence is never the answer.

Bet he's regretting some of his life choices now.

"You always a dick to strangers?" I ask him as I furiously try to think of a way out of this.

Could shoot him, of course. There's a gun on the floor. The dead woman must have dropped it there. But I can't move that far or Trinity will bleed out. Plus, Mr. Vain looks trigger happy enough to shoot me if I so much as fart without his permission.

My comment curls up his lips ever so slightly. And God, that pseudo-smile makes my blood run ice-cold.

"You don't know who I am?" He shifts his grip on Apollo, grabbing a fistful of his hair instead of the chokehold. He turns my brother's head to the side so he can stare at Apollo's face. "Trevor recognized me."

A shudder goes through Apollo.

No.

It can't be.

If this guy was involved with our captivity ten years ago, I would have remembered him. Which means he must be a new player in this fucked up game, but who? Is he Gabriel's replacement?

But doesn't matter. Whoever he is, he's about to kill one, if not all, of the people in this room.

Where the fuck are Rube and Zach?

Rube went into the hall looking for Apollo so he could get the address…

I lock eyes with the new Guardian. And it's as if he reads my motherfucking mind. I barely open my mouth before he turns and slams the door shut behind him.

But the lock's busted, so it pops open again just an inch.

"Rube! Zach! Help!" My throat burns how I yell, but fuck knows if they can hear me.

Pointless. They're already dead, Trinity says.

Christ, not now, babe. *Please*, not now.

Okay, fine, she says. *They're alive. They're just busy, right? Jerking off somewhere, having a puff, taking a dump.*

She's got a mouth on her, this one. I'll have to take her to task for it when we get out of this jam.

The Guardian sees the problem with the door the moment I do, though.

And that, finally, is when Apollo's balls decide to drop. Most of us had that happen during puberty. Nope…not him.

He slams his elbow into the Guardian's stomach.

Which, sadly, doesn't do much. It just makes the guy grimace and then pistol-whip him so hard he goes down like someone pulled the plug.

"Fuck you, you shit-eating cunt!" I yell.

The Guardian doesn't even look in my direction. I guess he's established I'm not going anywhere.

He walks over and picks up the chair by the dresser and jams it under the door handle.

Literally a second before something big and angry slams into it on the other side.

Fuck, we *both* get a fright.

The Guardian steps back, gun raised, and points it at the door.

He pulls the trigger. The shot goes off. A hole appears like magic in the center of the door.

Right where Rube's chest would have been.

The assault against the door stops. There's a heavy thump outside.

Not unlike a big body hitting the floor.

I'm starting to lose grip on reality. The world is shifting ever so slightly, like a roller coaster ride just starting up.

I look down at Trinity's ashen face. I don't know if she's still alive. I press my fingers to the artery on the side of her neck, but I can't feel anything.

"Get off her." The Guardian is closer now.

"Might as well shoot me," I tell him as I drop my head and look at him over the point of my shoulder. "Because that's the only way it's happening, you cunt."

"Hmm." He takes another step closer. "Sebastian, isn't it?"

The ground drops out beneath me. I shake my head, leaning back, trying to get away without taking my weight off Trinity's chest.

"Yes, that's right." The Guardian tilts his head a little, and his voice becomes husky. "I remember you. You were the little junkie."

He lifts his free hand, swipes it down in front of his face like mimes do. Happy/Sad. But his expression doesn't change except to become…hungrier.

"Always doped up," he says. "I'm not surprised you don't remember me."

"Guessing you had an uglier face back then," I tell him, but there's no strength in my voice.

Don't listen to him.

It doesn't matter.

All that matter is keeping—

"Not at all. But I had to change. You understand."

And then I do. Like a fucking lightning bolt hits my brain and implants the information there.

I look down at the dead body I'm leaning my knee on. Then up at him. "I don't see the resemblance."

He laughs and comes a little closer, but still too far away for me to attempt anything. "Why would you?" he asks, and then runs his hand through his hair like he's putting on the charm.

I want to throw up those fish tacos I ate seven weeks ago.

"She's not my daughter."

I narrow my eyes at her. "Right. She's Gabriel's. Guess she got her mom's good looks then."

Something touches his expression then. The faintest micro-movement around his eyes. A twitch of his lips.

"It was their idea, calling her Trinity," he says. His voice sounds a touch hollow now. "They thought we'd all raise her. The three of us."

His eyes hadn't exactly been cheery before, but they're dead cold now. He glances down at Trinity's body, then back up at me. "Monica would have aborted her like the others, but then that prick interfered."

As if my earlier revelation had taken up every bit of computing power, my brain fails to comprehend what he's saying.

The Guardian looks at Trinity again. "Her father was a pain in the ass, but he worshiped me. Do you have any idea the things people will do if they think you're a God amongst men?"

I open my mouth to say something brutal, but then there's a gun in my face. "It was rhetorical, Sebastian."

As his finger curls around the trigger, a distant wail catches both our attention.

Ambulance.

Police siren.

And that's not the only thing I notice. Apollo is picking himself up off the floor.

When the Guardian looks back at me, I show him my teeth. "Think you can get out of here in time?" I ask him.

His eyes narrow. He straightens the gun. His lips part, a particularly malicious gleam in his eyes as he starts to speak.

And then Apollo hits him over the head with the chair he quietly took out from under the door handle. When Keith Malone crumples to the ground, my body sags as if it wants to follow.

But I grit my teeth, gather saliva, and spit it on his slack face. "That was rhetorical, you sick fuck."

44
ZACH

At the top of the stairs, the hallway splits east to west. Rube and Cass head west, so Apollo and I take the east wing.

"Stay close," I murmur to Apollo. "And be quiet."

"You're the one talking," he whispers back.

I open the first door and we peek inside.

Crib.

Mobile with stuffed animals.

Gender-neutral geese dancing over the walls.

I start opening the closet doors to make sure no one's hiding inside one waiting to leap out at us. But the closets are empty. As in, there's not even a single diaper in sight.

This place creeps me the fuck out. It feels staged, like the owners moved out ages ago and the real estate agent set it up for an open house.

Who lived here? Where are they now?

"Next room," I murmur, backing up with my weapon still pointed, just in case someone appears out of thin air.

A gunshot sounds.

I spin around and face a locked door.

Apollo's not inside with me. Then I hear a key turning in the lock and my hair stands on end.

What the fuck?

"Apollo?" I run up and try the door handle.

Locked.

Christ. "Apollo!"

I know it wasn't him that locked me inside, but now I'm shitting myself wondering what happened to him. I bang on the door a few times, but that's not helping. I could shoot at the lock, but what are the chances of the bullet ricocheting and hitting me somewhere vital?

I start kicking the door, but it's sturdy as fuck.

"Apollo! What's the address?"

Rube.

"Reuben!" I yell. "Reuben, open up!"

But there's no response. What the fuck is going on out there?

Screw this. I step back, raise my gun—

"Rube! Zach! Help!"

I pause. That's Cass. But wasn't he just with Rube? What the—

Thud.

Thud.

The sound's coming from down the hall. Like someone's banging on something. I turn on my heel, scan the room. My eyes latch onto the window.

With every distant thud, my heart climbs another inch up my throat.

I shove my gun into my belt and hurry over.

I don't stop to think. I don't even allow myself to give the ground more than a passing glance.

My sight is fixed on a nearby tree. From what I saw before I looked away, there's a good yard of thin air between me and the closest bough.

But there's a gunfight going on, and my brothers are involved. I don't know who's on the winning side, or if there even *is* a winning side.

I bundle myself up tight, and then push away from the window as hard as I can.

My stomach slams into the bough. A stray branch scratches my face. I fumble, manage to get an arm slung over the bough, and hold on until I have my bearings.

I work my way to the main trunk and climb down. I drop down the last few feet, already running for the patio doors.

Something deep and dark and rectangular draws my eye.

A grave.

A *grave?*

I race upstairs, my legs almost giving out when I see Rube on the floor. I fall down beside him, and start panting as I hike up his shirt with a shaking hand.

Gutshot. Surprisingly little blood. Does that mean the bullet's still in there?

There's a crash from inside the room, but Rube needs me more right now.

Except...I don't have a fucking clue what to do.

A hand lands on my shoulder, trembling slightly. I look up into Apollo's face.

"Cass needs you," he says.

"But—"

"Go." He falls to his knees beside Reuben and starts ripping off a piece of his shirt. I stand on unsteady legs and half walk, half stumble into the room.

It's the one from the video.

But there's blood here now.

And three dead bodies.

Four if you count—

"No! Trinity!" I rush forward, but then Cass is in front of

me, driving me back. "No!" I try and shove him, but he somehow manages to herd me away from the bed. My back slams into a wall.

The sound of police sirens and ambulances want my attention, but I don't give it to them.

Cass clasps my head in his hands, wiping my face, forcing me to look at him. "Hey, bud. Hey. Over here."

We lock eyes.

"I did everything I could, okay? I tried to save her, but she's gone. She's *gone*. You read me?"

My heart stops beating. "CPR," I croak.

"Got no blood left," Cass says. He's grinning, but it's the kind of smile you see on a corpse where the fleshy bits of the face have been picked clean by scavengers. "It just kept oozing out. Can't put it back in, can I? So that's that. But listen, buddy, listen to me, okay?"

There's a heavy drone in my ears, which makes complying difficult, but I nod anyway. My eyes dart to the side as I try to look past him, but he tightens his grip on my face and sinks his fingertips into my scalp.

"Look, the police are going to be here in like...fucking *seconds*. All right? Now we need to do something very important. And we gonna have to do it really fast."

He steps back. Points.

A dark-haired man lays sprawled on the carpet. There's a gun near his right hand.

"We got to take this motherfucker downstairs. There's this big hole outside—"

"The grave."

Talking is good. Not looking at the bed, that's good too. Doing something that gets me out of this room? Even better.

"Yeah, the grave." Cass pats my chest. "Good. So, you grab his legs, yeah?"

Cass backs up, still grinning like a fucking Jack-O-Lantern, and grabs the guy's wrists.

"Come on, Zach. Stay with me."

I keep my eyes down. When my vision blurs, I blink them clear.

"We can do this."

I nod, not trusting myself to speak. But as soon as Cass breaks eye contact, my gaze flies to the bed.

She looks so serene.

So pale.

So fucking dead.

I blink again. My chest feels like it's caving in. Tighter and tighter and tighter. I try and breathe, try to clamp my mouth shut, but then another set of hot tears races down my cheeks. The salt in my mouth triggers a sob.

"No, n-no," Cass says, voice wobbling. "Fuck you, *Zachary*. You're grabbing his fucking legs, and we're putting him in that fucking grave!"

I choke, wipe my face on my shoulder, and lift the guy's feet.

He groans.

Maybe a normal guy would have dropped him. I don't. I hold on even fucking tighter. Because he undoubtedly had something to do with the dead girl on the bed, and that means I owe him a world of hurt.

A spasm goes through the guy's body, and then he lifts his head. He looks at me, dazed, unfocused.

There's something wrong with his eye.

Outside, in the hall, someone starts sobbing. Big, heavy, *ragged* sobs.

It takes me a few seconds to work it out.

Time where I'm holding back the ephemeral agony gouging out my lungs and stomach. Time where I'm moving back, dragging the guy's stomach over the pale blue carpet. Time where

I'm staring at that fucked up eye so I won't look up again and see Trinity on the bed and lose my shit.

The man twists in our grip. His strength is coming back. There's a wet slick on the back of his head. Splinters in his hair.

That's where the broken chair comes from.

"Doorway," Cass warns. "Take a left, bud."

I angle out the door.

Apollo's head is on Rube's chest. His blond hair shifts with every sob wracking his lean body. He's hugging Rube with his elbows, hands fisted in Rube's shirt.

The guy we're dragging begins fighting us. Cass's grin turns into a grimace. My arms are starting to burn from the weight, from keeping his ankles clasped when he tries to kick his legs.

He keeps bucking off the floor, forcing us to take his full weight instead of letting us drag him over the tiles. He sends a loathing glare at me over his shoulder, mouth twisted with frustration and fury.

And then I get what's wrong with his eye.

It happened a few times to Rube, and would always freak me out.

His contact has slipped. Like an eclipse, the dark lens creates a crescent from the lighter iris below.

I almost drop his legs.

But then I think he recognizes me too. And his face loses all color.

I don't blame him.

He knows what happened to my parents. Fuck, maybe he was even the one who found them.

Were they still in those chairs? No, wait…the chairs must have burned in the fire.

I honestly wish I could have stayed to see their faces.

See how they struggled to get free.

How their skin began blistering from the heat.

Fire cleanses.

It was the only thing that made sense. I was doing them a fucking favor. And, if it didn't work, then at least they'd already know what Hell felt like before they got there.

I walk faster.

The sirens are so much closer now.

"Hey, easy," Cass calls out.

So I rip the man's wrists out of his grip.

There's no time.

"Zach, wait!"

The man immediately flips onto his back and grabs a passing rail before I can haul him down the stairs.

We stop.

Stare at each other.

My Ghost's chest rises and falls, the action speeding up the longer I glare at him.

Trinity's stepfather.

Keith fucking Malone.

But he looks different now. Too different to account for age.

Plastic surgery then.

He really didn't want anyone figuring out he'd faked his own death.

Like Gabriel.

Like Trin—

Pain slices through me. My jaw clenches so hard the enamel on my teeth squeaks.

Cass stomps on Keith's hand. The man curls toward the pain, letting out a wordless yell.

I yank him down the stairs.

He tries to sit up, but his head still hits several of the stairs on the way down. Each time, he leaves a splotch of blood on the wood.

I angle him down the short landing, and then we go down the next flight.

Cass hurries after, stomping on his hands every time Keith manages to grab hold of something. He must already have several broken fingers—they jiggle around too loosely as we make our way downstairs.

Police lights paint the living room walls blue and red. Outside, car doors slam.

I grimace up at Cass. "Grab his fucking arms."

He does so immediately, deftly avoiding Keith's teeth when the man tries to bite him.

We hurry through the patio doors, Keith fighting us every step of the way. But Cass and I, we're filled with the Holy Spirit.

It gives us strength.

It guides our feet.

Keith gasps in pain when we drop him into the grave. It's only about five feet deep—I guess whoever was digging it didn't do all that well in school. But his body is cast in shadow when he rolls onto his side and coughs.

"Hurry," Cass says, a shovel already in his hands.

When the first spade of dirt hits Keith's face, he scrambles up and tries to claw his way out of the grave.

Cass slams his shovel against the back of Keith's head.

But not hard.

Just enough to send him toppling over. He lies there at the bottom, dazed, as we frantically pile more dirt over him.

I hear voices coming from inside. But no one's headed out back yet.

I guess there's enough to deal with inside.

We throw heaps of dirt around Keith's legs and torso, trying to weigh him down as much as possible. Keith comes to when dirt starts hitting his head again. He twists, spitting and cursing when a shovel of dirt hits his face. He pushes his hand down, face contorting as he tries to pull himself out of the dirt.

But maybe he's concussed, because he can't seem to drag himself free.

And then he screams for help.

I jump into the grave and stomp on his head. He goes still, and then starts shaking. I stay there, my foot on the top of his head, as Cass fills in more dirt.

Just before I climb out to help Cass, I crouch down and brush away dirt from his one eye. It trembles, but it doesn't open.

"See you in Hell, Keith Malone."

We shovel in as much dirt as we dare, toss the spades into the hole on top of him and then dart around the side of the house. We wash our hands and shake loose dirt off our clothes, and then enter through the front door.

As we step inside the living room, I see a pair of cops step out onto the patio.

A hand fumbles against my leg. Cass laces his fingers through mine. I look down, then up at his face.

He's staring after the cops, shoulders stiff, jaw bunched.

"If he's still alive…" Cass murmurs. Tears brim in his icy-blue eyes, turning them shiny as fucking marbles.

"Then we'll find him again." I squeeze his hand fuck hard. "And we'll dig him another fucking grave."

45

TRINITY

I'm blindfolded. Gagged. My hands bound behind my back. My bare feet scrape over an icy concrete floor as I shuffle around in utter darkness trying to figure out where the hell I am.

Panic ratchets up my heart rate to that of a hummingbird's.

I'm not alone in this dark.

I'll never find my way out.

Something follows me. I hear it crawling over the floor behind me.

Nails *scratch* on the concrete. Skin drags.

My foot slams into a mattress.

Before I can find my balance, I topple forward.

The bedding is wet and warm.

Someone bled here.

You, Trinity. That's your blood.

I push away the voice as I struggle frantically to stand. The thing crawling after me starts panting. Desperate as I am.

Finally I get to my feet. I surge forward, running as fast as I can.

Straight into someone standing in the dark. Strong arms

catch me before I can fall. They drag me close, and hold me tight.

It should have been comforting, but I know who these arms belong to, and I don't want to be anywhere near him.

My scream gets stuck in my throat. It's barely a wheeze. Fingers tangle in my hair and drag my head back. My blindfold is ripped off.

There's a click.

Light blooms, sickly yellow, from the bulb dangling above us.

I'm in the basement of 2142 Maude Street, but it's larger now. The floor is covered with dirty, blood-stained mattresses.

And there's a small, curled up body on each. Their shadows shift and dance as the light bulb swings left and right.

Almost makes them look alive.

I stare into my father's face, and Keith Malone looks down at me without expression.

Nails scrape against the floor. Plastic sheeting now—no longer concrete.

The panting comes closer.

I try to move away, but Keith is holding me too tight.

"You should be dead," he says. "I told them to kill you."

Nick and Jess. Are they here? With Keith's grip in my hair, I can't turn around to look. I can't even see how close the panting, crawling thing is that was following me in the dark.

"I will have to rectify that, child."

Keith's head snaps back. His mouth opens, but too wide.

Much too fucking wide.

A long, serpentine tongue uncoils and slaps onto my upturned face. I try to cringe away, but he's keeping me rooted to the spot.

His tongue leaves a layer of slime on my skin as it slithers down my neck, like a slug working its way down my skin. With a tug, he pulls down the front of my dress. I try to collapse in on myself, to hide my nakedness, but I can't. Not with my hands still bound.

His tongue creeps over my shoulder like a blind, wet snake. Searching. Hunting over my naked skin.

I try to scream, but I can't draw enough breath. My lungs are too tight.

The panting thing reaches my feet. Ragged nails scrape over my skin as it claws its way up my body.

It's smaller than me, but it's angry.

So fucking angry.

It wants to hurt anything, anyone.

Its hands grab my skirt as it tries to lift itself. As it tries to climb higher. My dress slides down to my hips and threatens to go all the way down my legs.

All the while that tongue leaves sticky trails over my breast, a nipple, the hollow in my throat.

The panting thing catches hold of my wrist. Drags itself up. The exertion makes it breathe faster. Like a dog back from a run. Quick and hard.

The sound comes closer as it crawls up my back.

Hair snags in my fingers.

And then I know what it is.

Who it is.

It had been lying on the mattress in that pitch-black basement. Already dead. That's what I'd been smelling. A girl with short hair, or a boy with long hair.

Dead.

Alone.

There in the dark.

Keith's tongue finds what it was looking for.

The panting thing claws my face, tearing out my gag.

A slick tongue forces its way deep into the hole in my chest, going all the way through to my back.

The pain is excruciating.

A scream tears apart my throat.

Cold, dead little fingers creep over my face and try to seal my lips.

"Ssh, Trinity," the child murmurs in my ear. "Don't let the bad man hear you."

My body jerks violently. I clap a hand over my chest, grimacing as I sit up in bed.

I dislodge two arms on the way. Apollo mumbles something under his breath as he turns and goes straight back to sleep.

Cass looks like he's still sleeping.

I shimmy out of bed as carefully as I can, and hurry out of the room. I pad down the stairs, take a left, and sprint into the nearest bathroom.

If the basin had been another foot away, I'd have missed it. I retch violently, repetitively, my eyes streaming with pain.

I shudder as I rinse out the sink, then my mouth.

Again.

That's the eighth night in a row.

I gargle half the bottle of mouth wash and stand at the foot of the stairs, staring into the dark.

But I don't want to go back to sleep. Not if that fucking thing is waiting to pounce on me as soon as I close my eyes.

I head downstairs and let myself out onto the patio.

The ocean sounds calm tonight. The crash and sigh of the waves are barely audible from where I'm standing.

I flinch when hands wrap around my upper arms.

"Same one?" Cass asks.

I had woken him.

"Yeah." I swipe my hair out of my face, put a hand over my chest. "It hurts more every time."

"Psychic pain," Cass says, coming to stand beside me and leaning his elbows on the railing. "Doctor said you're hundreds. That shit's healed."

I rub my palm into the scar just below my collarbone. "He also told me it wouldn't become infected, and it did. He also told me the scar would be barely noticeable." I turn to Cass and point at the dark, puckered mark on my skin. "This thing is visible from the fucking moon."

"Vain much, princess?" he says through a smirk, and reaches for me.

I step back. "I'm not kidding, Cass. It *hurts*. It feels…"

"Like it's happening again?" he asks, cocking his head. "You read those articles I sent you, right?"

I roll my eyes and go back to staring at the ocean. They've all been trying to help me through this, but I guess no one comes back from a near-death experience without a little emotional baggage. Me? I never pack light.

A scar.

PTSD.

So many triggers they have to line up.

I smile to myself.

I'm one of them now. The Brotherhood. Just as broken and fucked up as they are. All it took was getting raped and shot.

Kismet.

Cass slings an arm over my shoulder and draws me against his chest. He's wearing my pink robe, but didn't bother closing it up—his skin is cool and smooth and oh so delicious to touch. I slide my fingertips over his pecs and down his ribs, then circle his waist and squeeze him as I lay my head against his chest.

His heart thumps away quietly in his ribcage.

If it weren't for him, I wouldn't be alive.

Any of them.

But especially Cass.

I don't remember much of what happened in the blue room. My therapist said the memories might come back one day or never. I don't know if I want to know everything—my men already told me everything I need to know.

"Hey, I've got an idea," Cass murmurs into my ear. "Something to get you out of that pretty head of yours."

"We're not going to raid the fridge," I tell him, although secretly if he pushed me, I'd probably cave. I've already put on ten pounds—I'll be rolling around like one of those kids in Charlie and the Chocolate Factory if my men keep stuffing me with food.

"Not what I had in mind." Cass steps away from me and goes to the edge of the infinity pool.

He shrugs his shoulders. My pink satin robe slides down his back and pools by his feet.

Oh God, he was naked and I didn't even notice.

How could I not notice?

Because I was stuck in my head.

He takes his time getting in the pool, as if he knows how much it turns me on looking at his body. Every muscle is toned and lean, from his taut neck to his slim biceps, to his almost-eight-pack to his gorgeous ass.

"Is it cold?" I ask him, as he slips into the black pool.

"A little." He twirls around, sending ripples to all four sides. "Promise I'll keep you warm if you get in."

I glance up at the main bedroom's balcony. There are no lights on up there. Zach and Apollo must still be fast asleep.

"Five minutes," I tell him. "I don't want to be all groggy for the doctor's appointment tomorrow."

Cass holds up a hand, fingers spread. He watches me intently as I take off my vest and boxer shorts, and swims closer when I step hesitantly into the pool.

The water isn't as cold as I thought it would be, but I still let out a theatrical shiver when it hits my nipples.

"Oh, my poor baby girl," Cass murmurs, scooping me into his arms and spinning us around in the water.

He urges my legs around his waist, his hands lingering on my ass as we take another slow spin.

"You know that crap about how time heals all wounds?" he asks, putting his forehead against mine.

I nod, staring into his pale blue eyes.

"Well forget about that. You have us, okay? What we can't heal, we can easily make you forget." His lips brush my ear. My jaw. My cheek.

I turn, but he pulls back, teasing me with just a whisper of his lips before they're out of reach.

"Cass," I whine, tightening my thighs around his waist.

"Princess," he says, in much the same tone. "Don't be so demanding."

"I just want a kiss. But then we have to go to bed."

"And the demands just keep coming." He squeezes my ass with both hands, hard enough to make me draw a quick breath. "When will you learn?"

"Hopefully never." I try and chase his mouth, but he keeps moving his head away.

Just when I'm about to give up on our kiss, my ass hits the small island in the middle of the pool. During the day, there's a fountain that splashes into the pool but right now it's just a slab of stone.

Cass pushes me against the side, grabs my hair, and kisses me.

I melt against him, losing myself in the passion of his expert lips and forceful tongue.

He breaks off our kiss and then hoists me onto the edge before sliding his hands down the front of my body. Tweaking one nipple, then the other. Then his fingers glide down my stomach.

He's already wedged his body between my legs, but I spread them a little wider when he gets close.

"God, I fucking love it when you open your legs for me," he murmurs as he pushes up on his hands to give me a peck on the lips. "You're such a fast learner, my precious little slut."

He scoots me back, careful not to scrape my skin on the stone and reaches into the water to grab my leg. He lifts it, positioning my foot on the edge, kissing my knee as he stares up at me with a wicked gleam in his eyes.

"Cass..."

"What?"

"We shouldn't be—"

He slaps my pussy, and I cut off with a sigh.

"We should get back in bed," I continue hurriedly as he lifts my other leg, positions it on the other side of my body.

He ignores me, of course. He's too busy staring at my pussy. Giving my knee an absent, cat-like lick, he sticks his hand in the water and starts stroking his cock.

"We will, soon as I'm done with you."

"But the others—"

"Can have whatever's left." His eyes dart up to mine as he strokes my pussy with his fingertips.

"Fuck," I murmur, my eyelashes trembling as I fight for my

eyes not to close. If they did, it would be much too easy to surrender.

This is wrong.

It's not written in stone or anything, but when there's anything more than kissing, everyone's invited.

But Cass has been tempting me ever since my last bandage came off. Luring me away, kissing me until I'm breathless, and then trying to get into my pants.

I've fought him off more times than I can count, and I'm fucking proud of that.

But tonight...

He strokes my pussy, sending tingles up my body. I tangle my hands in his hair as he plants tiny kisses on my inner thighs, his eyes never leaving mine.

Like he's daring me to tell him to stop. Fuck, I want to. Because this feels so wrong—just the two of us, out here in the dark but so very exposed. All it would take is one of my men waking up and wandering onto the balcony for a smoke, and they'd know what we did.

Alone.

When he spreads my legs even wider, ducks down, and drags his tongue through my slit, I almost yank out all of his hair.

I force his mouth harder against my pussy, his tongue deeper. I lift my hips, and start rocking against his mouth, one hand behind me for balance, the other keeping his head exactly where I want it.

And fuck it feels good.

Diabolically good.

I never want it to end.

Seconds later, I'm already close to coming.

He draws back, licks his lips as he stares up at me. He slides two fingers inside me, beckoning. "Come on, Princess. You know you want to."

Oh God, I'm like fucking putty in his hands. He played the long game and I guess he finally won. I don't have the willpower to resist him anymore.

He licks my pussy again, his fingers still deep inside me, teasing me. Then he starts sliding them in and out. "This could be my cock," he murmurs. "Stretching you. Filling you."

I shake my head. "We can't."

His eyes narrow. "That's not the right answer, Princess."

"Cass, come on—"

He grabs me around the waist and tugs me off the island. His mouth grinds against mine as he drags me back to the edge of the pool.

And I fall for it.

Because I think he's accepted my decision.

We climb out of the pool. He leads me back into the house, not bothering to pick up my robe, not letting me stop for my clothes.

But we don't go upstairs.

He yanks me away from the stairs when I head for them. When I resist, just for a second, he picks me off my feet and carries me to a chaise lounge in the living room.

"Hey, I thought we were—"

"Sorry, my precious little cock tease." He kisses me again, hard, and drops me on the couch. "This is happening."

I push up onto my elbows. "But it's not—"

He grabs my hair, yanks back my head. "Say 'wrong' one more time…"

I stare at him, my jaw bunched.

They treated me like a glass figurine for the last few months. This is the first time one of them is getting even a little rough with me.

Thank *fucking* God.

"It's wrong," I tell him.

He shows me his teeth. "Then I don't want to be right."

Cass straddles me so fast I don't even have time to fight him. He grabs my wrists, slamming them into the chair above my head. Then he claims my mouth again, kissing me like he hates the fact that I turn him on this much.

And I can feel just how much he wants me. Every inch of his cock is rock hard as it slides over my belly.

He shoves a hand between my legs and follows with a knee.

I have no choice but to let him in.

As soon as both his legs are between mine, he goes to his knees and rakes his eyes over my exposed body.

He slaps my pussy hard enough to make me gasp, and then thrusts a finger inside me.

"You're not even wet enough for them, why the fuck do you want to go upstairs?" he says.

I open my mouth, but he doesn't give me a chance to speak.

His lips are on mine, bruising hard, and then his hand is over my slit. He squeezes, massages me, puts pressure on my clit with the base of his palm.

I moan into his mouth, my legs falling open for him.

"That's better," he whispers.

His fingers spread my pussy open. He dips his hips, dragging the crown of his cock over my dripping slit.

"Getting there."

He presses the tip of his dick against my entrance, and then pulls back to smear my arousal over my clit.

The touch is so light, but still electrifying. I lift my hips, trying to increase the pressure, but he just chuckles at me and nips my breast.

I press my nipple into his mouth, and he teases it with his teeth, his hot, erratic breaths puffing against my skin as he slides his cock along my slit.

"Fuck, please," I moan. "Just…"

"Say it, and I'll consider it."

"Just fuck me."

"Hard?"

"Yes!"

"Not slow?"

I groan. "Yes, slow."

"So slow and hard?"

"Cass, fuck…please."

I'm about to start sobbing.

He lets go of my wrists. Sits back on his heels. Strokes his dick and studies me. Then he turns his head a little and says, "What do you think, boys? Hard and fast, or soft and slow?"

I jerk under him, my eyes darting to the dark pools of shadow in the living room.

Zach and Apollo step forward. They're still dressed in their pajamas—a pair of boxers for Zach, and a vest and jocks for Apollo.

They're both hard. The lust in their eyes is unmistakable.

Color blazes over my cheeks. Cass slaps my pussy again. "Eyes up here, Trin."

My eyes fly back to him. "Cass—"

"Let them watch," he says, putting his head to the side. "Maybe if you give them a good show, they'll still want you when I'm done."

When he forces the first inch of cock inside me, everything else ceases to exist. My back arches, a soft sigh escaping my lips. He teases me, keeping just an inch of his dick inside me as he strums my clit.

I'm so fucking close to coming I almost unravel the second he finally thrusts into me.

I let out a breathless moan, scraping my nails down his arm.

He folds down, catching my lips with his. His kiss is deep

and soulful as he slowly starts fucking me with every inch of his cock.

Slow.

Hard.

His kiss intoxicates me to the point where the room starts spinning. I stab my nails into his back, then his ass, trying to get him to grind harder against me.

He groans, his lips trembling against mine. "Jesus, princess, you're holding onto me so fucking tight."

He's heavy, but deliciously so. And when he starts moving again, it's slow and steady.

"Are you going to come for me?" he whispers.

"Yes."

"Then come, princess. I want to feel you coming all over my cock."

He kisses me again, and slides a hand between us. He massages my clit with his thumb, slowing down until he's barely moving.

Then he rams into me, filling me with every inch of his dick.

Again.

Again.

But he doesn't surrender my mouth. Doesn't stop teasing my clit.

When I come, it's with a shudder and an explosion of bliss deep inside my core.

He pounds into me, and then his cum fills me. He thrusts again, grunting against my lips, like he wants to get even deeper.

Everything down there tingles furiously when he pulls out. He keeps stroking my clit, each caress sending new tendrils of pleasure through my body.

He gives me a last kiss, soft and gentle, as he climbs off me. I lose myself in his mouth, my legs falling open. His cum leaks out of me, and I don't even care if Zach and Apollo see.

He's still kissing me when the couch sinks down between my legs. I try and look, but he grabs my chin and forces me to keep kissing him. And he never stops massaging my clit.

A cock presses against my entrance.

I groan, shift. I want to know who it is, but he won't let me.

But at soon as that first thrust slams into me, I know.

I gasp as Zach fucks me, so hard I can't kiss Cass back anymore. But he doesn't seem to care. He just rains kisses on my lips and chin until I push him away.

It's not fair.

He had me all to himself.

When I face Zach, he stops fucking me. But his cock is still buried in me to the hilt. My eyes flutter, but I force them wide. I grab his shoulder, urge him down.

He moves stiffly, like he's resisting me.

But he's going to have everything, whether he wants it or not.

I slide my fingers in his hair and rock my hips against him, urging him to fuck me again. "Don't stop," I whisper. "You can fuck me as hard as you want."

There's a moment's hesitation, and then he ducks forward and kisses me. His cock draws out, but it slams back a second later.

Pain, pleasure—they mix and swirl around inside me in a dizzying fog.

We can barely keep our lips together, but it doesn't matter. Just the heat of his breath and the caress of his mouth against mine is enough.

That way, he can breathe in every gasp and catch every moan I make as he punishes me.

"Are you going to come for me too?" he asks, breathless, fervent.

"I don't know," I tell him. This is fucking torture of the best kind, but whether I can come when he's fucking me so hard is anyone's guess.

"Make it happen, little girl," he growls. He straightens, grabs my wrist, and slaps my hand between my legs. "And hurry, because I'm not waiting for you."

He grabs my hips, adding even more force to his powerful thrusts.

"Christ, Zach, you're going to break her," Apollo says.

Zach grabs my hand again, and forces me to touch myself. "You never done this before or something?"

Tears leak from my eyes, but I don't know if it's shame or terror or pain or pleasure.

I don't even care.

Cass strokes my hair. "Come on, baby girl."

I touch myself, start massaging my clit.

"Harder," Cass whispers.

Zach's fingers dimple into my hips. I massage a little harder, my mouth falling open as that tiny nub starts sending urgent pleasure signals soaring through my body.

"That's it," Zach says. "Now faster, sweetheart."

I speed up. My head pushes back into the couch. I start moaning and rocking as I lose control over my body.

"Look at me," Zach snaps.

I force my eyes open, but they're blurry as fuck. He starts slowing, but each thrust is now more violent than the last. The impact of our hipbones meeting goes through my body like an aftershock.

"Fuck," he growls. "You'd better come with me." He grinds into me, filling every inch of me with his cock.

I let out a breathless yell, my back arching off the couch as I climax.

"God," he groans. "You're so fucking tight."

One last thrust has my mind coming loose. Zach fills me

with his load, and it dribbles down my slit as he pulls out. When he slams back I let out a sob.

He sits back, stroking a last bit of cum from his cock as he watches me shivering under him.

Then he reaches out blindly and grabs hold of Apollo. "You're up."

I lift my legs, squeezing my thighs together. Apollo hesitates, eyes going wide. He opens his mouth as if to ask if I'm okay, and I let my legs fall open again.

He's between them a second later. His cock slides inside me while Zach's cum is still leaking out.

This couch is ruined.

But I don't give a fuck.

I push onto my elbows, let Cass smooth sweat-slicked hair from my face, and then grab Apollo's head for a kiss.

Apollo thrusts deeper into me. Deeper. Deeper. I lift my legs and wrap them around his waist, and force him in the last bit.

"I love you, Trinity," he murmurs.

"I love you too," I whisper back.

We meld together as he gives me a deep, breathless kiss. He pulls back, thrusts into me again.

"But...uh..."

I frown. "What?"

He gives me a grin. "Doggy style?"

I need their help to flip over. My legs are rubber and my knees jelly. But they get me on my hands and knees, and make me share kisses between Zach and Cass as Apollo rubs his cock over my pussy, hunting out my slit.

When he thrusts into me, I let out a strangled gasp of pleasure.

Zach reaches for my clit, but Apollo slaps his hand away. "Mine." It's the closest to a growl I've ever heard coming from his sweet mouth.

I laugh, and that earns me a hard slap to my ass. I moan and rest my head on the couch like the good girl I am.

Apollo thanks me with a groan and a series of hard, deep thrusts that send me spiraling toward another climax.

He comes before I do, giving my ass another hard slap. But he stays inside me as he starts strumming my clit. I push my legs a little further apart, groaning into the cushion as my climax speeds closer.

"What the fuck is going on?"

Apollo yanks his dick out of me. I go onto my knees, grabbing on the back of the couch for support as I try and focus across the living room floor.

"Do you know what fucking time it is?" Reuben growls.

"Half-past three?" Cass says.

"We've got to be at the doctor in five hours."

He's wearing a thick robe, and when he walks closer, it's with a heavy limp. His hair is disheveled, his eyes darkly shadowed.

"Rube, we can expla—" Apollo begins, but cuts off and scrambles off the couch when Rube gets closer.

"This is what you four do when I'm out of it?" he demands, waving a hand in my general direction. "You all fuck each other?"

"Sometimes I read," Cass says.

"Enough!" Rube looks at me, disapproval stark in his eyes. "What do you have to say for yourself?"

I blink up at him, look away, and then start wagging my hips.

Honestly, my brain is mush. If I could have talked my way out of this I would have, but…I've just been fucked seven ways from Sunday.

A big, warm hand caresses my ass.

"Think this is going to fix anything?" Rube asks. "A quick fuck, and all is forgiven?"

"Buddy, you're usually out cold by now," Cass says. "We could have been doing this on top of you and you wouldn't have woken up."

"Doctor said no pills tonight." Rube strokes my ass again. "And no sex, either."

He slaps me.

Fucking hard.

I whimper as my arousal—and possibly three different men's cum—trickles down my inner thigh.

"That's why we didn't—"

"Shut up and hold this."

I look up in time to see Rube handing his robe to Cass. Then he clicks his fingers at Apollo. "Get back in her."

"Man, I would? But..." Apollo cups his hands over his dick and takes a step back. "You scared the bejesus out of me."

"I'll do her," Zach says. "But only if you fucking promise not to rip out those stitches again."

That's the problem with Rube. He thinks he's invincible. *Unbreakable.*

Zach thrusts into me, no teasing, not even a warning. My mouth opens in a gasp, and that's when Rube forces the crown of his cock between my lips.

He was in surgery for nine hours, and walking a week later. That same month, he had to go back in because he'd torn something important—because he'd been fucking me like a goddamn stallion despite the doctor's orders.

The only way we could get him to start healing was to insist the doctor give him a prescription for sleeping pills. And I tried to stay out of his way as much as possible.

Still, it's taken him twice as long to heal as it should have, and if the doctor doesn't like what he sees tomorrow, he could be on bed rest for another week.

So I suck his cock while Zach fucks me from behind, and we

put on a good show so that when he comes, Rube doesn't feel left out.

Soon, everything will be back to normal.

No more sneaking around.

No more pills.

Reuben wraps my curls around his fist, guiding his dick deeper into my mouth. "Did they make you come?" he asks.

I look up at him, wide-eyed as I nod.

"Was it good?"

Another nod.

"I don't believe you."

I groan as Cass's fingers trail down my stomach, heading for my clit.

"No, no," Rube murmurs, when I try and move away from his touch. "You said you could handle all four of us." He grabs the base of his cock and forces another inch of himself down my throat. "So handle us, my girl."

When Zach's had his share of my ass, he moves beside Rube. He hasn't come again, and I know why.

My men think I'm even prettier when I'm covered with their cum.

So as Rube's dick starts throbbing in my mouth, and the grip in my hair tightens, Zach starts jerking off beside him, biting his lip as he stares down at me with pure adoration.

Cass shoves his cock into my slit, because I guess they can't help filling every single one of my holes.

And Apollo teases me toward another climax with his fingers.

We don't all come at once…but it's pretty damn close.

And as my climax is tearing through me, Rube demands I look up at him so he can watch me swallow down every drop of his cum.

Side by side, he and Zach are like night and day.

His green eyes so bright, where Zach's are always shadowed.

Light and dark.

All my men have that in them. Both the light *and* the dark.

Thankfully, I've seen more of their light shine through these past few days. I'm hoping, soon, that light will vanquish the dark.

It has to.

The police found enough evidence in Keith Malone's safe house to convict hundreds of child molesters across the country, and lay charges against thousands more. It was the biggest bust in sex-trafficking history.

Keith Malone was dead when they finally excavated the grave. It wasn't that they didn't find a freshly filled-in grave suspicious. The cops were just…distracted.

Kismet.

We brought closure to hundreds of families. Even a decade later, it could still help them heal. The task force assigned to the case is working around the clock to find the rest of the houses still out there.

We brought light to the shadows.

But we also brought hope. And that, I think, is the most important thing.

Because without hope, what is there to look forward to but endless night?

The End

If you love dark reverse harem bully romances, then be sure to check out my latest series, Serpents of Cinderhart.

They call them the Serpents.

Knox, Mason, Silas.

These sick, twisted psychos are the untouchable elites at Cinderhart Academy.

I'd never get involved with such dangerous guys despite how gorgeous, rich, and influential they are.

But after I witness them committing a sadistic crime, I'm dragged kicking and screaming into their dark, depraved world.

If they plan to break me, they're late to the party.

Nim Winters isn't the same girl who stumbled onto their crime scene a few months ago.

I have nothing to left to lose.

The Serpents? They have everything...but not for long.

Can I send you my secret dark romance novella that's never been published...?

Join my VIP newsletter and you'll receive your own exclusive copy of My Darling, and I'll keep you up to date with my new releases and promos!

https://authorloganfox.com/my-darling-signup

MORE BY LOGAN FOX

For more books by this author, reading order, playlists, trigger warnings, socials, and more...please visit:

https://authorloganfox.com

www.ingramcontent.com/pod-product-compliance
Lightning Source LLC
Chambersburg PA
CBHW070203120726
47909CB00001B/231